*Lincoln Center in July*

*And Other Stories*

Roy Lisker

© 2016 by Roy Lisker
Book design © 2016 by Sagging Meniscus Press

All Rights Reserved.

Set in Williams Caslon Text with LaTeX.
Printed in the United States of America.

ISBN: 978-1-944697-04-4 (paperback)
ISBN: 978-1-944697-05-1 (ebook)
Library of Congress Control Number: 2016936265

*Recent Advances in the Measurement of* $\pi$ was originally published in the Journal of Irreproducible Results.

Sagging Meniscus Press
web: http://www.saggingmeniscus.com/
email: info@saggingmeniscus.com

*Voi che sapete, che cosa è amor . . .*

# Table of Contents

| | |
|---|---|
| Introduction *by Jacob Smullyan* | vii |
| Sam The Messiah Man | 1 |
| Willy van Fritz | 17 |
| Lincoln Center in July | 23 |
| Logan Airport | 35 |
| Amplitude of the Cosmos | 51 |
| The Tale of the Guru | 67 |
| Three Weddings | 81 |
| Sea Urchins | 89 |
| The Revelation of Doctor Snew | 133 |
| Recent Advances in the Measurement of $\pi$ | 167 |

| | |
|---|---|
| The Hotel Quagmire | 173 |
| The Governments of Chelm | 187 |
|     Introduction | 187 |
|     The Council of the Wise Elders | 190 |
|     A Question of Logic | 191 |
|     The Cowherd's Complaint | 191 |
|     The Tenant's Complaint | 193 |
|     The Schnorrer's Tale | 196 |
|     A Discourse on Government | 203 |
|     A Free Society isn't a Free Lunch | 204 |
|     The Fortunes of War | 207 |
|     Tyranny, on Delivery | 208 |
|     On Widows, Goats and Other Matters | 209 |
|     And Why Not? | 215 |
|     What's in a Name? | 216 |
|     Identity Crisis | 219 |
|     Reinventing Socialism | 221 |
|     In Pursuit of Happiness | 224 |
|     Concluding Remarks | 227 |

# Introduction

The career of Roy Lisker has been one of the most exciting and distinctive chapters in American letters, while leaving (as of yet) almost no mark in its official history. That this dichotomy exists is a reflection both of the noble and apparently absurd intransigence of the author in being himself—in fact, in being a person in a world of people striving with all their might to be non-persons—and of the perverse standards of the publishing and academic industry in the United States.

Lisker has led a life of creative ferment in many spheres. First and foremost a writer, he has worked prolifically in every imaginable literary form; done original work in mathematics and physics; performed music and poetry in the streets of the U.S. and Europe; composed music; and, inseparably from his other activities, been a political activist, which led to his imprisonment for non-violent protest against the Vietnam War. A key characteristic of his work and life is that it is fully and naturally expressed in multiple dimensions, resisting professional specialization. He is one of the few intellectuals today who bring together, without cant, deep sympathy for and knowledge of both the humanities and sciences.

Born in Philadelphia in 1938, he entered a graduate math program at the University of Pennsylvania at the age of sixteen, but in his second year, he felt powerfully called to an artistic vocation; though music was his deepest love, his diversity of interests required the medium of language, and he devoted himself to writing. Several stories in this volume date from this period.

## INTRODUCTION BY JACOB SMULLYAN

In 1965, in a landmark protest covered on the front page of the New York Times, he and four other anti-war activists were arrested for burning their draft cards in New York City's Union Square. In 1967, with his case still on appeal, he left for France and remained there for over four years. It was an extraordinarily productive time in his life, and he was well-received in France: his first novel was published by Gallimard, Sartre's journal *Les Temps Modernes* published several of his articles, and Editions Max Eschig some of his musical compositions. However, he returned to the U.S. in 1972, as he had always planned, to serve a six month sentence in Allenwood Penitentiary.

For most of the next two decades, he led a largely itinerant lifestyle, staying especially in university towns (Boulder, Cambridge, Berkeley, New Paltz, Chicago, St. Louis...) and publishing his own work in newsletters available for private subscription: first *New Universe Weekly* and then its successor *Ferment*. These newsletters had a small but distinguished base of subscribers, including at various times E.O. Wilson, Milton Babbitt, Howard Zinn, Noam Chomsky, and Thomas Kuhn. Attempts to find a conventional publisher in the U.S. led nowhere.

To say the least, Lisker made very little money from his self-published zine. He usually scrounged a living by staying with friends, busking with a violin, selling a few self-published books or cards on campus or in public places, occasionally working odd jobs (such as grading papers for the physics department at Berkeley). But much of the time he was as close to penniless as a person in twentieth-century urban America could be. He countered these difficulties with great resilience and personal energy, and an obstinate refusal to give up his personal freedom or dim his creative flame.

*Ferment* contained every sort of writing: accounts of scientific conferences (no doubt the most entertaining accounts of such events ever written); muckraking journalistic investigations; history (including memorable studies in the history of mathematics, such as the work for which he is best known,

*The Quest for Grothendieck*); critical essays on theater, film, poetry, and music; a searing, unsparing memoir; serialized novels; short stories; original work in mathematics, physics, philosophy, and psychology; travel writing, poetry, drawings, recreational mathematics . . . a vast body of work with inexhaustible variety of form, reflecting endless curiosity and an irrepressible creative vitality.

When he inherited a small amount of money in the 2000s, he was able to return to France for periods of months at a time. Once more, he was received in France very differently than in the U.S. On his visits, he was given an office at the Institute Poincaré, where he spent part of his time studying statistical mechanics; he was invited to give presentations at IRCAM on math and music; public readings of his plays were produced. All of this occurred almost without preparation, simply because he was a productive intellectual: there was no necessity of "proving" that the work was valuable through a method of validation external to the work itself. When his money ran out, he would return home to Middletown, Connecticut, where he lives, still, in supportive housing, most of the tenants of which are handicapped in one way or another. Lisker, too, is handicapped, from a worldly point of view—by his intelligence, and by not being able to bear submitting to the consensually enforced tedium and betrayal of everyday life. This handicap, from another point of view, is a measure of the real seriousness of his mission—his own (and our) spiritual survival in a society based fundamentally on an ethic of spiritual self-destruction.

The stories collected here are a small part of his enormous output, but are representative of several important strands in his work that were present from the beginning: satire; a zest for playful formal experiment; the recurring themes of politics, music, mathematics, and the role of the frustrated outsider. While written for the most part early in his career, they have all been significantly revised in later years, some of them (like *Sam The Messiah Man*, the recitation of which is a long-standing holiday tradition) many times.

Many of the stories—*Amplitude of the Cosmos, Sam The Messiah Man, Lincoln Center In July, Willy van Fritz, Three Weddings*—deal with music, almost to the point of obsession—and indeed, obsession and madness follow upon music in one way or another in all of them. Several others reflect his scientific interests: *Sea Urchins* and *The Revelation of Dr. Snew* both satirize the spiritual emptiness and careerism of the scientific world; *The Hotel Quagmire* and *Recent Advances in the Measurement of* $\pi$ are hilarious examples of a genre of mathematical spoof unique to him, in which the means of math and science are grotesquely misapplied. In the gleefully experimental *Logan Airport*, math also makes a hallucinatory cameo in a nightmarish survey of the modern world's inhuman environments. *The Tale of the Guru* is, properly speaking, a short play, and has been staged delightfully as such; but we include it because, as a virtuosic etude in nested narrative layers, it works equally well as a play for reading, and it also represents another genre in which Lisker excels, the fable. Also a fable is the novella *The Governments of Chelm,* in which the legendary village of fools provides an opportunity to demonstrate the futility of all systems of government.

In Lisker's work, as in life, the quest for personal fulfillment—whether through art, mathematics, beauty, or sheer human decency—is in perpetual conflict with social forces that deny it, shut it out, or commodify it to deprive it of meaning. While his own personal refusal to acquiesce to those forces has come at considerable cost to his own comfort and led to his being imprisoned, marginalized, and ignored, Lisker has never been defeated in his main purpose as an artist, nor has he ever dropped the torch of inspiration and good humor which shines so brightly in these stories.

*—Jacob Smullyan*
*April, 2016*

# Lincoln Center in July

*And Other Stories*

# Sam The Messiah Man

IVE A.M.: the early morning of December 15, 1985. Frosty and still. Walking about the living-room in his bedclothes, Sam Goldberg, violinist, vacantly absorbed the miraculous snow-flake ballets descending from the high heavens to their earthly melt. Gazing through the tall French windows of his stately house in Concord, Massachusetts, Sam watched the streetlights flicker and go out. Plenty of time remained before he would be going down through the basement to the garage to warm up the car.

The drive to Logan Airport to catch the plane to Denver would begin at 7:30. After arranging to park his car there for ten days, he would board the flight to Denver. He was expected there before noon (local time) to preside over a performance of Handel's *Messiah* with the Colorado Symphony Orchestra.

"Breakfast is ready, Sam!"

"Be there in a minute, Sharon!" Sam returned to the bathroom and washed up at the sink. The heavy demand for his talents would keep him in the West for the next eight days. Then he was due back in the Boston area for the Christmas Day concert with the Boston Symphony Orchestra. He and Sharon looked forward to spending the rest of that day with their three children, Abe, Simon, and Rebecca, all grown to maturity with their own families and concerns. He'd already reserved a table for the family at an upscale kosher restaurant in Brookline.

A brief respite! After Christmas, Sam wasn't expected home again until January 11th. The interim would send him trekking through snowstorms to engagements across the country and a few in Canada and England.

Sam dried his face with a towel, threw on a bathrobe and slippers, and shuffled into the dining-room. Walking to the fireplace he paused to adjust the Hanukkah decorations on the mantelpiece. Once again he compared his watch with the reading from a small pendulum clock: 5:30 AM.

As he lowered himself into a chair at the dinner table, Sam emitted a fervent sigh of contentment. The aroma of coffee and clatter of dishware signaled Sharon's imminent arrival. While he waited, Sam re-lived (as he was so fond of doing) his graduation, in June of 1946, at the top of his class at the Curtis Institute of Music in Philadelphia, when so many honors had been heaped upon him. He chuckled at the high hopes that teachers, family and fellow students alike had placed in him, and simpered as he contemplated, once more, the cleverness with which he had disappointed them all!

Even Sam could not resist dropping a few tears as the faces of the teachers beloved of his youth rose up again before his mind's eye: kind, dumpy, and wise Professor Baumgartner, chairman of Violin; the brilliant, exquisitely groomed Professor Spinelli, Composition; Professor Lutoslowski, always in a hurry, never on time: Piano. Sam's laugh combined a mixture of sympathy and scorn.

Each and every one wanted him to work like a horse at the plough and starve for Art! But *he* (Sam Goldberg, violinist) had forever laid to rest their old-fogey European Conservatory foolishness! He had done the unforgivable and *thrived!* Sam shook a fist.

Sam's plan to retire in five years had already been laid out to the last detail. It would bring to an end a very successful, in fact extraordinary career. Age had not mistreated him. He was in good health for a man in his sixties, a bit overweight, his glasses stronger, his hearing unimpaired. The tonsure of silver hair stretching behind his ears and around the back of his head only added further distinction to his standing as a respected senior musician.

Sharon, sad and unsmiling (she rarely was anything else) came in from the kitchen dragging a cart holding cereal, coffee and eggs.

"Like Jascha Heifetz!" Sam cried, talking out loud to himself—"like Jascha Heifetz!" He was reminding himself that he lived like a celebrity through doing the bare minimum of work.

"I probably earn more money, I bet you," he gloated, "in *real* dollars, than Baumgartner, Spinelli and Lutoslowski ever did— all put together! . . . And in America!" he cackled, so loudly that even Sharon, who had lost most of her hearing over the decade, could hear him:

*"MONEY'S where it's AT! MONEY'S WHAT COUNTS!"*

"Eat up, Sam," Sharon chided, " . . . you have to leave soon."

His smug reflections continued in silence: "What was my secret of success?" It was not the first time he'd asked himself this essentially rhetorical question: "Cleverness! And, well . . . A *total lack of ambition* . . . Then . . . *A HARD-NOSED PHILOSOPHY OF LIFE!* . . . A capacity for *realism!* Far beyond that of any musician I know about."

"Sam! . . . Sam!" he congratulated himself, "You've got that primitive grasp on the verities of life that puts *you* in the company of the likes of the Rockefellers, Vanderbilts, Gettys . . . " And he smirked.

Sharon watched him with concern. He didn't realize that he was getting old, but to her the symptoms were obvious. It worried her that he might not even make it through this season. When he settled in again, sometime after January 11th, she was going to pressure him into retiring right away. They had enough money; it was only force of habit that kept him at an occupation that was no longer required of him.

Or was he, perhaps, being driven by something else? Some personal demon, perhaps, some inner compulsion? No one understands what motivates an artist. She certainly didn't understand Sam, and she'd been married to him for 32 years.

# SAM THE MESSIAH MAN

❉ ❉ ❉

Within his first year as a student at Curtis Institute of Music in Philadelphia in 1943, Sam already understood that the listening public has rejected most of the classical music written in the 20th century. As he told his doctor:

"You couldn't feed a synagogue rat on the income from contemporary music!"

By his third year at Curtis he'd realized that concert audiences have little use for most of the traditional classical repertoire as well. How often did one see an announcement of *Schumann's* Violin Concerto on a poster outside of a symphony hall? *Salieri's* operas? *Hummel's* piano concertos? The String Quartets of *Mendelssohn*? Any symphony of Dvořák's except the *New World*?

It was patently obvious that the audiences at classical music concerts, by and large, only want to hear a small number of established masterpieces played over and over again in exactly the same way.

The reality was enough to dampen the spirits of any aspiring artist, one still young enough to think of a career in music as a lifelong adventure.

Popular music was an alternative of course, yet it held no appeal for him: "Why," Sam argued, "should I devote my artistic life to playing music I don't like?"

Indeed, for a short time, Sam considered dropping out of the Conservatory altogether and enrolling in one of Philadelphia's world-famous medical schools.

Then Sam's imagination went to work, and in due course he discovered a silver lining within the dark cloud of professional classical music.

Any qualified musician, through mastering a few shrewdly chosen well-worn standards (the "war-horses"), could forever afterwards chuck out the sentimental garbage about snubbing the Philistines, shocking the *bourgeoisie,* suffering in garrets and *working for nothing,* and live out his allotted span of days surrounded by all the trappings of comfort and wealth. The promotional work involved would be more in the nature of a hobby: cultivating the agents, institutions and grateful audiences that would reward him handsomely for the dependable and undeviating rendition of the *tried-and-trusted*.

For his senior honors recital at the Curtis Institute of Music in May of 1946, Sam played the Paganini Concerto in E♭, the Wieniawski Concerto in D minor and the Bartok Unaccompanied Violin Sonata. Technically, these are among the most fiendishly difficult pieces ever written for the violin. He was never to play them again. By graduation day, Sam had narrowed down the list of pieces he intended to play *for the rest of his life* to a single indestructible paradigm: the first violin part of the orchestral score of Handel's *Messiah*, a piece of music technically accessible to any talented elementary school student after a few years of study of the celebrated Suzuki violin method.

Here it is important to note that, for accomplished musicians, there are no easy pieces in the classical repertoire. Mozart's violin concertos are an excellent example. There is little in them to appeal to the virtuoso. They lack all the gymnastic tricks one finds in the concertos by Paganini, Tchaikovsky or Sibelius; yet they aren't any easier to perform in public. A Mozart concerto is a guarantee for any performer of total exposure on every single note. He deliberately avoids using any of the gimmicks—popularized by Vivaldi, Tartini and others—that make the facile appear complicated. One finds in them no displays of brilliant effects that could be used to effectively cover up faulty intonation, bad phrasing or poor musicianship.

What applies to Mozart is also true of Handel. Even so simple a score as the first violin part of Handel's *Messiah* will resound, when played by a musician at Sam's level, as far above the renditions of your generic orchestra violinist, as the ravishing bouquet of vintage Château Lafite Rothschild wine will soar above the sour aftertaste of Gallo Red!

# SAM THE MESSIAH MAN

Sam therefore devoted four years, from 1947 to 1950, to the attainment of absolute mastery of the *Messiah* score. Every note, every tempo, every dynamic was committed to memory, bowings and fingerings constantly upgraded and revised (and in fact such experimentation with minor technical details continued all through his career). He bought all the recordings; studied the musicologists; analyzed the entire *Messiah* score—not just the violin parts—theoretically, historically, and artistically. Ultimately he knew every note of every part of the *Messiah* score, orchestra, chorus, and vocal soloists, as thoroughly as the world's finest conductors.

During the years it took him to acquire this proficiency, Sam supported himself by freelancing. Several orchestras wanted to make him their permanent concertmaster. He turned them all down; he *knew* what he wanted. Eventually he was able to convince all the prime movers in the music industry that his presence on the stage as *Messiah* concertmaster galvanized orchestras and audiences in a way that no-one had ever imagined possible.

Mind you, this was a young man, still in his twenties. Once he started playing, everything came together; the effect was dazzling. Musicians, bored to tears through having played the *Messiah* a hundred times over, suddenly discovered new excitement in its pages. To watch Sam at the helm was to be witness to a revelation! What the orchestral sound gained in homogeneity, sophistication and style was truly incredible. Conductors were known to comment that Sam's presence on stage made them superfluous: he knew the score so much better than they did!

By the early 50s, Sam could—and did—call the shots. He never played anything but this one piece, even for pleasure, even in his own home; never accepted a position lower than concertmaster; never gave interviews; or solo recitals; or lessons. (He did, however, love to give autographs. Sam appeared to revel in being seen as something of a character.) In 1963, a few days before the Kennedy assassination, his combined bank accounts passed the million dollar mark. Financial insecurity henceforth became a thing of the past; while wise investments protected his old age. By his own lights his crowning achievement had been the creation of a brand new profession within music: roving *Messiah* concertmaster!

The basic routine that had evolved over the 50s would serve him for the rest of his career. For most of January to mid-March, and the 6 months from May to November, Sam's fingers did not so much as graze the strings of either of his two prized Old Italian Masters violins. His Guarnarius, purchased during a sudden drop in the market for old instruments, was appraised in the 80s at $2 million. Two weeks' steady training in November, and again in March, sufficed for the cruel workloads of Christmas and Easter.

Between Thanksgiving and Twelfth Night and again for one month around Easter holidays (we're speaking of a maximum of 80 days) Sam slogged over 150 gigs! By the mid-70s his fees were averaging $3,000 per concert, while his yearly income was never less than $500,000. And rising with inflation!

Sam never disputed his friends and associates when they criticized him for having no ambition. He had no more desire to be super-rich than he did to be a great violinist. His goal in life, oft proclaimed with fatuous unction to friend, family and associate as "Sam's practical philosophy," was to do as little work as possible, yet live like royalty. It just happened to be the case, that this intention had, over four decades, translated itself into three months of back-breaking labor followed by nine months of delicious hibernation.

Sam was enormously proud of himself, and there is no doubt that he ought to be given credit for shrewdness: if there is one musical masterpiece that the world will continue to demand after a billion replays, it is Handel's *Messiah*. Handel's *Messiah* will outlast McDonald's hamburgers. Sam's nest-egg was indestructible as long as Christianity remained a force on this planet; nor was he about to lose any sleep worrying about the possibility of its sudden demise.

## SAM THE MESSIAH MAN

Of course, after 40 years in the music profession Sam hardly needed to hustle. Within the world of the performing arts everyone knew him as "Sam, the Messiah Man." Many anecdotes about him were in circulation. One of them, which is probably apocryphal, centers on a New York booking agency. Every year shortly before 11 AM on the third Monday in September, the entire staff gathers around the telephone. As they wait they place bets on the exact minute when Sam's call will come over the line. Sam always calls between 11 and 11:15. In the first ten years (so the story goes) he introduced himself with *"Hello. This is Sam. What's the Messiah been up to?"* Then he drops the *"This is Sam"* bit. Finally, after a decade or so, somebody picks up the receiver and barks (to the tune of "Yes, we have no bananas"): "Messiahs for Hire, Incorporated!"

Trade humor.

❋ ❋ ❋

Christmas Day in Boston, 1985. The *Messiah* concert of the Boston Symphony Orchestra was scheduled for the 3 o'clock matinee. A steady snowfall had begun early in the afternoon. The wind was high, the day bitterly cold. At 2 PM, true to form, Sam Goldberg's Lincoln Continental pulled up in front of the stage entrance on the north side of Symphony Hall. He stepped swiftly out the front door, retrieved his instrument case from the back seat, then handed the keys to the doorman to park the car in a lot on the other side of Massachusetts Avenue.

The previous 24 hours had strained even Sam's resources to the utmost. The ordeal had begun the day before with a flight from Denver to St. Louis to perform at a gigantic midnight mass concluding an Evangelical Congress at the St. Louis Convention Center. What sleep he'd been able to get that night had been done on the plane: immediately after the concert in St. Louis he'd flown to New York, arriving at La Guardia Airport in time to preside over a 9 AM *Messiah* concert at Columbia University's Union Theological Seminary.

8

His brother, a rabbi on the faculty, had been sitting in the audience. Although everyone else stood up during the Hallelujah Chorus, he'd remained seated. This breach of protocol may have reflected religious scruples, or, more likely, had been intended as a criticism of Sam's way of life. He couldn't wait around to find out: a chartered limousine took him to Newark Airport; there he boarded the 45-minute Continental Airlines shuttle to Boston. Sam had raced his car from Logan Airport through heavy Christmas Day traffic to get to Symphony Hall on time.

Nor did his commitment end with this matinee performance. At 1 A.M. that night another flight was booked to take him back to Chicago. Then onwards to Detroit and Ann Arbor, Michigan, and St. Paul, Minnesota: eight engagements in all, between December 24th and 27th!

A vortex of snow whirled like a tower in his wake, as Sam hurried through the stage entrance of Symphony Hall. A doorman cleared the way; Sam returned no greetings. During the holiday season one could not have uncovered so much as a mustard seed of benevolence in his calculating heart: these were *the most lucrative days* of the year. From the long travail beginning with the midnight mass the night before, and ending with a guest appearance with Pinchas Zuckerman's chamber orchestra in St. Paul, Sam raked in thirty thousand dollars! At the 1985 Consumer Price Index!

We interrupt this narrative to recall the list of principles that make up what Sam referred to as his "practical philosophy":

NO AMBITION

GOOD CONTACTS

PRECISION SCHEDULING

UNRIVALLED EXCELLENCE

*and*

A HARD-NOSED PHILOSOPHY OF LIFE!

## SAM THE MESSIAH MAN

Sam deposited his hat, coat, scarf and gloves in the cloakroom, then dashed into the Men's Room for some quick grooming. Within 15 minutes of his arrival he was in the wings, pacing the musician's lounge. The priceless Guarnerius violin was withdrawn from its case, the strings tuned, the bow tightened, the hair rosined. Warming up with scales or passage-work hardly seemed necessary: had he not already played the score twice over in less than 16 hours? Nor did he need to review the slight variants in the editions employed in St. Louis, New York and Boston: Sam knew them all.

A droll recording of the serenade from Don Giovanni, played on chimes and broadcast on loudspeakers throughout Symphony Hall, recalled the audience to its seats. The din of conversation subsided as the musicians began walking onto the stage in small groups. As the lights dimmed, Sam entered through the curtains at the left, followed by the Japanese conductor, Seiji Ozawa, now in his 14th year as permanent conductor of the Boston Symphony Orchestra.

With the consummate stage presence of a veteran of four decades of public service, Sam returned the applause from an eager audience by a deep bow at the waist. He placed a thin handkerchief on his left shoulder. His ear picked up the ambiguous "concert A" from the oboe. Following minute adjustments on his strings, he transmitted the ground pitch to the rest of the orchestra. Fans waved to him from the darkened auditorium. Turning to face them, Sam winked!

Once comfortably installed in the concertmaster's chair, Sam's gaze casually roamed over the ranges of sentimental pseudo-Greek decorative bas-reliefs along the edges of the ceiling. He remembered reading how Isadora Duncan had behaved at the time of her disastrous appearance in Symphony Hall in 1922. Ripping open her blouse to expose her bare breasts, she'd pointed to these same sculptures and cried to an astonished audience:

*"You! . . . You worship plaster Gods!"*

To himself Sam thought, "I wonder how much *she* left in *her* bank account?" And he smirked.

Orchestra musicians treasure their ancient jokes: one of them tells of a viola player who dreams that he's sitting in an orchestra, playing the Brahms *Requiem*. Waking up he finds himself sitting an orchestra, playing the Brahms *Requiem*.

But 40 years of conditioning had placed Sam far beyond the protagonist of this dour anecdote, far beyond either dreaming or sleeping, trance or even hypnosis. Sam's mental state was closer to that of the workers on automobile assembly lines who condition themselves to totally block out their minds while on the job. One might indeed characterize Sam as someone who, to a consummate degree, had fashioned himself into the perfect artifact of modern capitalism: a technician ridiculously overtrained for the production of a single absurdly specialized task.

One is therefore in a position to appreciate his distress when, beginning with the fugue that enters midway through the Overture, Sam acknowledged the encroachment of a relentless, annoying yet strangely fascinating train of thought. This time, despite his many years of conditioning, his mind *refused* to shut down on command. With an obstinate energy that caught him off balance, he found himself picking up and pursuing a meditation that had begun the night before in St. Louis while waiting out an endless peroration on Divine Intervention and the Virgin Birth. By the time of the entry of the first tenor recitative, *Comfort Ye My People*, a host of nagging reflections had swollen to the proportions of an obsession. Incredibly, no noticeable effects were apparent in his playing. Blindfolded, drugged, even comatose, Sam could still churn out a *Messiah* without fault or blemish. And this is what Sam was thinking:

"*Now, you take this man, Jesus. Just a man, mind you. Remember: just—a—Man! I'm a Jew (they don't let you forget it)... You're never going to get me to believe the Christians' 'Son of God' cockamamie... Between you, me, and the metronome, believing in God is already a crock, if you know what I mean. I've never met anyone who ever made a dime crying Hallelujah*

and crawling before an old man with a beard, begging for forgiveness . . . So! I'm a lousy Jew, too, all right? So why should I worry about his so-called Son, I ask you? . . . But you know, his birth was a good thing for me. Hey! I've made a fat income from it all my life, and look at it this way: it's funny when you think about it, but Christmas carols are like a kind of soup kitchen for jazz musicians . . . for musicians in general . . . Look, even a street musician can earn a living over Christmas! . . . and his death (Jesus's that is) gave us Easter, too, a real blessing, a mitzvah! . . . And, as a matter of fact, the goyim (forgive me, no offense intended!) consider his Death more important than his Birth, otherwise there wouldn't be any religion . . . and, say, when you really come down to it . . . "
Sam reflected, with a disturbing momentum that caught him off guard:

" . . . the way this man, Jesus, died, couldn't have been an accident . . . He was just a man, remember; just a man . . . A man, not God . . . how does it go? for the Holy Scriptures say that He rose up in the flesh and appeared to his disciples after three days . . . and they believed in Him . . . and again on the road to Emmaus . . . and only doubting Thomas refused to believe . . . until he touched the wounds . . . what utter rubbish! Then the early Christians went out into the desert, lived like hermits . . . and the martyrs were persecuted by Rome, which eventually acknowledges Christianity as its state religion . . . and it takes root in the two Empires, East and West . . . The collapse of the Roman Empire ushers in the Dark Ages . . . and the Christian Faith (with a little help from Charlemagne) conquers Europe . . . ultimately it spreads all over the world . . . "

Startled, Sam shook his head as if waking from a dream: *"How did I get onto this?"* Yet he soon fell back into the same train of thought: " . . . *fast track to the 18th century. George, the German monarch invited into England, brings Handel with him . . . Of course Handel conquers the musical world . . . and King George the First commissions the* **Messiah** *(or maybe it was George the Second . . . I don't think it was George the Third, that's the American Revolution . . . what do I know? I'm not a musicologist! I'm not even* *a violinist when you come down to it, or rather I'm a funny kind of violinist . . . ) so that millions of Christians around the world would flock to performances of the* Messiah *at Christmas and Easter, year after year for centuries . . . so that I, Sam Goldberg, could draw a guaranteed income for forty years, without having to learn a single God-damned new piece of music! or pretend that I really enjoy living like an artist, that is to say like a dog, or be forced against my will to be creative, or show initiative, or invent some kind of ambition in this* miserable! Cut-throat! Ruthless! Vicious! Wretched! Rat Race of a World!"

Sam's violin obbligato, composed by himself 30 years earlier to accompany the alto aria "He Was Despised And Rejected, A Man of Sorrows And Acquainted With Grief," was always the high point of his concerts. Over the years Sam had built up a loyal following that attended them solely to be transported by the sound of his lyric violin sobbing above the vocalist. As he began to draw the soft strains that raised the illusion of an amber glow over the trembling strings, Sam could scarcely restrain himself from crying out:

"*What* all *of this means is that Christ died for* me—*for me* alone! *Christ had to die so that Sam Goldberg, violinist, could live!*"

Like the sun emerging from the edge of a vanishing storm-cloud, Sam's stiff grimace crinkled across his face. Smug satisfaction rippled from ear to ear. He admired the cleverness he'd shown in reaching this conclusion. It was time once again to hew the line: his special relationship to Christ could be debated in his nine months of leisure. Calling upon almost half a century of conditioning, Sam once again totally emptied out his mind.

Yet: with an upsurge of mounting horror, Sam found himself, *for the first time in all his days as a* Messiah *concertmaster,* thinking about the *meaning of the words written in the libretto!*

"*. . . He was despised and rejected, a Man of Sorrows and acquainted with grief . . .* "

Responding to a strange agony moving through the depths of his interior oppression, Sam moaned softly to himself:

"I, too, am acquainted with grief! Didn't Judy, my daughter, die in a car accident when she was only 15? And when my mother died while I was on tour, I couldn't miss even a single day to be at her bedside . . . it didn't matter that I loved her as much as any son can love a mother, she had to die alone . . . And the doctors say there's trouble with my heart . . . They'll soak me for all the money I ever made, then throw my body into an unmarked grave, like Mozart! And property values are dropping in Concord . . . too many ethnics, like Sharon and me. We'll have to move—in our 70s! And Sharon, I know she doesn't love me, I've known it for many years . . . "

Sam wept copiously. Engrossed in their work, none of the musicians seated at the adjacent stands paid him any attention.

"Despised . . . Rejected . . . Rejected of Men! That describes me exactly, just as it did that man, Jesus . . . He gave his face to the smiters! And Oh, don't I know what that means! I know how they all hate me! Me, Sam Goldberg, the Messiah Man! because I graduated at the top of my class, and got rich through mastering a single score and playing it for the rest of my career! Oh they hate me all right!"

Like a moth returning to the scorching flame, his mind feasted obsessively on its torment:

"I am Sam Goldberg, the Messiah Man, despised and rejected of men, a man of sorrows and acquainted with grief! Behold and see, if there be any sorrow, like unto my sorrow!"

By a powerful effort of will Sam managed to pull himself together. Anyone observing him at that moment would have recognized that he was in the grips of a major emotional crisis. But why should anyone have suspected that something was amiss? Although he was sitting at the front desk, the audience couldn't see his face very well. The other musicians were too busy. His violin playing was, if possible, above even his normal standard of flawless perfection.

Yet somewhere in the middle of the chorus that begins "The Lord Gave The Word," there came that irrevocable moment when the deep truth he'd sought through these two long hours of misery exploded into consciousness, when Sam's suffering psyche was rent by the force of a grandiose revelation. It happened at the end of a long interior discourse that went something like this:

"*Jesus was a Man of Sorrows . . . I, too, am a Man of Sorrows . . . Jesus has been called 'The Messiah' . . . I am called 'The Messiah Man' . . . and Jesus died for Sam Goldberg alone, so that Sam Goldberg could live!*

" *. . . What does this mean? . . . What can this* possibly *mean? Hmmm . . . Jesus was born (Behold, a Virgin shall conceive!); Jesus preached to the multitudes; those who had ears to hear, heard; all others understood not . . . He healed the lame and the blind, raised the dead . . . He suffered and died on the Cross, the Prince of Peace . . . Afterwards his disciples proclaimed the teachings of their beloved Rabbi . . . What happened next? The Temple in Jerusalem destroyed by the Romans in 70 A.D., the Jews were dispersed, my ancestors among them. Miraculously, Constantine, the Roman Emperor, converts to Christianity; when was that, A.D. . . . 336 . . . Then the controversies, the schisms, the persecution of heretics, the long line of Popes. Feudalism, the Middle Age, death and destruction everywhere. Yet at the same time, the creation of our magnificent European classical music! . . . which develops, very slowly, under the patronage of the Roman church . . . the Protestant Reformation in the 16th century . . . Luther, Calvin . . . the Church of England, Henry the Eight . . . Queen Elizabeth! The golden age of English music and letters . . . until Cromwell and the Puritans ruin music in England . . . Then the Restoration chases out the Puritans and brings music back into the churches . . . What next? William of Orange, the Dutch invasion . . . The Glorious Revolution! . . . 1688 . . .*

"*Starting in the 18th century, Parliament offers the English crown to Georg Ludwig, Elector of Hanover . . . He orders Georg Friedrich Handel to join him in 1712 . . . who composes the Messiah in . . . 1741! Which is performed for the first time in Dublin, Ireland, on April 13th 1742! It all holds together . . .* "

Bewildered, Sam paused. Blind instinct alone kept him at the violin, while his mind raced ahead:

# SAM THE MESSIAH MAN

*"Mozart arranges the score for large orchestra. A Messiah cult evolves around Christmas and Easter, along with evergreen trees, wreaths, bunnies, turkeys, cranberry sauce, sweet potatoes, reindeer, Santa Claus! To the sole end that Sam Goldberg, violinist, also a Jew, could* KNOW! FULLNESS! OF LIFE!"

There was not a minute to be lost. As the Hallelujah Chorus burst over Symphony Hall, Sam sprang to his feet, strode to the front of the stage, and cried:

"I! AM JESUS CHRIST! I! *Sam Goldberg (violinist) am* GOD'S! OWN! SON! *God so loved the world that he sent* me, *Sam Goldberg (violinist), his only begotten Son! so that* YE MIGHT KNOW ETERNAL LIFE!!"

On its feet, bellowing out the Hallelujah Chorus at the top of its lungs, the audience saw little of this. But Sam's wild antics were being played out in full view of the entire Boston Symphony Orchestra. Seiji Ozawa indicated to the startled musicians that they should continue to go on playing as if nothing were the matter. In his 35 years as a conductor, he'd dealt with every kind of crisis. He paused just long enough to bend down to the principal cellist and instruct him to rush offstage, alert the security guards and telephone for an ambulance. The curtains would come down and Sam hustled off stage at the end of the Hallelujah Chorus. For the moment there was nothing to be done: Sam had to be allowed to rave at liberty.

Seiji Ozawa reflected that his father, a devout Buddhist, would have provided the apt proverb. "They all crack up in this racket!" he murmured, bitterly, under his breath in Japanese: "Each in his own way, sooner or later, they All—Go—Down!"

*Berkeley, 1986*

# Willy van Fritz

ITH HIS WIFE holding onto his right arm and leading the way, Willy van Fritz, the great maestro and composer, the virtuoso, burst into the clubroom! He strode through the noisy gathering on a route that took him directly to the great Steinway concert grand piano which, recently cleaned and re-tuned, seemed to be waiting for him. Bending down, he adjusted the height of the stool. He removed his jacket, rolled up his shirt-cuffs. Waving good-bye to his wife who had wandered off to mingle with the crowd, Willy sat down before the piano and—*Bang! Bang! Bang!*—churned up a fiendish ruckus.

The invited guests milled about in small circles on the thick Oriental rugs, inventing idle chatter as best they could, valiant in their efforts to ignore him. The reception was an exhibition opening, a *vernissage* for a certain mediocre though fashionable society painter. He could be seen, a tall, frail man in a dashing pinstripe, his hair wispy like a bush crocheted of silver threads, fortyish, ample of means and of astounding ancestry, waltzing about the room while putting forth a face upon which he'd slapped a grimace of simpering affectation.

The thought of raising some sort of objection never entered anyone's mind. Van Fritz was a great man and entitled to his eccentricities. There were even those who, despite the fact that their heads bulged above their necks, blood-red from the agony and strain, claimed to enjoy listening to his playing. Willy's wife stood by the punch bowl on the long oak table placed parallel to the big stone fireplace, distracting persons in her vicinity with nonsensical and idle commentary.

Nor did it seem unexpected (though it must undoubtedly have been irksome to several of them) when strings began to snap and wood crunch as Willy, his long mane wild and flying lion-like about, his lips slobbering with foam, his feverish face clammy with cold sweat, threw off the final vestiges of restraint, losing himself completely in the morass of his inspiration, and ploughed into the keyboard with all his might!

Eventually, as was bound to happen, his antics became unbearable to everyone. Each note emanating anew from the stringboard sounded its own autonomous calumny. The very air seemed to be suffocating from the endless reverberations of curses and oaths.

Even then, no-one dared suggest the slightest criticism of Willy's behavior. People seemed unable in fact to leave the room, either singly or in droves. They knew it would make a bad scene. Well! He stopped, anyway. Bending over to reach down to the briefcase at his feet, van Fritz pulled up half a dozen pads of blank music paper. Forthwith he gave himself over to composition, throwing notes onto the pages with amazing rapidity, using the fantastic collection of pens he'd tucked away in his jacket and vest pockets. Swearing to frighten the devil, van Fritz covered sheet after sheet with weird scribblings, crumpled them up into tight wads, then threw them back over his head into the room.

What, pray, was one to make of all this? As some of the guests crowded around the piano to watch the genius at work, others got down on their hands and knees, crawling about on the floor to retrieve the scraps. Apart from their brilliance, which was universally acknowledged, opinions differed greatly as to the proper interpretation of these random fancies. On both sides of each page one uncovered a chaotic jumble of symbols, among them such things as upside-down or mirror-inverted clef signs; absurd combinations of sharps and flats conforming to no known system of tonal organization; arbitrary numbers of ledger lines to a staff; lute tablature; Labanotation; words from over a dozen languages; mathematical symbols; and even some Egyptian hieroglyphics. There wasn't a single person in the room apart from Willy himself who could claim to understand what they meant, yet as the wads of paper flew thicker and faster, descending in regular volleys like hail or snow, almost everybody began dashing wildly around the room catching them from the air and stuffing them in their pockets. Only the painter, in whose honor the reception had ostensibly been organized, staunchly maintained a stoic if pitiful indifference. With relentless cadence, these scorched tokens of Willy's inflamed imagination continued to pour forth until all the pads were empty. Whereupon he once again turned his attention to the piano to savagely bang away, reducing the noble instrument to a pitiable shambles.

There was a general sense by now that they'd had enough. Most of the guests would have quickly made their excuses and left, had not the hosts prevailed upon them to stay for the refreshments that were about to be served. Shortly afterwards, liveried caterers entered the clubroom, laying out plates holding canapés, crumpets and crackers, neat little triangular sandwiches filled with spreads and patés, pastries, saucers of heaped olives, tomatoes small and tight as marbles, frayed celery stalks, tea, coffee, punch, Chablis. Hannalore van Fritz made her apologies to the painter who, though he affected to acknowledge her, was not able totally to conceal his irritation. There was nothing he could do. It was generally accepted that Willy's conduct was a textbook case of Promethean genius floating on a sea of infantile exhibitionism. Such insights made it that much easier to put up with him just a little longer. Above the rumble of conversation one heard the results of further experiments, exotic musical horrors dense with bone-wracking trills, unclassifiable dissonances, chilling modulations, as Willy van Fritz, ranging up and down the compass of the keyboard like an unshackled lunatic, shouted and sputtered obscenities in an unbroken stream.

## WILLY VAN FRITZ

The guests strolled around on chaotic trajectories, compulsively stuffing food down their throats, chattering trivia. Piercing the cacophony, a woman's voice rose to a terrifying shriek.

Everyone—not excepting Willy—froze. The matter appears to have been this, more or less: Willy's wife and the painter had gotten caught up in an altercation concerning the canapé recipes; or it may have been the prices of his paintings; or it may have been something else. Whatever it was, it ended with him taking out some kind of Moroccan dagger with a jeweled hilt and running it forcefully through her chest until it poked through on the other side.

The clubroom fell silent as fear and confusion took possession of the multitudes. Nobody was in disagreement over the circumstances of her death, although many details of the situation could be disputed. The painter, in some sense still the guest of honor, stood apart, neither remorseful nor guilty, at most embarrassed, perhaps awkward, the gory knife gripped firmly in his right hand, wiping away some of the bloodstains that had gotten onto his suit with a handkerchief from which there emanated a faint odor of lavender. Men rushed about every which way, stressing their self-importance, as they will do in such situations. Many of the women fainted; they were carried to couches and laid out, their dresses unbuttoned, their temples stroked with ice-cubes taken from the punch-bowls.

Now windows were thrown open so that people could stand in the casements and shout into the streets for help. The painter lay unresisting, having been seized and flattened onto the carpet, emitting vindictive chuckles, although probably uncomfortable with four men squatting on his arms and legs. As they berated him for his criminality, they also used the opportunity to let him know in what low esteem they held his artwork.

"Willy," one of them snorted, "Now; there's a *real* artist!"

Only then did van Fritz got up off the piano stool. The way was cleared before him as he slowly walked the room's long diagonal to arrive at the crumpled corpse of his wife. For ten minutes he just stood there without uttering a word, observing her curiously. Tears spurted from his eyes and he was heard to emit a deep sigh. Finally he nodded his head, made an about turn and went back to the piano. Visibly shaken but not about to be upstaged, Willy reached for a sledgehammer leaning conveniently against the wall, grappled it in his two hands, and began breaking down the piano, first crushing it in two, then pounding it to bits!

Panic descended universally. Terrified crowds surged through the exits—it was about time!—not pausing to say their goodbyes, forgetting their coats in the vestry, allowing the prisoner to get away, leaving the body of van Fritz's wife abandoned and soaking in a widening pool of blood. Willy alone remained, standing before the ruined hulk of the piano, his chest heaving, his arms hanging like a gorilla's, his face crimson with power and rage, aggressive, triumphant, the veritable anger of the Almighty, indeed as Samson himself must have looked when he routed, single-handedly, the Philistines. He stalked and stomped about the room like a heavy beast for a while, until he grew tired of it. Then he picked up his hat, coat and cane, and went home.

The next morning an ambulance arrived and a crew of workmen entered the building. The clubroom was thoroughly disinfected and cleaned and the body transported to the morgue. Restoration costs were conservatively estimated upward of seventy-five thousand dollars, and it is little wonder that the next meeting of the board of directors should have been entirely taken up with the question of where to raise the money. After proposals of subscriptions, benefit concerts and grant applications had been passed around, somebody made the suggestion of calling up Willy van Fritz himself to ask for his ideas. To ask him for a direct contribution was out of the question. He was known to be so poor that he scarcely had enough money to pay for a new pair of shoes, let alone cover the cost of a grand piano.

Yet even as they were debating the matter, Willy himself telephoned to offer his support! He would gladly commit himself to the composition of a symphonic masterpiece, based on the tragic events of that afternoon and dedicated to his wife. He assured them that performances of it around the world would bring in thousands of dollars. Anything left over from the cost of the damages he would gladly turn over to the family of his in-laws, he himself despising the very institution of money.

Willy's orchestral tableau in five movements, *Eternally Forlorn Love,* is now performed almost as often as the Blue Danube. The new piano, a Bösendorfer, arrived last autumn. It is both bigger and better than its predecessor. Willy is not likely to ever have a chance to play on it, as he is permanently banned from the premises. He considers this affront deeply wounding to his vanity and a monument to human ingratitude unparalleled in history.

*Philadelphia, 1958*

# Lincoln Center in July

ULY 12, 1976. The humidity was oppressive beyond the limit of nature's rights over mankind. A board of lights, flashing on the Prudential Building's facade blocking traffic to the north, monitored the temperature through a series of spontaneous adjustments: at 2:25 it stood at 98 degrees; in the next half hour it rose to 100; shortly before 4 PM it registered 104.

From where he had stationed himself Frederick Ross could observe clouds of smoke and ash mixed with cinders swelling over the regiments of skyscrapers, empty and desolate as craters on the moon, on Eighth Avenue one mile away to the south. The debris of the fire settled in lean pillows over their naked floors, their rusted girders reflecting the occasional dull flicker coming from the flames. An effect, he concluded, which might also be explained by buckling through the action of heat.

Indifferent to this dreadful parameter Frederick Ross stood in the shadow of the 72nd Street branch of the Manufacturer's Hanover Trust Bank and, numbed by stoic conditioning, played the violin. He was in his early thirties, lanky, nervous, dressed in jeans and a blue-green striped shirt, with a shock of dark curly hair that kept falling over his brow and had to be pushed back at awkward moments. A fair violinist at best. Leaving the New England Conservatory after two years only added to his difficulties. Musical ambition remained undiminished. The decisive factor.

The music stand to his right held sheet music of works by Bach, Vivaldi and Kreisler, while his violin case, open on the sidewalk before him, held the spare change thrown in his direction by the public. The top of the case, made from a leather-like copper-bright substance, had been decorated in acrylics around its central bulge with a delicate fringe of flowers and leaves.

This graceful decoration had been the idea of a friend, a painter enamored of mixed media, one of his co-worker's at the music store, Patelson's at 56th St. and 7th Avenue, where Ross put in two days each week. She had thrilled to the challenge of executing a masterpiece on the surface of a violin case. Her enthusiasm had crested then died away after enhancing the contours of its lid. This may, after all, have been wise: a tasteless ostentation, verging on vulgarity, could have been risked by an injudicious display of ornamentation. Frederick for his part would not have wanted anything to interfere with his proselytizing efforts in the high service of classical art.

Then again, like so many of the artists of Fred's acquaintance, she may have simply been high on inspiration but short on determination. He was not ungrateful: the graceful suggestion of lingering embellishment evoked nostalgia and elegance, a fantasy that both violin and case might have been rescued from some baroque villa surrounded by vistas of cerulean blue sky and labyrinthine vineyards in full view of the Mediterranean.

Ross may have been benighted, perhaps a trifle dense, certainly obstinate to imagine that his devotion to serious music was being picked up by the odd handfuls of heat-stunned pedestrians who, briefly, crossed within reach of his performance. Few were inclined to be generous even in fair weather. The squadrons of the work force, city office workers staggering wretchedly through thermal tidal waves to return to their—*at least!*—respectable jobs in air-conditioned offices, were astonished to encounter Frederick Ross in rolled-up shirt sleeves, his sallow face covered with a lather of sweat, functioning, so it appeared, on blind energy alone. Encouragement and appreciation were hardly to be expected: the reactions of the public veered rather in the direction of fear. What could possibly motivate this cheerless young man to labor—and with such ferocity—out on this sidewalk Inferno?

His dynamism did not inspire others, it only depressed them. Let it be granted, that Frederick may have gladdened a few potential victims of heat stroke via his sterling message of mind over matter. Unlike the vendors of lemonade or hot-dogs, nothing he offered had to be paid for. He could not have been making more than $3.00 an hour. Quarters dropped into his case with the stinginess of beads of moisture sweated out of desert rocks. Nervy types gyrated past him bent over the case ignored him counted his coins ambled down the street laughing.

The record states, however, that his efforts did not go entirely unrecognized. Lifting his gaze, ever so transiently, from the score of the E-major violin concerto of the eminent Bach, Fred took note of several picturesque faces turned in his direction, all beaming admiration without a trace of dissimulation across the traffic heaving along Broadway in both directions. Four steaming jack-hammer operators naked from the waist up, their bodies slicked with water, black streaks of tar and mud, had silenced their machines through a wordless consensus at the same time, to acknowledge kinship with the shy, bespectacled fellow proletarian on the sidewalk. He, like they, also despised the limitations of the flesh! Were anyone to ask their opinion they would concur: Frederick Ross belonged to the fraternity of real men!

Fire engines hurtled by in spiked intervals. Others, bleating like scared goats, followed soon afterwards down Columbus Avenue, their message alarmed and shrill. More trucks raced uptown, speeding directly past him then turning the traffic island to continue back down on the other side of Broadway.

Ross surrendered: even he could now no longer withstand the combined pressure of weltering heat public indifference mayhem economic disaster nightmare. The time was 4 o'clock.

He laid the violin carefully back into its case, draped a green, flower-print shawl over it, then snapped the locks. Pedestrians glanced down at him, sideways, with contempt. They despised him for giving up. They had despised him for continuing. He was an easy victim, a foil for the ambient hostility and broiling tempers of the equatorial day. His earnings for the afternoon came to $10; a few dollars of pocket change to take back to the Lower East Side, with enough for a sandwich and soda at the lunch counter of the Ansonia Hotel. He enjoyed chatting with its Greek counter girl, known on occasion to drift into humming delightful folk melodies.

Frederick Ross left the Ansonia around 4:30. A breeze, tantalizing rather than refreshing, heralded the evening. He fell into a leisurely stroll down Broadway towards the ASCAP building at the confluence with Eighth Avenue, just across the street from Lincoln Center. New York City mythology would have us believe that a superior class of highly cultivated people circulated through this area, loosely designated *Lincoln Square* by contractors and realtors. Direct experience had made him skeptical. He did concede that it might still be worth his while to play for a few hours, after the streets had cooled off and provided the fire were brought under control. He paused in the vicinity of the Juilliard School of Music, sitting down on one of the stone benches in front of Avery Fisher Hall.

Metal poles rooted in the sidewalks at this corner mount a thicket of billboards filled with concert announcements. He read them with the obsessiveness to be found only in the incurable music fanatic. Although he affected to despise both Juilliard and Lincoln Center as embodiments of all the forces in the musical establishment which, by his lights, were blocking his pursuit of a normal musical career, he experienced a vicarious, almost masochistic, excitement from the over-blown publicity provided for famous concert artists. During the season he attended as many concerts as he could. Street-wise New York City musicians have little trouble in obtaining cheap, often free, concert tickets.

Resuming his promenade he entered onto the spacious arena of buildings and esplanades feeding into Lincoln Center Plaza. Arriving at the great fountain before the Metropolitan Opera

House, Ross acknowledged further indications that the fire, still visible beyond the outlines of the buildings of Fordham University, was not resigned to fading away. A suspension of cinders defiled the spectrum of the waning day. Billows of smoke poured from some locale behind the Lincoln Center Bandshell, roughly in the direction of Roosevelt Hospital. The emergency could be serious, he reflected, taking a traditional comfort in the relativity of all catastrophe.

Dizziness assailed him with the suddenness of a shock-wave. It had become imperative that he step indoors to seek relief from the intense humidity, preferably in some establishment with reliable air-conditioning. In this neighborhood the only real choice was the coffee shop of the Empire Hotel, less than a block away, across the traffic island at 65th Street.

From the elegant hotel lobby Ross passed through a corridor into a room filled with props more appropriate to a typical small town bar and grill. Against the mirror behind the saddle-soaped counter stood liquors bottled in moon-rock canisters. Formica paneling and screens reflected silver glitter. Wrought-iron chandeliers supported electric candles that dispersed a dull, not even sinister illumination. Below these lay a floor tessellated by hexagonal ceramic tiles resembling cracking mud flats. He descended into the restaurant-café and took up a seat at the counter.

The restaurant was dark, cool, even chilly, but comfortable. All the same, it was only a matter of time before he would get up to leave: the atmosphere of the Empire Hotel café quickly became oppressive. Slaughterhouse red leather upholstery covered the bench seats in narrow, confining booths. The less inhibiting coffee counter supported a clientele mixing Empire Hotel residents, many of them musicians on tour, with the transient snobs flocking to this neighborhood to inhale the cologne of its manifold cultural attractions. A raised peristyle in the foreground of the café terrace lay prone, gripped in the embrace of a great picture window. The window ruined the terrace: it gave one the odd sensation of being trapped on a

Cinemascope screen. Hardly even a facsimile, even ersatz, of a Montparnasse café; merely noisy and unsettling. Clients who moved onto the terrace, enchanted by the dream of savoring a hand-me-down European charm, found themselves paying for overpriced ambiance lacking even the familiar satisfactions of old New York.

His discouragement could not have been more complete. He had to be a fool, he told himself, to want to continue to do battle with the City for a handful of pennies. His goal for that day had been to raise enough money for one of his rare lessons from the violin teacher he went to on Riverside Avenue, a genial gifted 72-year old Viennese woman who had been in this country since the 30s. Yet he'd earned barely enough to take the subway back to the Lower East Side.

The waiters knew Ross and were friendly to him. One of them came over after a short time, slid him a free ginger ale, and counseled him not to lose heart: a dance concert at the New York State Theater was scheduled to let out at 6:00. Only tourists went to dance concerts in New York at the height of the summer. Lovers of the fine arts, for sure, and with money to burn!

Ross thanked him for the information. He felt much better after a few minutes and, despite his aversion to the setting, remained there for almost an hour. The time passed quickly, chatting with the waiters and the person on the right, a cellist who sincerely wished he could do something for him and did not see anything odd or unusual about Ross's profession. Hanging around the restaurants in this area was sometimes useful for picking up information about teaching jobs, freelance gigs, and other potluck musical work. The cellist did not need to tell him what he already knew: that he had the talent and the musicality, but not enough of the training and none of the discipline for a full musical career.

Frederick Ross walked back out onto the street at about a quarter to six. From the moment he opened the door he found himself being carried along as if by compulsion across the rushing of traffic. The facade of the ASCAP building stretches the full length of 65th on the east side of Broadway. Like a 20-story battleship smokestack, its central core squats atop a prognathous marquee displaying the enchiseled initials "A.S.C.A.P." A procession of coarse-grained unsurfaced pillars concentrated around the front entrance before splitting into chains marching away in both directions. Behind and between the columns on both sides of the entrance stood the tables and chairs of high-class restaurants. In keeping with the predilection to commercial overkill that has made us renowned among nations, name and decor proclaim these establishments to be inflated caricatures of European prototypes. One discovered the *Fiorello* to the right of the marquee. *Cleo's*, more elaborate, more cosmopolitan (which does not prevent it from being the more humdrum of the two), lay further down the street in the opposite direction. Between Cleo's and the ASCAP entrance stood an unadorned sandwich shop which did a brisk business from office workers on their lunch breaks.

This location, in front of the sandwich shop but beyond the pillars and exposed to the street, was the only realistic choice of place for street performance in Lincoln Square. To stand right in front of the Lincoln Center Plaza across the street (or on the Plaza itself) was out of the question—not that Ross hadn't tried them! Although he could not expect to be welcome in front of Fiorello's or Cleo's, he was actually encouraged to stand before the sandwich shop. Its proprietor found Ross's image, combined with his solid musical taste, good for business. For him, coffee was always on the house, and at least once a week he found himself treated to sandwiches.

The dance concert audience had just begun to emerge from the doors of the New York State Theater. It fanned out onto Lincoln Center Plaza, descended its broad steps into the street in a doughy mass, then dispersed in the manifold directions available to it at this complex intersection. Among its members a reliable percentage would cross Eighth Avenue, traversing the traffic island to the east side of Broadway to be serenaded by Frederick Ross as they wandered uptown.

His rejuvenated spirits translated themselves spontaneously into his playing, now more lyrical, electric, accurate. The wailings of fire engines were becoming sporadic, the din of traffic in abeyance. At last he could hear himself play! Certainly he was producing a far better, more professional product than the tinny Bach he'd been reduced to grinding out at the height of the afternoon heat wave. He opened up with the first movement of Mozart's 4th Violin Concerto, followed by the 5th. (This choice was enough already to reveal that his opinion of his own playing did not entirely correspond with his real abilities. Only virtuosos dare perform Mozart's 5th in public.) With the swelling of the crowds he might realistically anticipate making some money.

Frederick Ross had yet to learn that his fate was not of the kind that makes men millionaires. Anyone engaged in the promotion of a craft on the streets of a large city can tell you about the deadly tightness of provincial tourists. Their numbers, combined with their remarkable appetite for getting rid of huge amounts of cash, conceal other less ingratiating traits. They descend on the commercial areas of the Big City, dragging along with them hosts of preconceptions about con-men and hustlers and beggars. They imagine themselves very clever in being able to detect them. For these minions the ambulant musician, the hawker of hand-made jewelry, the sidewalk chalk artist, even the hot-dog and pretzel vendors, are objects of suspicion. It is reasonable to surmise that the presence of this mentality will be found in roughly the same proportion among the crowds of visitors in every major cosmopolitan center.

As with the contours of their stomachs, there is a mushrooming tendency in their distribution curve around middle-age. The elderly have their relative tolerance, while children and students may be attracted to street artists out of curiosity; although, despite its legendary glamour, one should not overstate the case for youth. All street artists have had the experience of being cut to the quick by some scrubbed, callow, insolent collegiate type racing through the district to rubbish a century note on alcohol, prostitutes, grass, cocaine, discotheques, fancy restaurants or other gilt-edged trips, sneering with contempt at the people who live or work there.

Frederick Ross was able to get in about twenty minutes of uninterrupted playing before the mutterings from the crowd crossed the threshold of consciousness: "Get a job"; "Go back to school"; "Jackass"; "Bum"; "You're hurting my ears!"; "Squeak! Squeak!"; "Ouch! Stop!" Insults had almost no effect on him. Even a hostile response was better than nothing. He detected a genuine clash of values within them, a vicarious recognition. It was the unalterable, stolid indifference that rolled past him in unbroken wavefronts of unimpeachable solidarity that provoked his reaction of impotent fury. Anything giving true insight into the workings of the city's heart was brutally rejected. Brought together by the dream of savoring the tart vitality of the great metropolis, this debris of provincial America swirled its ignorance down the street. They moved in unison, these congregations of slack bodies, sour dispositions self-righteous with mediocrity, impelled by some mindless shuffling momentum towards the horizon in both directions.

The restaurant terraces had begun to fill up. Distributed among their customers, like wriggling splotches of color in a dingy sea, Frederick Ross could identify the faces of music lovers, people who recognized him for what he was and set some value on his efforts. Some of them smiled at him in such a way as to indicate that they knew he was playing Mozart; although it quickly became obvious that this recent, more cultivated, clientele were as little disposed to part with their dimes and quarters as the boors, for whom he might just as well have been grinding out meaningless noise. Frederick Ross gripped his violin by its neck and hurled it through the air. It was a petulant impulse, beyond his control, like the rash action of the movie hero who slaps the cad that insults his girl-friend; or the pianist who bangs shut the piano lid and walks off stage in protest against a discourteous audience; perhaps somewhat like the slamming down of the telephone receiver at the conclusion of a fruitless discussion. Frederick Ross had not been a willing participant in the act. As he had not made the decision to initiate it, there had been no time for its prevention through inhibition or restraint.

Hard stares filled with shock and pain turned in his direction.

Empty faces gaped wide as intellects unused to reflection tried to make sense of this astonishing deed. Had everyone just witnessed the spectacle of some crude individual trying to wreck a priceless musical instrument?

*. . . A viola was it, or a violin? What was that thing he'd been playing on anyway? . . .*

*. . . He had to be one of those local characters you hear about. That's how bad things have gotten in our own time. See how our glorious classical music is treated like trash! . . .*

*. . . Well, if you ask me, it's worse even than that. In fact, this individual is mounting his idea of a demonstration against the sanctity of Art! I would classify him as a public menace. You hear about those things these days: John Cage . . . Dada . . . Deconstructionism . . . ? I don't know what you call them, it's uncivilized, that's what it is . . .*

*. . . What nerve! Someone ought to give him a good talking-too. He's ruining the, how shall I put it, the bouquet of our delicious afternoon at the ballet! Such brutish conduct shouldn't be allowed to poison our refined pleasures, our cozy, insipid dreams, our gauzy fabric of soporific delight! . . .*

*. . . Hey, we're paying out six dollars for our goblets of wine, twenty dollars for the entrées, four dollar for each bowl of garden salad! I've been told you can buy a new car for the cost of some of those violins! . . .*

*. . . But really, when you come down to it, it's the whole idea of the thing! If you ask me, he's out to destroy Western Civilization! Hasn't somebody gone for a policeman? I'd do it myself except that the Florentine pasta will get cold . . .*

No one passed Frederick Ross a quarter. No one offered him a sip from a glass of wine, or even a glass of water. No one told him of a friend connected with a group or orchestra that might have work for him, or of some wedding where musicians were needed. No one in fact so much as spoke to him. Within the vapid faces that stocked the terraces on both sides as if under the command of some film director, hostility and fear were focused on him and him alone.

The violin had flipped in mid-air, landing belly-downwards; the fall had been broken by the arch of its bridge. The A-string had snapped. Otherwise it was undamaged. Those cheap factory instruments can be remarkably tough. Ross would never have brought his real instrument out onto the street. He picked it up gently and, very carefully, wrapped it in its green flower-printed shawl. Then he placed it, lovingly, correctly, in its case. The tension of the horsehair of the bow was slackened, the bow then being inserted between the clasps on the velvet upholstery inside the lid. The locks were snapped in place. The music stand was folded, then dropped into the briefcase. His sheet music was placed alongside the pages of a music-copying assignment due in a few days.

To the couple sitting close by, at a table to his left, still staring at him with suspicion yet into whose faces a predisposition for drowsiness had already begun to creep, he shook his fist and screamed:

> "You'd let a man starve but you're outraged when he damages a wooden box!!"

They averted their eyes, from embarrassment—yet, who knows, from honest shame?

Frederick Ross collected his gear stiffened his body walked self-conscious exhausted yet proud five blocks in the direction of the subway entrance at Columbus Circle. He needed to return home quickly to wash up and prepare for the lesson he was giving later that night. Provided the student kept

## LINCOLN CENTER IN JULY

his appointment. Across the street, on an electric bulletin board fastened onto the wall of the Empire Hotel, the blinking neon lights presented its opinion to the world: 94° Fahrenheit. Somewhere along Ninth Avenue, the clang of a fire truck.

*Hudson Valley, 1979*

# Logan Airport

ALKING through corridors. The same corridor endlessly repeated. The architecture sags, following the contours of faulted basements. Each step through the labyrinth throws you further off balance. Cheap construction is everywhere in evidence. Obese pillars, identical dowels turned out in series on the same lathe. Unsurfaceable cinderblock, cement walkways stained grey by the rains. The long unbroken ribbon of glass spreads in a single sheet extending for a quarter mile in either direction. It reflect the glare from a sun that is not our sun, a universe that is not our universe.

Multitudes of identical rubber mats mark the units of distance along your path. A double-ply shatterproof glass door opens and you enter the hall, to confront a mechanical doll in blue uniform seated behind a bone-white counter of abnormal length. Signs in gargantuan letters stand poised above her head:

> *ALLEGHENY AIRLINES*
> *AMERICAN AIRLINES*
> *DELTA AIRLINES*

It ought not be said that her face is entirely without expression. What it does express cannot be translated into recognizable terms. Neither love nor hate nor any obvious sentiment reveal their presence. She looks much as she is supposed to look. She looks as if she were receiving instructions from the omniscient forces.

## LOGAN AIRPORT

We are in a world governed by attendants wearing starched unwrinkled blue green gray red uniforms and who do not share in our humanity. Although not machines, their souls are made of a substance essentially different from our own. Along with the over-groomed and over-simplified personnel, you notice a handful of passengers milling about the waxed micaceous floor. They contribute to the sense of desolation that is produced by too small a number of persons in a cavernous space designed for large crowds.

And if, in addition, it is impossible to state which are the living, and which the dead?

It is time to ask for help: the Trans-World Airlines plane landed on schedule, but your friend was not on it. A short stubby girl, her head crowned with scalloped curls, her age fixed by company policy to within a shade of 21, nods in the direction of Traveler's Aid. In the metallic clip of her voice you hear the distant resonance of a cosmic tapedeck.

"You go out that door take the airport bus travel in cloverleaves around various dreary immense piles of porous concrete until if you are lucky the bus stops before an amorphous block of stone metal and glass identified as the International Airport. You are advised to step down there. The bus costs a dollar."

Her delivery is that of an automaton skilled in obedience: facial movements, arm wavings, language, vocal levels, swaying of the head and neck, have cooperated in mechanical synchronism. Hired for sex appeal, there is nothing even remotely human, let alone sensual, about her. She is one of the Airport's many appendages. And you hold her culpable for the theft of the dollar. You set out on a search for another opinion. You wander the endless carpets, like rivers of raspberry sherbet, coursing through these sterile canyons.

Information booths have been spaced every hundred yards or so. Their design is such as to permit the general public to ask if they might have been designed to anticipate the control panels of future jumbo jets. From their switchboards, zombie-eyes of frosted hue blink on and off. The black youngster behind the counter models a smart uniform destined eventually to be worn by the cafeteria help in space stations. He sits alone and presses buttons with futile gestures, communicating information with the lifeless air with which he came into the world. Word for word he recites the same statement beeped to you a moment ago by the young lady at Allegheny Airlines.

Each of them transmits on a different sound track from the same speaker system. You make a silly fuss about the dollar, although you don't know why you bother. At the sound of your voice the person next to you in line turns faintly hostile. The Information Officer smiles at your little joke: what an amusing idea that one, to walk!

"It is not advised. The International Airport is so far away." He shakes his head, a condescending twinkle in his eye: "And you may get lost!" You walk away turn at right angles grope towards the pleated rubber mat before the exits. The doors slice open and you re-enter the little village of pavements ramps pillars towers bare cinderblock walls tarmacs alleys roads.

One cannot determine the origins of the winds, nor their contents distilling onto our flesh. They have the taste of acid in them of distant refineries sterile wastelands without a trace of vegetation. This landscape (which it would be foolish to disobey), has intimidated the 30 or so persons collected at the Bus Stop into silence. Not one had had the slightest suspicion before coming here that an airport could be such grim business.

Overhead on the high ramps cars race like bullets. Planes scream in birth torment. We are nowhere; the planes are going nowhere. There must however be some relationship between these nameless labyrinths and those bellowing birds the stink of slaughterhouses in their wakes. Their insensible alienation sharpened by their inflexible sense of direction, they perambulate in geodesics about the globe. Rocking clouds dangle in the skies like synthetic rubber bubbles hanging from the high ceilings of bankrupt factories.

Natty buses hump along the concrete roads, idiotic like

the go-carts on an asylum golf-course. An Avis bus, a freak vehicle, spins down the road, weaving between columns and clumsy at the turns. The people seated inside have pleated their flesh bent their bones in obedience to postulates of truncated space-time; the buggy is too long too squat its face smashed in its puff roof pointlessly straddling a beer-bellied frame like a dunce's cap. A Budget moving van, a Hertz bus, and yet another grotesque vehicle used for transporting luggage follow in regular succession. There can no longer be any doubt that we are in a world ruled by robots, electro-mechanical servo-goons energized by distant dynamos. The realisation that you are never going to get out of here is just beginning to make itself felt. Maybe; if you had the money for a plane ticket. Which you haven't. Under the circumstances it makes just about as much sense to continue on to the International Airport to inquire about your friend. The bus pulls over to the curb and comes to a halt.

We pile on together: a middle-aged Blue Cross office worker with a heart condition; his wife; two women, violinists, their instrument cases covered with leather and slung over their shoulders; a blond secretary; a soldier in the army of some anonymous nation. You shove a dollar at the driver make your way to the back of the bus stop at the first available seat. Somehow you manage to squeeze yourself between the flabby body of a businessman and a globe-trotting youth, his backpack resting on the floor between his legs, the filth of 6 nations under his armpits.

The secretary does not have the exact change for the bus. She has no intention of giving the bus driver a five-dollar bill for a trip that she believes will only take five minutes. Were she to learn that the trip will last forever, she might withdraw her objections. Then again it might not make the least difference. What she really wants is to get the soldier to make change for her. He doesn't feel like being helpful. Or perhaps he hasn't got the change. Or perhaps he does have the change but doesn't want to part with it. Or it may simply be that he doesn't hear her request. His basic attitude, inferred from his posture, seems to be that there must be very little intersection between civilian and military life.

You rise from your seat walk over offer her the money. It is vehemently rejected. You are of no interest to her; any dealings with you beyond the absolutely unavoidable might compromise her standing in society the respect of her friends her job. The soldier belongs to a different category. She will do anything to please him.

All the driver wants is the bus fare.

You return to your seat shove yourself between the oblate banker to your right and the unwashed vagabond to your left. You find yourself staring with exaggerated interest at the advertising filling the sequences of cardboard rectangles at the border between the walls and ceiling. A toothpaste ad . . . or might it not be propaganda for the toothbrush? From the mouth of a bent tube a white turd bulges gleaming onto the horizontal obsidian bristles of a plastic green armature.

At the far right of the field reclines the snoring head of some Caribbeano. To his left, the carousers at two different parties. They chant the same message to a notated fragment of song:

"MY BEER IS RHINEGOLD THE DRY BEER!"

The sybarites are portrayed in simian caricatures, as if the consumption of Rhinegold beer somehow makes it easier to wallow in animality. To the right of the Rhinegold song the taxpayers of this municipality have paid for an inducement to the public to visit its closest Off Track Betting Center and gamble on the horses. Above the retouched photo-montage of a foolishly happy country gentleman in foolish Harris tweeds leading his confused horse by the reins, one finds a cautionary note in the tiniest print: the address and telephone number of Gambler's Anonymous.

But how can we have come so quickly to 96th and Broadway?

You leap off the seat rush through the door of the Uptown IRT, terrified lest they slam shut like Siegfried's sword slicing you in two. Out of the doors of the 7th Avenue local into the bowels of hell! You move through a contaminated nightmare garlanded with steep runways iron bars, gassy pools of blackish density punctured by bitter sunlight. Slimy homunculi cast shadows long as solemn subdominant ninth chords moted with billions of transgalactic vermin. The denizens of this underworld move quickly with familiar domesticated gestures of terror, making way silently as you pass, though you remain invisible to them.

The roar of traffic overhead is deafening in its relentlessness. With a leap, like a rat ejected from its embankment by the floods, you burst from the loins of the subway onto New York's Upper West Side!

*CUCHIFRITOS...*
*PIÑA COLADA...*
*ARROZ Y FRIJOLES...*

You stroll up the Broadway's West Side at the height of the blazing afternoon past aggregates of immigrants derelicts street vendors harried musicians students persons on the lam executives working folk huddled in doughnut shops over dirty coffee counters. New York's excitement is ever sordid; persons without needle marks on their arms have them on their brains. Flesh flicks and Chinese restaurants. People pushing and shoving and stepping all over one another. That's New York!

A shabby newspaper kiosk shelters in the pocket of a bank building's enclosing wall. Though it is summer and mid-day, a naked light bulb burns perpetually, like a lighthouse beacon. The New York Times, The Village Voice, Daily News and other traditional rags rest on piles falling in complete disarray about the sidewalk. One finds papers from every country in the world; you buy a dozen. Framed in a rickety casement, a flabby dwarf, like driftwood washed up from distant shores, squats atop a steep tripod. Weighted down by the years, he wears a green cap and, although shrewd, has little time for imagination. The

Rhinegold sits, in the form of the Nibelungen ring, securely tucked up his anus. You retire into a café, order a coffee, sit down at a table and begin to read. On the front page of every paper there is a picture of some street or landscape inclined at a steep angle. You study these carefully. Inclined streets are more meaningful; descended with urgency, climbed with purpose, they bestow on one a sense of accomplishment . . . *climbing after midnight in the company of friends along Circle Road the hairpin turn winding about Montreal's West Mountain urging ourselves via steep pathways lined with Gothic estates ponderous monuments to supercharged dreams descending in summer noon down the hills of San Francisco humming with traffic crowds restaurants shops stalls and residences scattered like loess on eroded mountainsides skating volcanic flows vomited from deep recesses of Earth tumbling down the slopes of Montmartre over the causeways of the Sacre-Coeur through canyons and gullies to the plains of Clichy Pigalle Barbes rue de la Goutte d'Or revving a motorbike over the peaks of the Massif Centrale down through the Rhône Valley Valence Avignon Aix Marseilles through Provence to the Pyrenees bathing in rejuvenating streams of Mount Canigou carrying me through Collioure Port Vendres Banyuls Cerbère Mediterranean sunscapes over Moorish castles weaving the knotted macramé of medieval streets of Barcelona . . .*

We hiked up Tibadabo mountain to the magnificent vistas at the summit. The carnival park, somber artifact from the future in antiquated Spain, was closed for the summer holidays when, searching for the friend who was supposed to have met us at the El Prat de Llobregat airport, we climbed up to it on a broiling August afternoon. Had I not been as tight as any other American tourist we might have spared ourselves the labor by spending a few hundred pesetas on the Funicular. Nervously fingering the porcelain crucifix dangling from a chain around her neck nestled on her busom, the shy barmaid from the red-light district seated beside me looked out over slopes dense with vegetation.

*Or are we not in reality inching our way up the Butte Montmartre?* There is some support to this hypothesis: with

## LOGAN AIRPORT

some astonishment we regard an unruly conclave of two dozen French university professors sitting and standing about our trolley car gobbling away like indignant turkeys. Crouching under the seat at the far corner of the car, one can make out the contours of the sinister Orson Lime; he has hidden himself well. He comes to us via the Ferris Wheel in the Vienna Prater courtesy of Flughafen Wien Schiphol Gatwick Logan Newark Reykjavik Charles de Gaulle. His glare is all malevolence; he plays the blue zither.

The polemic proceeds apace. The acrimonious gibberish of the schoolmasters fills the tiny cell. They speak a pastiche of greekisms, concepts coined in British and German universities, and low Paris argot. They are analyzing the syntactic form of the construction of the question of whether a truly engaged Marxist would worry about whether the psycho-analysis of literature is more important than the psycho-analysis of life; and various forms of the contrapositive. Not only are they prepared to kill for their beliefs, they have already done so: two professors from tiny villages in the Gironne, both decorated with the Legion d'Honneur, lie stretched across the stalls of the ferris-funicular, their skulls bashed in with paving-stones from the Barricades of May '68.

Russian soldiers stand about the car, scratching their bald heads. They stick their Kalashnikovs through the windows and amuse themselves shooting down seagulls arriving over the Seine from the Danube. The soldiers keep their distance from the squabbling professors. They listen with great respect; they have been brought up to revere French culture, which always relates to revolution. Orson Lime emerges from his hiding place to peddle morphine about the compartment.

The diapered baby howls "Buvez Cinzano" from a green poster covered with scatological graffitti. Context is all; I lay my hands on the shoulders of the Spanish barmaid rip her blouse from neck to waist bury my head between bared breasts leaping like nubile lambs, the scent of *Sardinas a la Planta* mixing with the pungency of cooked wine. There is commotion and clatter.

We hear the din of approaching riot but ignore it. The car wrenches itself around a tight corner, creaking like an old invalid, slams to a halt shuddering in staccato volleys proceeding from front to back. Lights blink on and off: the Metro has completed the gruesome route from Pigalle to Étoile. The doors fly open; aromas of jet-liner exhausts fill the compartment.

In the turmoil and confusion you made your apologies tore your head from the barmaid's busom flew through the door to the platform collided with a wild dishevelled hag flailing an accordion. Long knotted tresses teeming with mites covered a ravaged and debauched face. The many layers of rags draped about her carcass shook with rage. Knocking over two bankers, a retired general and three North African rug merchants you dashed up the stairs to emerge onto the Place de l'Étoile. Then you rushed across traffic to the arcades of Le Drugstore where, from a secret booth known only to yourself and a few intimates, you placed a free call to Boston's Logan Airport.

Like kayaks bucking the rapids three Citroëns, beige, blue and red cut through the traffic gyrating the Arc de Triomphe and rose against the fierce currents entering by all directions made their way to the Parc Monceau. Behind the steering wheel of each coupé sat a young architect, each a recent graduate from some college in California. They were late for a conference, an important meeting, the purpose of which being to determine the quickest and cheapest way to pave over the Parc Monceau, setting for much French literature, some gorgeous scenes out of Proust for example. It was unfortunate, though inevitable, that the park would be at the ideal location for the parking lot and shopping Mall necessitated by a shrinking economy in a world of limited options. The Mall was expected to be completely modern, the height of modernity, indeed an exact copy of the one the architects inspected just the year before in Hyannis on Cape Cod.

No cause for alarm! The Mall would also be distinctively French, the contours of the proposed complex following the lines of a pentarhomboidaldodecahedron, the alleyways between the buildings anointed with charming names like *Chausée Mozart, rue Michel-Ange, Place Cervantes, Impasse Proust* . . .

Buses cars jeeps trucks motorcycles bicycles Velosolexes horse-carts joggers pedestrians stride the 12 lanes of the Champs-Élysées in all directions growling blazing hissing wrestling murdering slamming shouting spitting cursing. The grinding of metals sound like the howls of dogs pushed through meat-grinders. 3 motorbikes and their drivers, mashed to a bloodied paste by savage truckdrivers, are being swept against the sidewalks of the grandiose boulevard. The traffic, waved to all points of the compass by the gendarmerie, fans out in long strings like gobs of chewing gum from the mouths of spiteful children.

A tap on the shoulder from behind. You turned around to confront a rotund individual in drab suit and tie, crunching maniacally on the stem of a pipe the ashes from which dripped down your shirt front. His wire-framed glasses lenses round and huge, stood poised to fall off the rim of his nose. Bull neck and protruding belly lay hidden beneath the crests and furrows of his flowing red beard. A small though heavy box, some kind of high-tech gadget, was tightly gripped between his flaccid palms. Alternately garrulous and obnoxious, he turned out to be an internationally recognized physicist speaking a highly educated broken English with a foreign accent that was unmistakably non-French. For the last two hours he'd been searching for the physics labs in the neighborhood of rue Pierre Curie and the rue d'Ulm.

"Id moast be in dis' place, No? Nearly datza big brick house over dere—vat you 'tink?" He pointed to the Arc de Triomphe.

You tried to explain to the nerd that the distance from the Place de l'Étoile to the Rue d'Ulm is not less than 6 kilometers. Predictably he erupted in hysterical fury. The do-hickey, I learned, was a bomb. I transliterate:

"State of the art: a 'quark' bomb! Quark bombs consume everything in quarter acre around detonation point! The blast area hangs on as Black Hole for next 25 billion years. If bomb explodes during conversation, entire Champs-Élysées get sucked into vacuum! Could been defused in labs on rue d'Ulm. Now too late. Vat in hell you me expect to do!?" he screamed.

You then advised him to run to the Parc Monceau and make a gift of the bomb to the gathering of architects. As a Black Hole, the Parc Monceau would at least never have to suffer the indignity of becoming a shopping mall! When he returned you invited him to join with you to take in a film at the Cinemathèque in the Palais Chaillot.

The auditorium darkens; the film begins. A middle-aged man walks a 10-speed whitegreen bicycle up Chestnut Street on Boston's Beacon Hill. The time of year is late September; leaves brown and yellow fall about him in the frail mists. He leans against a knobbly lamppost stares up at the sky counts the doors and windows of a jetliner passing directly overhead. The plane is bound for Logan Airport. Later that evening he will be riding his bicycle over there to meet a friend. The bicycle is turned around as he prepares the descent to Charles Street.

On the way down he stops to chat with a brittle dowager who has poked her head through an opened window, its panes fashioned of antique colonial glass. A crooked finger supports a custom-decorated Chinese teacup filled with anisette. Six cats pile over her head and shoulders. They are fatter than laughing Buddhas, but they are not laughing. They regard the cyclist with profound mistrust. Two of them have eyes missing one is part reptile another is burnt to a crisp the rest have lost their tails. Carrying on a conversation with this woman is difficult as she refuses to understand any language other than the one invented by Jonathan Edwards and brought to perfection by Oliver Wendell Holmes.

Biding her a fond farewell the cyclist leaps onto the handlebars to tumble down the long steep street to certain death at the other end.

The woman will no doubt chain her bicycle to the back fender of a delivery van after its driver assures her that it will not be moving for the rest of the morning. She will then descend a staircase and enter the pastry shop below ground level which at that time will probably be managed by a Norwegian couple. Her waitress, a girl in her mid-twenties of glacial mien, buries her scalp beneath a haystack wig lifted from a department store mannequin, mannequin eyes of Carrera marble, Carrera marble breasts pointed like guided missiles. Disdain on her brow, her mouth indifferent; with a deft swipe she will shear off a slice of cheesecake, placed it on a crinkled paper plate, and push it over the counter in the woman's direction.

After paying one expects that the bicyclist will move on, draw coffee from an urn at the far end of the counter, sit down behind a square table set in the most obscure recess in the crowded room. Hardly will she be seated when a suspiciously distinguished Old World gentleman, rendered ever so much more suspect by a top hat and frayed hand-me-down rumpled suit, will certainly reach over from his table to hers to pass her the morning edition of the Boston Globe. A felt pen will have been used to encircle a message in the Classified Ads with a thick smear. It was in this way that the woman will learn that her friend was slated be on the first plane arriving at Logan Airport that afternoon at 4.

Her further instructions are explicit. She is to finish her snack without making herself conspicuous, then move to the part of the room indicated by the tip of the umbrella of the elderly refugee. This duly noted, she will toss a grateful nod in his direction for having, at last, given her the information sought these long months. Glancing through the ground-level windows of the pastry shop just long enough to see the delivery van dragging her bicycle through the streets of Beacon Hill, the woman will stand up and make her way to the Ladies' Room down a narrow staircase illuminated by a large and dull red lightbulb.

Logan Airport: the lounge. Without a doubt this must be the right place. You notice the violinists seated together on a bench, violin cases and bodies ineluctably locked in a disjointed

Cubist embrace. Your passage is blocked by yet another turnstile. It requests a quarter; a roving secret agent gives you one and you pass into Logan Airport. With a grimace you collect three suitcases jostle with the crowds irritably descend the escalator to the lower levels freedom. Anxiously you await your friend. There is so much to tell! You reach the bottom of the escalator enter another lounge sit down to wait.

I could not be there to meet her. For three hours I found myself trapped underground between Government Center and Kenmore Square, on the B-train of the Green Line. It was lamentable that a thrill murderer boarded the train shortly after I did and sank a shiv through the neckbone of a weary business executive—who may not have had too many reasons for living anyway. Then he pushed past me into the window seat next to mine, brought out a second knife from the instep of a leather cowboy boot and regarded me with malevolent fascination.

Our society tends to think of aggressiveness as rather a good thing. In the case of this tragic youth it was linked with traits of a decidedly less desirable nature. He squirmed in his seat reamed his ears with the eraser end of a pencil threw out Christ's, damn's and shit's in quick succession with appalling vehemence smoked spat on the floor farted cried cock sucker, mother fucker and son of a bitch. With the point of his knife he pryed loose a bit of wisdom tooth from the back of his mouth and spat it out directly in front of me on the floor. Where else did I want him to put it? he seemed to say.

Interpreting my prolonged silence as a sign that I might possibly be afraid of him he said:

"*YouZE SAW WHUT I JUST DUHN to dat UDDER GUY I bet? I mean like DIDn't youZE . . . HUUUHNN?*"

In the pair of seats just in front of ours a proper Bostonian from Beacon Hill sat with her entourage, half a dozen cats that crawled over her head and shoulders. In the crook of the index finger of her right hand she held an custom-made Chinese teacup filled with anisette. I leaned forward onto the metal bar at the top of her seat and asked her for advice.

"Don't you know?" she crowed, "I've always thought that dealing with unwanted bores was everyone's first lesson in life! My dear," she went on, turning around to make me the present of a calico cat, "You must put the CHILL on him!!!"

Leaning back into my seat, I regarded him with astonishment, as one might contemplate a piece of rotten meat on display in a grocery counter:

"PAWdon me—SIR! Are you, by the most imprAWBable kAUHMbination of circumstAWHNces, ahdRESSING mE?"

So I takes de cat up from dis here bozo's lap and GETOUTTADUH train at Borstun eUnervoisity, cause uh duh Diffuhrentshel Geometry seminar. Dis here moron what's givin dis lecture or class or seminar or fucken COKEquillIUM ain't nothin' butta dumb mudder-fucker widduh fat ass ennuh bushel'uh beard all ovuh his rotten dirty little face. Dey flies him here over here fromuh shack up innuh Payruvhian Andes justuh givus dis here SHIT about Abstract Geoidiocy!!

Hey! You wunna know sompin'? He must be duh same meatball I seed gettin' offa Trans-fucken Woild Airlines dis morning at Logan! Well, hez some kinda big shot I guess, even dough his shit don't stink no better'n mine!

DEFINITIONS: *Let M be a manifold, O and A two arbitrary points on the manifold, their coordinates specified relative to a stationary reference frame.*

*Let K be the collection of all infinitesimal displacements with origin at O.*

*Let X be the sub-collection of all members of K which, when extended, intersect A. We will say that M is geodesically proper if every such sub-collection contains at least one non-infinite member.*

POSTULATE: *The Earth, as defined through the researches of Erastothenes Strabo Columbus Magellan Lindbergh and others, is geode-ically proper.*

THEOREM: *There exists a preferred direction along which any airplane departing from the airport in Lima, Peru at a positive*

*velocity, will arrive at Boston's Logan airport in a finite amount of time.*
PROOF: *I myself am here giving this lecture.*

When I hears dat stuff what makes me vomit I breaks up his schtupid lecture cause I wanna drag duh asshole outta dis here lecture hall soz I can stomp all over his face!

"*Haz it ever occoid to youze,*" I yells, "*dat youze don't make no discrimination between duh Lie algebras uv duh vector fields, and duh symplectic manifolds uv duh differential forms!! Huh, schtupid assed mudder fucker?*"

Snifflin' likeuh goat in heat, duh honored goofball leers at me like I'm some kinna whore's douchebag! But he answers duh question. Ain't no jerk-off gonna come five tousand miles justuh scratch his balls when he could be sittin' at home fuckin' a llama!

"*Sir! Only Mayans worry about things like that! We Incas, you see, are renowned engineers, not nit-picking mathematicians!!*"

It was at this point that I ran out of the room. Not because I was offended mind you—though I must say it is a bit odd at a science conference to see someone ramming a switchblade through the ribs of a colleague over a mere disagreement in terminology—I left because I remembered that a friend of mine was due to arrive in less than an hour at Logan Airport and that I'd promised to meet her.

At the entranceway I ran into a man and a woman, a pair of specialists in dynamical systems from Moscow University, and a departmental secretary, another woman. They beseeched me to drive them to Logan Airport: they were fleeing the country. We crossed Commonwealth Avenue, walked quickly to a parking lot near Kenmore Square and got into my car.

Having driven onto Tremont Street escape is impossible. Pyres of chain-linked 10-speed bicycles block all the streets surrounding Boston Commons. Angry university students (of which Boston shelters over a hundred thousand) crouch behind barricades erected at all the street corners. Next to them sit accumulated stockpiles of cobblestones tear gas canisters flares

## LOGAN AIRPORT

baseball bats Molotov cocktails. It all seems a bit odd for Boston.

Bombs burst trails of smoke obscure the view chants of solidarity rise up shouting cries of agony moans. Enraged students surround the car dent the roof puncture the tires set it on fire roll it down the street towards the police phalanxes in riot gear deployed in defensive positions all along State Street. The car explodes: the women the men the cat are incinerated in microseconds their interleaved ashes lifted by billowing winds and gently deposited over Greater Boston. Thick banks of ash accumulate around Logan Airport over the runways the planes the ramps the buggies the beings vehicles the buildings the lawns.

The mobile staircase is rolled across the tarmac to the entrance of the plane. You descend. The middle-aged woman at your back is bossy, bad-tempered. She pushes you along with the point of her suitcase. Just ahead of you stands an elderly minister of some eminently respectable sect its headquarters on Beacon Hill. He is in poor health and you don't want to collide into him.

Gripping the railing you examine the traceries of ramps and runways stretching endlessly towards the horizon. Cars race up and down the roadways like frenzied cockroaches. Helicopters lift from invisible beaches to hover expectantly over the runways. Hyperboloid cooling towers dot the landscape. They give off a savage roar as the winds suck into them. Clouds swell; disappear. Planes skitter off to the abyss.

Two pale suns are setting in the West. The clocks will never function again. Nor were they ever intended to.

Entering the lounge of the International Airport you sit down to wait.

*Hudson Valley, 1978*

# Amplitude of the Cosmos

s the beautiful blue dawn rose over the banks of green Volkswagen vans parked alongside all the curbs of Brattleboro, Vermont, Brahms sang down from heaven, and all was definitely a bit sinister with the world, Dietrich Zinzindorf, an Austrian émigré cellist with a sinister smile, and whistling selections from Brahms, drove his green Volkswagen van through the narrow, twisting streets of Brattleboro, Vermont in the early dawn.

Was it because he wanted to rouse the uncouth laggards slumbering inside their hillside condominiums, that he pressed the heel of his right hand against the car horn so that it blared over the village like the violin score for Schönberg's String Trio as played by a beautiful and wickedly aggressive Japanese woman violinist? Or was Dietrich Zinzindorf merely fleeing the inevitable crumbling of the North American pre-Cambrian shield, ancient core of the entire continental mass? The dull glow hovering ever over the crumbling archways of picturesque Brattleboro ejaculated the sperm of madness.

After circumnavigating several mountains, a green Volkswagen van driven by an Austrian émigré cellist, sinisterly smiling and whistling snatches of Brahms, stood before the gates of the Yankee Pilgrim nuclear power plant. Parking the vehicle alongside the curb, he opened the can of kippered herrings and uncovered the mounds of old bagel crusts he'd put aside for breakfast. He munched over his meal with deliberate care. Sticking his left hand in the left pocket of his blue orlon trench coat, he foraged among the colonies of head-lice for a shredded pocket score of the Brahms F-minor Quintet. Then, blowing away the vermin, he settled into his reading.

Around the same time that the beautiful blue dawn rose over the banks of green Volkswagen vans parked alongside all the curbs of Brattleboro, Vermont (while Brahms sang down from heaven (and all was definitely a bit sinister with the world)), Jean-François Aspèrge, an embittered and chronically unemployed celesta player, a man deeply jealous of all successful concert artists, sat at the table nearest the entrance of the bakeshop underneath Brattleboro's most picturesque crumbling archway. As he munched over his mound of old bagel crusts, he cursed the Marlboro Music Festival in a bizarre mixture of French, Russian and Malayalam.

In the coal-black depths of the previous night, for their concert in the Marlboro College concert barn-auditorium, the beautiful and wickedly aggressive Japanese woman violinist Mitzi Kagami, the Austrian émigré cellist, Dietrich Zinzindorf, and warmed-over Death had, while cursing the North American pre-Cambrian shield under their breaths in a mixture of German, Japanese and Medieval Church Latin, whistled the Schönberg String Trio. Midway through the piece Death stalked out of the barn, ejaculating the sperm of madness. Over their audience, from the crumbling recesses of her coal-black eyes, Mitzi Kagami (who had, only that afternoon, rejected the marriage proposal of a diamond merchant from Malaysia) flashed glances of surly contempt.

All this and more—and much more—was on Jean-François' mind.

Murder was on his mind. Murder, and revenge, and blood! At odd moments, he would suddenly shout *"Blut! Blut!"*, imagining himself in the last act of Alban Berg's *Wozzeck*. Jean-François had convinced himself beyond the shadow of a doubt that the beautiful and wickedly aggressive Japanese woman violinist Mitzi Kagami was sleeping with the Austrian émigré cellist, Dietrich Zinzindorf of the sinister smile. He had formed the determination to assassinate them in their beds (or bed, as the case may be). Indeed, he had already chosen his murder weapon: a razor-sharp hunk of obsidian torn from the nearest extrusion of the North American pre-Cambrian shield, ancient core of the entire continental mass.

Joyous with anticipation, Jean-François wept tears of beautiful blue dawn. Sticking his left hand in the left pocket of his blue orlon trench coat, he foraged among the colonies of head-lice for a shredded pocket score of the *Marteau Sans Maître* of Pierre Boulez. Blowing away the vermin, he settled into his reading.

It was somewhere around the time when Dietrich Zinzindorf, finishing the last of the kippered herrings and smiling sinisterly, was preparing to turn his green Volkswagen van around to make the return trip to Marlboro, Vermont; when the concert-barn was being vacuumed clean of head-lice, old bagel crusts and shredded pocket scores; when Brahms sang down from heaven (though all remained definitely a bit sinister with the world), that warmed-over Death, shrouded in a flowing burnoose, walked out of the best bookstore on Brattleboro, Vermont's main thoroughfare and stalked its streets, all of them lined with banks of green Volkswagen vans parked alongside all the curbs.

Brattleboro snorted in derision. Green Volkswagen vans over all Vermont belched kippered herrings, their motors snarling the strains of Brahms' Alto Rhapsody. Rivers ran red with Austrian émigré cellists. Wandering through picturesque crumbling archways, the eyeballs of Brattleboro's most abandoned alleycat ejaculated, from their coal-black depths, the sperm of madness.

And it must have been just then that Jean-François, the embittered, chronically unemployed celesta player, deeply jealous of all successful concert artists, rose, crouching, swiveling and sniveling—rose from the table nearest the entrance of the bake-shop beneath Brattleboro's most picturesque archway— and dashed up the street without paying his bill!

## AMPLITUDE OF THE COSMOS

As through the frosted window-panes of the bake-shop, with the sneer of contempt he reserved for all musicians, the baker watched his flight, Jean-François jiffied up the narrow streets of Brattleboro, Vermont in the beautiful blue dawn. He quickly displaced the unnerving silence of this mountain village and its host of uncouth slumbering laggards, and stumbled almost the entire way up the mountain to Marlboro College, God bless it. The wild whistlings of willowy winds swirled Schönberg through his hair. From their crumbling depths, his coal-black eyes ejaculated the sperm of madness.

Less than a mile from the entrance to the college Jean-François discovered an extrusion of the North American pre-Cambrian shield, ancient core of the entire continental mass. Scraping his knees raw on the compacted earth, he knelt beside the rock. Gnashing his teeth, he produced a sound very like the correct German pronunciation of *"Immer leise wird mein Schlummer ein,"* while the howl that was ripped from his guts might have been taken directly from the third movement of Schönberg's String Trio. Jean-François tore off a hunk of obsidian from the rock and jammed it into his belt. Then he arose, crouching, swiveling and sniveling, and bent his jealous, embittered, chronically unemployed bones up the slopes of the mountain towards Marlboro College, God bless it.

In a recess of the dingy basement of the best bookstore on Brattleboro's main thoroughfare, an obscure young and disgruntled salesclerk (surrounded by books that, crammed with facts and figures, stressed the necessity of immediate direct action to save the environment or what was left of it) took up the lotus position to peruse them with grim irony. In a studio apartment above the store, an aggressive though not very wicked, and certainly not beautiful coloratura soprano practiced high C# all afternoon long.

The bookstore salesclerk's heart and soul were dedicated to promoting ways to abolish nuclear power. Even the uncouth laggards slumbering within their hillside condominiums know that Brattleboro, Vermont is surrounded by nuclear power plants on all points of the compass; though only a few of them also know that they are fueled yearly with uranium pellets unloaded from green Volkswagen vans driven by individuals with sinister smiles whistling snatches of Brahms. In the winds that blow the topsoil from the rare outcroppings of the North American pre-Cambrian shield in this region, one may at times hear the voices of electric utility executives whining for their megabucks. Along the terraces of the surrounding mountains ingloriously revel the wastedumps of progress.

He was fully aware of the fact that very few successful concert artists give a damn about nuclear power, or any other political issue for that matter. In and around the Brattleboro area he knew of but three such individuals: first an embittered, chronically unemployed celesta player, deeply jealous of all successful concert artists. He had encountered him one morning in the beautiful blue dawn sitting in the bake-shop underneath the most picturesque crumbling archway in the village.

Then an Austrian émigré, whose smile had something sinister in it, obviously obsessed with Brahms. In the depths of a certain coal-black night he had given the salesclerk a lift in his green van (a green Volkswagen) from the Marlboro Music Festival back to his dingy garret in Brattleboro.

Finally there was a beautiful, aggressively wicked Japanese woman violinist. She had come into the bookstore one afternoon to pick up a book she'd ordered, a collection of recipes for kippered herrings.

Had their fates been kinder, had other initiatives been attempted which could have brought them together long enough to reveal their political affinities, how much cruel carnage could have been avoided! Who is to say? Yet, inexorably, before the night was out, the haft of the obsidian blade was destined to glint above the singing strings of the violin like the sunlight off the hoods of a thousand green Volkswagen vans, the guts of the cellist would ejaculate the sperm of madness, and the head-lice of the celesta player were fated to wallow in the kippered herring trough. All in vain (from a certain point of view); for the inevitable crumbling of the North American pre-Cambrian shield, ancient core of the entire continental mass, was not to be delayed, even by an instant.

❈ ❈ ❈

Mitzi Kagami stood on the stage of the Marlboro College concert-barn practicing the first movement of the Prokofiev Violin Concerto in D. Brahms sang down to her from heaven (though all remained definitely a bit sinister with the world). Her gold and silver bangles glinted in the sunlight pouring in through the panes of glass dense with the shadows of silhouetted birds.

The sky, as a stiff chilly breeze emerging from the whale-runs of the Far North flounced the hedges and trees on the Marlboro College campus, melted like burning wax.

Her bow rasped on the E-string like an obsidian blade across the carapace of an arthropod and, uncontrollably, she yawned. Pondering once again, as she did every afternoon at about three, the intrinsic banality of existence in general and the worthlessness of the human race in particular, her bow creamed off a hefty *smorzando* from the creamy, dreamy Prokofiev concerto, played as she alone could do it, with all the beauty, aggressivity and wickedness in her nature.

Mitzi's growing fame did not permit her to waste even a second of valuable practice time: as her arms schnoodled Prokofiev, her bare feet skipped to the rhythm of the opening movement of the Schönberg String Trio. Neither would she permit her mind to rot, like the North American pre-Cambrian shield, in idleness. Even as she practiced Prokofiev, waltzed Schönberg and flickered the picturesque eyelids of coal-black eyes lodged in the crumbling recesses of her eye-sockets, black as night, she was setting her mind busily to work thinking of ways to promote the elimination of nuclear power. The construction of nuclear power plants had to be stopped if Prokofiev were not to have composed music in vain. She had, alas, all too often seen the reveling of the inglorious wastedumps of progress, nor would she ever become resigned to the spectre of a world ejaculating the sperm of madness.

The sky, as a stiff chilly breeze emerging from the whale-runs of the Far North flounced the hedges and trees on the Marlboro College campus, melted like burning wax. Violinist Alexander Schneider spoke to pianist Rudolf Serkin in Brahms. Serkin replied in Brahms. Beneath the trees outside the campus refectory David Soyer, cellist, explained Brahms to violinist Isidore Cohen. In a secluded forest niche, hidden from the eyes of mankind, bass player Joseph Levine knelt on a carpet of pine needles and worshipped Brahms.

The night air, wild with the shrillings of costly violins, was. Sitting on the face of a large rock outside the concert barn (coincidentally yet another rare regional outcropping of the North American pre-Cambrian shield (ancient core of the entire continental mass)), warmed-over Death in Harlequin masquerade, rollicking like a ourang-outang, blew mournful melodies on a shakuhachi through his nostrils. Music lovers flounced through the double-doored entranceway in a frequently modulated stream. Odors of licorice clung to the warm interior of the concert-barn, the accumulated residue of a hundred Mozart clarinet concertos.

The major work on this night's program, Schönberg's String Trio, had been sandwiched between von Suppé's *Light Cavalry Overture* and the Brahms F-minor Quintet. Alexander Schneider and Isidore Cohen teamed up for the violin part, Leonard Rose grappled with the ghost of Pablo Casals for possession of the cello, while the viola part was handed to the 193rd person entering in through the front door. It was entirely owing to this strange ritual, the momentary brain child of a Marlboro Festival director, that the young, sparsely bearded and disgruntled bookstore salesclerk was wrenched from his accustomed obscurity into world prominence. This was not due to his viola playing (his sour disposition having so affected his hearing that he could play no musical instruments), but because of his impassioned speech against nuclear power, flashbacks of which would emerge in the nightmares of the audience over the next two years.

Even as this concert perambulated its inexorable trajectory, a green Volkswagen van hurtled down Interstate 91. Its passengers, an Austrian émigré cellist (a man obsessed with Brahms who tended to smile in rather sinister ways), and the wickedly aggressive and beautiful Japanese woman violinist, Mitzi Kagami, were bound for Amherst, Massachusetts. Fleeing premonitions of panic, they moved towards a still greater madness. Their dinner, 16 tofu cubes, a bucket of sprouts and a bottle of rancid white wine, was consumed in the open countryside under the full moon, beneath baobab trees whenever they could find them, otherwise on the park benches of small towns where the great clocks in the towers of deserted City Halls bonged the tormented hours.

They were in love! Wild, enraptured, sicky love, of the kind that occurs but once in a lifetime, if at all. Amherst had been chosen for this wild flight from reality owing to Mitzi's passionate attachment to the poetry of Emily Dickinson. Across the lanes of Interstate 91, lizards, under the gleaming headlights of the green Volkswagen van, scissored ecstatically in extended ensembles. In the coal-black night, over the inglorious reveling of the waste-dumps of progress and above the mountain peaks scarcely visible in the great distance, forked lightning ejaculated the sperm of madness.

At 2 AM the van entered the desolate wastelands of Amherst, Massachusetts. Parking the vehicle alongside the curb, the musician lovers brought their instrument cases with them and opened them up, for donations, on the most deserted sidewalk in town (which at that hour could have been anywhere). Under the light of a full moon almost entirely obscured by the fleeing of bats from a hundred church belfries, they performed the Kodaly Duo for cello and violin. The ghost of Emily Dickinson, shivering and sobbing in gossamer moonlight beams, prophesied the imminent crumbling of the North American pre-Cambrian shield, ancient core of the entire continental mass.

Their recital concluded, cellist and violinist replaced their instruments in their cases and drove to the corridors of the sub-sub-sub-basement of the Student Union building of the University of Massachusetts. This labyrinthine complex of tunnels stays open all through the night. Lingering in the cafeteria just long enough to finish off the bottle of rancid white wine, they walked arm-in-arm, dragging their instrument cases behind them, through the halls then up four flights to the lobby of the university hotel which squats atop the student union like a lost Eskimo on the coasts of Baffin Island.

The rooms of the hotel of the University of Massachusetts in Amherst, Massachusetts are simply palatial! They can be rented at prices perfectly consonant with the parameters of liberal hypocrisy imposed on any modern university feasting at the public trough. Indeed, one might call them veritable butter baths of luxury. The wall paper is tastefully ornate, with replicating patterns of schools of kippered herrings and lox. Long sound-smothering curtains cover floor-to-ceiling bulletproof windows like hangings over the picturesque crumbling archways of ancient temple vaults. The beds are regal, even grand, their springs so supple that their mattresses begin bouncing even before one rolls into them. The ambiance resembles that of a space capsule destined for distant, better worlds. The most commanding presence in all the rooms is that of the color television set which hangs suspended from the ceiling on long translucent Teflon fibers, God bless them.

Their mutual intention was to engage in fornication and related disgusting acts, such as eating one another's mounds of bagel crusts and grooming each other for head-lice. Yet neither reckless inseminations nor any other kinds of spicy ruttings were destined to occur in the seamy pulchritude of the hotel at

## AMPLITUDE OF THE COSMOS

U Mass. In a tiny isolated office of the U. Mass. MassPIRG (at U. Mass. Amherst (in Amherst, Mass.)), Jean-François Aspèrge sat on a green leather couch, its upholstery torn in many places. Attempts at sleep being largely unsuccessful, he arose frequently throughout the night. Not wishing to sit around and rot, like the North American pre-Cambrian shield, in idleness, he'd used up the time by practicing his celesta exercises. His wrists were strengthened by bonging spoons on the radiators. The music that emerged—the celesta score of Bartok's *Music for Celesta, Strings and Percussion*—radiated through the oleaginous mass of concrete that passes for a college hotel (squatting atop the student union building like the cracked eyeballs of Amherst's most abandoned alleycat) as forked lightning will revel ingloriously through wastedumps of progress. The bonging of Jean-François spoons, rasping on the couple's nerves like an obsidian razor on the carapace of an arthropod, drove them wild with pentatonic agony. These Hungarian melodies resonated at much the same frequencies as most of the electronic gadgetry in the building, with the result that all the color televisions were turned on full blast. Sleepless and wretched, the lovers found themselves forced to watch reruns of reruns of Late Late Late Shows of movies from the 40s. It was outrageous, it was utterly intolerable, and that in spite of the fact that the room's seamy pulchritude cost not a penny more than what was perfectly consonant with the obligations of liberal hypocrisy imposed on a modern university feasting at the public trough.

The tiny room in which Jean-François Aspèrge made largely unsuccessful attempts at sleeping, and failing that trained his musician's wrists by the bonging of spoons on its radiators, was the headquarters of the Massachusetts Public Interest Research Group at U. Mass., situated in a narrow second-floor corridor amidst a crowd of other political advocacy organizations. That afternoon Jean-François had conned the activists at MassPIRG into letting him crash on their couch, by pretending to be an organizer for the Clamshell Alliance who happened to be hitch-hiking to a sit-down demonstration in front of the nuclear power plant in Seabrook, New Hampshire. Among the students present in the office at the time, only one had suspected that he might really be an embittered, chronically unemployed celesta player deeply jealous of all successful concert artists; but her opinion was ignored. Essentially Jean-François had not been deceitful, not in the long run, since he was, heart and soul, fundamentally opposed to the advancement of nuclear power. Had it not been his misfortune to be driven by two dominating passions, first his ferocious hostility towards Mitzi and Dietrich's sicky love, secondly his unachievable dream, so abused and frustrated that it had swollen to an incurable pathology, to be recognized as a true professional concert artist, he would most certainly have made good on his commitment to go to Seabrook.

All of the offices were separated from one another by windowed panels. The entrance to the darkened corridor was secured at the front end by a door opening onto a balcony. Directly before the balcony on the ground floor of the student union stood the student bookstore, where one might expect to find many books that, crammed with facts and figures, stressed the necessity of immediate direct action if the environment, or what was left of it, is to be saved. Although this door was kept locked at night, it was opened at two hour intervals by a security guard with a flashlight whose job it was to patrol the corridor just in case beatniks, homeless radicals, or borderline psychotic musicians might try to crash out on the couches of the numerous on-campus political advocacy groups.

Jean-François was therefore obliged at two hour intervals to put aside his spoons and to appear to be doing some paperwork relating to the struggle against nuclear power. Nor was this pretense: U. Mass. MassPIRG at Amherst, Mass. had in fact given him a sheaf of documents relating to its investigations into fraud and conspiracy in the management of nuclear power plants which he had promised to edit before leaving, a decision that was not up to him, but would be governed by the perambulations of the cellist, Dietrich Zinzindorf of the sinister smile, and of the beautiful Mitzi Kagami who, with much wickedness, and aggressively, played the violin.

Evidence was tightly scribbled over these pages showing that there existed a conspiracy of manufacturers, owners, and operators of nuclear utilities to take over the world. Specifically: the nuclear power industry had elaborated a strategy for international blackmail, based on the threat of a meltdown at the Yankee Pilgrim plant near Brattleboro, Vermont within the year.

The consequences of such a deed were unthinkable. To avoid them, mankind had to relinquish control over the planet to a consortium formed by General Electric, Westinghouse, Con Edison and Hydro-Quebec. One can readily picture the smoke-filled caucus rooms in which these executives, munching over their stingily hoarded mounds of old bagel crusts, sparks sharp as flakes of obsidian spurting from the coal-black recesses of their crumbling eye-sockets, and ejaculating the sperm of madness, concocted such schemes. Among other things, they had neglected to take into account the inevitable crumbling of the North American pre-Cambrian shield, ancient core of the entire continental mass. Yet it was all there, right on the pages before Jean-François in horrendous black and white.

Action focused on a certain, in the beautiful blue dawn, green Volkswagen van driven by an Austrian émigré cellist, a somewhat sinister individual who whistled snatches of Brahms. Under the guise of delivering crates of kippered herrings to the Yankee Pilgrim plant cafeteria, he would actually be bringing in canisters filled with pellets of neutrino paste compacted under enormous pressure. Immediately after their delivery, the nuclear consortium intended to announce its ultimatum to mankind.

Under gossamer moonlight beams, warmed-over Death, shrouded in reams of computer printout, wandered the open countryside between Brattleboro, Vermont and Amherst, Massachusetts. Resting in the shade of spreading baobab trees wherever he could find them, otherwise on the park benches of small towns where great clocks in the towers of deserted City Halls bonged the tormented hours, he twanged the *Dies Irae* on a Jew's harp:

>*Boing! Boing! Boing! Boing!*
>*Boing! Boing! Boing! Boing!*

❊ ❊ ❊

The concert in the concert-barn auditorium of the Marlboro Music Festival drew—at long last—to its blissful close. Afterwards a reception designed for the constructive mingling of both audience and musicians was held in the Green Room. Caterers had prepared a spread composed of mounds of old bagel crusts, plates of kippered herrings, lox, buckets of bean sprouts, and rancid white wine collected from the remnants of bottles left over from previous festivals.

Pompous, stiff and ridiculous, Alexander Schneider, Isidore Cohen, Leonard Rose, the ghost of Pablo Casals and the obscure and disgruntled, young and bearded bookstore clerk moved through the crowd, imbibing its praises as nothing more than the fulfillment of its natural obligations. Warmed-over Death, in Harlequin guise, hitting at his exposed teeth with xylophone sticks, chortled at them through the frosted window-panes in unseemly fashion, but they were too pre-occupied to notice or care.

Sitting down on a torn couch upholstered in green leather, surrounded by its admirers, the ghost of Pablo Casals hummed his celebrated *Song of the Birds*. In a secluded forest niche, hidden from the eyes of mankind, ghostly birds chirped the *Song of the Pablo Casals*. Alexander Schneider and Isidore Cohen exchanged tips on the effective production of a violin *schmorzando*. Leonard Rose, producing multi-phonics through the f-holes of his instrument, was playing both solo parts of the Brahms Double Concerto for Violin and Cello.

## AMPLITUDE OF THE COSMOS

Finalizing their strategies for international blackmail in a dingy corner of the room, trustees of the Yankee Pilgrim plant sucked the marrow from the bones of Kentucky Fried Chicken dinners. Snorting in derision, the North American pre-Cambrian shield buckled and groaned, leaving six hundred Eskimos on the coasts of Baffin Island homeless and wet.

The young bookstore salesclerk, no less obscure (nor less sparsely bearded) for having performed that night in the Schönberg String Trio, took up the lotus position in a conspicuous location near the cabal of utility executives and, although everyone knew he was eavesdropping, affected the perusal, with grim irony, of a textbook on nuclear engineering. Later than night he would be telegraphing their plots, sub-plots and counter-plots in code from his garret apartment above Brattleboro, Vermont's best bookstore, located on a Main Street lined with banks of Green Volkswagen vans parked alongside all its curbs, to the offices of U. Mass. MassPIRG at the University of Massachusetts in Amherst, Mass.

And so it was that, to the sound of the celesta part of Bartok's *Music for Celesta, Strings and Percussion* bonged on MassPIRG's radiators; to the wretchedness of the bagel swapping, frustrated fornication and head-lice grooming of the sicky musician couple, Mitzi and Dietrich; to the endless reruns of reruns of Late Late Late Shows of movies of the 40s; to the grisly hummings of the ghost of Pablo Casals and the reverential chirpings of the birds; to the sounds of the xylophone teeth, Jew's harp and shakuhachi playing of warmed-over Death; to the fleeing of bats from a hundred church belfries as the great clocks in the towers of deserted City Halls bonged the tormented hours; to the evil schemes of nuclear power executives; to the sobbings, in gossamer moonlight beams, of the ghost of Emily Dickinson; and to the inevitable crumbling of the North American pre-Cambrian shield, ancient core of the entire continental mass; and lastly, but not least, to the dull glow of the coal-black eye-sockets of the eyes, black as night, of Brattleboro's most abandoned alleycat which, under its most picturesque crumbling archway, ejaculated the sperm of madness, the night, black as coal and drawing to its blissful close, was.

As Brahms sang down from heaven (and all continued to remain definitely a bit sinister with the world), the embittered, chronically unemployed and deeply jealous Jean-François Aspèrge wended his sad way up the mountain slopes towards Marlboro College. Gleaming in the beautiful blue dawn like the glintings of sunlight off the hoods of a thousand green Volkswagen vans, Marlboro College snarled, cursed, belched and indicated in a great many other ways that it welcomed this intruder about as much as it needed another Brahms F-minor string quintet, this sinister madman flapping his arms and crying "*Blut! Blut!*" like someone living the last act of Alban Berg's *Wozzeck*, the grey matter behind his eyes crumbling like the ancient archways of picturesque Brattleboro, Vermont.

Munching over his hoard of old bagel crusts, Jean-François sat down on the face of a large rock, coincidentally another rare outcropping of the North American pre-Cambrian shield (ancient core of the entire continental mass). His mind was soon steeped in contemplation. He was debating the relative merits of twin hypotheses: that he was either schizophrenic or paranoid.

*Berkeley, 1985*

*AMPLITUDE OF THE COSMOS*

# The Tale of the Guru

*A Recitation for Voices of Humans and Jungle Creatures*

### Narrator's (Flat) Voice:

WORLDLY-WISE One, once upon a time in a little village in India, there was a GURU. And this Guru met with a class of children under the shade of the spreading Bo Tree. One day he told them this story:

### Guru's (Earthy) Voice:

Once! O young innocents! O Children of the Gods! Once so very long ago! Once upon a time, there was: a JUNGLE! And in this Jungle there lived: an ELEPHANT! And while he was walking about one day (in the Jungle, mind you!) he met: a MONKEY!

NOW: What do you think of that? And this . . . Monkey . . . well; he wanted to speak to this Elephant. Indeed, he actually stepped in the Elephant's path and stopped him! And he said:

### Monkey's (Squeaky) Voice:

Memsahib Elephant! Do not continue to go the way you are going! Do not go that way! No! No! No! By all means, do not go that way! No! No! No! Never go that way!

# THE TALE OF THE GURU

### Guru:

Well, my Children: imagine the reaction of that old Elephant. Put yourselves in his boots! The Elephant looked at the Monkey in utter amazement, and said:

### Elephant's (Slow Rumbling) Voice:

Oh Monkey: what is the matter? Why can't I go this way? I ALWAYS go this way!

### Guru:

But the Monkey had a ready answer for that one:

### Monkey:

O venerable long-nosed one! Do not continue to go on that way you were going! Even if you were going that way, even if you ALWAYS go that way, do not, do not, do not, do not go that way! Let me tell you the story of *THE LION AND THE JACKAL*!

Once upon a time, O Elephant, a LION was bouncing around in the jungle, this very same jungle, this one here . . . when, lo and behold, he met: A JACKAL! Oh Memsahib Elephant: believe me when I tell you that this Lion was very hungry, hungrier than the famished gazelles at the time of the monsoon floods; and he would fain have eaten this Jackal! And so, he grabbed the Jackal in its paws and pinned it to the ground! But the Jackal said:

### Jackal's (Rasping) Voice:

O Lion! Spare my life! Hear my story!

### Monkey:

To which replied the Lion:

### Lion's (Roaring) Voice:

Huhhhn! Jackal?!! Make it snappy! I'm hungry!

GURU:

But the Lion was fond of a good story and he released him. Then the Monkey said:

MONKEY:

The Jackal said:

JACKAL:

Once, O LION! Once upon a time in a distant kingdom, there lived . . . a KING!

LION:

What wuz duh king's name? Huhhh? Jackal!

JACKAL:

The king's name . . . er . . . ah . . . the king's name . . . was . . . RAJA! Raja ruled over vast dominions, filled with many happy subjects! At the court of this Raja, mind you, were many retainers, menservants and maidservants, couriers and courtiers, knights and princes, knaves and fools, and a beautiful wife as well, and many Concubines, including one favorite Concubine, whose name was . . .

NARRATOR:

But then, O Worldly-Wise One, the Children cried all together at once:

CHILDREN (CHILDISH HIGH-PITCHED VOICES):

What's a Concubine?

GURU:

A Concubine, is the second, or third, or fourth wife, and so on and so forth, of a king. They are not for the likes of you or me, which is as it should be. It is best that the subject be avoided altogether. So, my very young ones, let me go on . . . where was I? . . .

# THE TALE OF THE GURU

### Children (All shouting):
The Jackal said!

### Guru:
Yes. Thank you. Well, the Jackal said:

### Jackal:
Therefore towards his wife and all his Concubines, did this king, RAJA, manifest much connubial bliss; and they, also, manifested much connubial bliss towards him! Yet, alas: for one day his favorite Concubine did something that very much offended him, and he waxed sore wroth:

### Elephant:
Oh, Monkey!

### Guru:
said the Elephant,

### Elephant:
Do not make this tale too long sad, or too sad, for I must soon be going!

### Monkey:
It's a sad tale for sure. It really is! Boy, is it sad! I'll grant you that much! It's very, very sad! But it's also very good, very good! It's a very, very good tale! Even that Lion himself thought it was a good story when the Jackal told it to him, and I'm sure you'll agree with me that it's a very good story when I tell you what the Jackal told the Lion. Have no doubt about it, I can assure you . . . !

### Elephant:
Enough, Monkey! All right! Proceed if you must.

### Guru:
sighed the Elephant. But, my Children, is it possible that this

story may well be too long and too sad for you at your tender age?

### Narrator:
said the Guru, stopping his recitation, O worldly-wise one. But they cried out as with a single voice:

### Children:
No! No! No No No!

No No! No No!

No! More story! More! More! More!

### Guru:
Very well then: The Monkey said to the Elephant:

### Monkey:
The Jackal said to the Lion:

### Jackal:
The King said to his Concubine most favored in the land:

### Raja (Booming accusing voice):
O My Concubine! You have much offended me! For, as it is written in some book of wisdom: "A naughty Concubine is worse than a bed of straw and the taste of stale chapattis!"

### Jackal:
To which the Concubine replied:

### Monkey:
—but just then, I hate to say it, I really do, but just then the Lion interrupted the Jackal and frightened him half to death, by asking:

### Lion:
Dis CON'-CU-BINE, wuz she pretty, Huhhhn? JACKAL!!

# THE TALE OF THE GURU

### Monkey:

The Jackal was really annoyed, I don't think you need to be told that. But, Elephant you know as well as I do, you know how it goes, if the Jackal didn't keep the Lion amused all the time, he became dinner! In less time than it takes to say "Mahabalipuram!" So he said:

### Jackal:

O, Lion! She was like unto the moon at midnight! Her eyes sparkled like the stars in the eastern sky, not any eastern sky either, but that sky which one may see in winter through the dews-swept dawn over Uttar Pradesh! Her teeth were whiter than the Elephant tusks of Bengal . . .

### Elephant:

I would be *very* careful, Monkey, in what you say.

### Monkey:

Begging your pardon, Elephant; you know how vulgar those low-class Jackals are. Well, the Jackal continued:

### Jackal:

Her cheeks, O Lion, lit up the heavens like torches blazing in the courtyards of Madras at the festival of Dipavali! And, Lion, if you will allow me to continue with my story, the Concubine asked the king, Raja:

### Guru:

But just then the Elephant himself interrupted the Monkey to ask:

### Elephant:

My memory is very good, Monkey, and I am certain that you never told me the name of this Concubine.

### Monkey:

Right you are, Elephant! Let me think. The Concubine's name

was—Lakshmi. That was her name all right! Lakshmi!

**CHILDREN:**

Lakshmi! Lakshmi!

**NARRATOR:**

cried the Children. And they would have continued to cry out her name, perhaps forever, had not the Guru silenced them by many stern admonitions gleaned from the Vedas on the obligations of students in the company of a teacher. Then the Guru said:

**GURU:**

The Monkey said:

**MONKEY:**

The Jackal said:

**JACKAL:**

The Concubine said:

**MONKEY:**

But once again, begging your pardon, Elephant, the Lion stopped the Jackal, and asked:

**LION:**

Whut wuz her name, Huhhhn! Jackal!

**JACKAL:**

Her name, O Lion, was LAKSHMI!

**WORLDLY-WISE ONE:**

But I already know that!

**NARRATOR:**

Of course you do, Worldly-Wise One: but the Lion didn't. In fact the children themselves interrupted the Guru once again, and complained:

# THE TALE OF THE GURU

**CHILDREN:**
We all know her name is Lakshmi!

**GURU:**
Yes—

**NARRATOR:**
said the Guru,

**GURU:**
—but it was the Lion, not you, who did not know her name, at least not until then. Well, the Monkey said:

**MONKEY:**
The Jackal said:

**JACKAL:**
The Concubine said:

**LAKSHMI (SWEET, TEARFUL VOICE):**
O my powerful Lord, in what fashion have I been the occasion of thy great displeasure?

**JACKAL:**
And the king replied:

**RAJA:**
Dare you deny that I saw you, just the other day, wandering about in the woods? Why were you not in the palace, attending to your duties?

**CONCUBINE:**
O Sire! I beg you to forgive me! I was merely picking flowers for your birthday, a mere two days hence! Do not forget, my beloved Lord, what many a wise sage of yore has said:

"Those blessed beings who engage in innocent occupations will never know grief, woe, weeping, sorrow, mourning, lamentation or remorse!"

RAJA:

That is true, indeed,

JACKAL:

the king agreed,

RAJA:

but the holy books also tell us that "The wise horse does not run until the master commands!" and in fact, I even recall having seen it written down somewhere that, "Even the waters of the Ganges dare not rise in flood against the word of Brahma!" You have been disobedient, my naughty Concubine, and you will be punished!"

JACKAL:

The king's heart was filled with vexation, and could not be appeased until this unfortunate, beautiful Concubine was driven from his court!

ELEPHANT:

That was an unjust king, so to abuse a good and innocent Concubine!

MONKEY:

Truly said, Elephant! and his own death was terrible and horrible! We should never forget what the ancients have written: "Virtue is its own reward," and, "A living dog is actually much better off than a dead king!"

ELEPHANT:

Forsooth, Monkey! Most wisely spoken, for it has also been said that "One cannot hope to escape the consequences of evil deeds even in the clefts of high mountains," and, furthermore, that "The glittering chariot of this world is like unto a vain bauble, whose axles forever screech: *ME . . . !! ME . . . !!*"

# THE TALE OF THE GURU

### JACKAL:

The poor rejected Concubine had nowhere to go. She wandered through the jungle picking berries, raw fruits, and wild herbs. It came about one afternoon that, sitting alone within the branches of a banyan tree, weeping and sighing for her change of state, she met a SNAKE!

### CONCUBINE:

Oh, Snake!

### JACKAL:

said the Concubine—

### MONKEY:

said the Jackal—

### GURU:

said the Monkey—

### NARRATOR:

said the Guru, O Worldly-Wise One—

### CONCUBINE:

My name is . . .

### WORLDLY-WISE ONE:

I hate to interrupt, Narrator, but that's rather a scary story to tell to Children, don't you think? There are lots of different kinds of Snakes in India. I mean, it could have been anything from a harmless garter Snake to a king cobra or, for all we know, a starving boa constrictor!

### NARRATOR:

Indian tradition, O Worldly-Wise One, generally portrays Snakes in benevolent rather than venomous roles. I doubt very much that the Guru had a boa constrictor in mind. It's a fair guess that we're dealing with a common variety of water

Snake. These are not dangerous but have been known to grow to enormous sizes. Take it from me, those Children weren't frightened by the arrival of the Snake. Well, to get on with it, the Guru said:

GURU:

The Monkey said—

MONKEY:

The Jackal said—

JACKAL:

Lakshmi said:

CONCUBINE:

Oh, Snake! Just a short time ago, I was among the favored of the land! But now I have been sent away and forced to live in the jungle, and I don't know what will become of me!

SNAKE (SNAKY VOICE):

Do not grieve!

JACKAL:

said the Snake,

MONKEY:

said the Snake,

GURU:

said the Snake,

NARRATOR:

said the Snake,

SNAKE:

All things come and go! It is the way of the world! Who can know what the morrow will bring? I myself have lived to see slaves exalted and kings thrown down, the rich made beggars and beggars rich! Indeed, if I bethink me not amiss, has it not been said by some venerated sage of ancient Punjab that, "A little while and the bird is on the wing!"? Do not disdain those who remind us that "The wise do not grieve!" Of all these wise old sayings, that of which I most treasure is this one: "He who never complains, will never complain, that others complain against him, saying, 'He complains too much!!' "

GURU:

Take heed, little Children,

NARRATOR:

said the Guru,

GURU:

Although these words were uttered by simple jungle creatures, they are filled with ancient wisdom, and you must commit them to memory—and to your hearts! Well, as I was saying, the, er, Snake said,

CHILDREN:

The Monkey! The Monkey!

GURU:

I beg your pardon; right you are! So, the Monkey said to the Elephant!

MONKEY:

The Jackal said to the Lion!

JACKAL:

The Snake said to the Concubine!

SNAKE:

Dry your tears, most estimable lady! Your eyes will once again sparkle like mist over Himalayan peaks! Your breath shall once again be like the soothing ocean breezes guiding the dainty fishing vessels along the coast of Malabar! Your lips, once again—how shall I say it—shall twinkle like rubies in the turbans of the Nizams of Hyderabad! Be my guest!

### JACKAL:

So the Snake took Lakshmi to his cave and gave her the remains of a boar, and afterwards she lived with him for many weeks until she found a home with her own species! Nor did he touch a single one of her bracelets and bangles, although it is well known that snakes are greedy for gold and jewels, but preserved them in a heap to serve as her dowry in a splendid marriage held the following year to a high caste prince, and attended by three rajas of Peshawar and the Rani of Gujarat!

### MONKEY:

Then the Jackal shut up. The Lion stared at him a good five minutes, before he roared:

### LION:

Iz dat all, Jackal? Why, I oughta eat you up right now!

### JACKAL:

Oh Lion! Lion! There is a moral to this fable, which is, that all creatures may be of use to one another! Sire! Look down the road aways, and you will see an Elephant, certainly a better meal for you than my emaciated carcass. As he has just been listening to a very very long story told him by a foolish Monkey, he is completely confused and will offer you no resistance!

### MONKEY:

And the moral, oh Elephant, of this story is,

### GURU:

said the Monkey:

### MONKEY:

that if you had walked along this road you would have met, right away, and absolutely for certain, I guarantee you, an honest-too-goodness crouching Lion, who is just waiting to gobble you up,

# THE TALE OF THE GURU

for he postponed his lunch for a long time to listen to a very, very long, boring and confusing story being told him by a stupid Jackal!

### GURU:
The Elephant was grateful to the Monkey for saving his life and gave him a shower from his trunk. And, my Children, the moral of this story is, that I am now a very, very old man, who is not sure of what he is saying half the time.

### NARRATOR:
And the moral of this whole convoluted, digressive, confusing and essentially meaningless fable, O Worldly-Wise One, is that we are all living in a fable of Monkeys and Elephants, Jackals and Lions, Snakes, Kings, Concubines and Snakes, Gurus, Children, Narrators and Worldly-Wise Ones! Be steadfast in your devotion and never stray from the path of goodness.

### WORLDLY-WISE ONE:
Golly-gee! Thanks!

*MacDowell Colony, 1962*

# Three Weddings

## I.

THESE things were reputed to have happened at a wedding in our district a few years ago. The bride came from one of the wealthy families established among us for over a century. Where the bridegroom came from, or whom he was related to, I don't know, save that he was young, just out of law school and that (it was generally believed) a brilliant career lay ahead of him.

What is certain is that the town hall's ballroom had been rented for the celebration to follow the wedding ceremony. Reports state that the bride's father, a prominent banker, had stood, bursting with pride, at the front gate to greet each of the guests as they came into the driveway.

In spite of the large amount of hearsay, there is a general concurrence on the essentials: in the interval between the first and second courses, before all the soup plates had been collected and the main course about to be served, a band of roving musicians appeared at the front gates with an offer to provide music for the night's dancing. By all accounts these musicians comprised a motley assortment of displaced vagabonds, both men and women. Included among them were gypsies, klezmers, tinkers, black jazz artists and buskers.

Clods of dirt from all the nations on Earth clung to their dilapidated shoes and boots. Their costuming, also, was exceedingly strange: comical hats, both large and small, hanks of fur stitched to their garments; waistcoats of several centuries' vintage held together by belts, shoelaces or bits of string; ribbons and loose bits of fabric dangling every which way; particolored vests, breeches with rents, perruques and wigs, torn rags mixed together with costly satins and silks. Rare gems were sometimes to be seen sparkling within the clutter of cheap trinkets of plastic, paste, wire or glass. Everything they owned gave the impression of having been stolen. Their instrument cases lay heaped up in a farm cart that had been dragged through the mud and onto the lawn: 6 violins, 3 violas, 2 cellos, a bass, an oboe, flute, 2 clarinets, bassoon, bagpipes, saxophones, keyboards, guitars, a zither, a marimba and a great range of percussion. None of their instruments were electrified.

The bride's father intended to reject their offer. Hospitality required only that before sending them on their way they be invited to partake of a glass of brandy; it would have struck the guests as hard-hearted were he to do otherwise, given that the snows had fallen earlier than usual that year and the musicians were miserably poor and far from being adequately clothed for the weather.

Had not the bridegroom taken it upon himself to offer to pay them for one dance before leaving, they would no doubt have gone off and we would never have heard of them again. The overpowering effect made on the assembly by this superior, well-disciplined ensemble, all professionals, some of them unquestionably musicians of genius, stirred up a clamour in the hall that they be engaged on the spot. Finally the bride's father had to relent.

The contract was hurriedly drawn up and signed, and the tribe of rootless derelicts climbed onto the ballroom stage to begin arranging chairs and music stands in the semi-circular formation of an orchestra. This finished, they sat in silence, waiting for a signal from the conductor.

This came during the serving of the beverages and dessert.

Once launched, it seemed that no force existed on earth able to control or contain their fury. The orchestra never rested and scarcely paused. The guests, drowsy with drink and bloated to satiety, rose staggering from the tables, to be drawn irresistibly into the dance. The music's wild sensuality acted on the reflexes of the dancers like whips on the backs of galloping horses. The melodies themselves were peculiar yet not unfamiliar, conforming to no known system of music, rather to some very ancient way of organizing sound, older perhaps than the races of musicians playing them. Laughter, song and dance persisted from one end of the ballroom to the other, from hour to hour, licking the walls and ceilings like the flames of a roaring bonfire until well into the night. Guttural cries rising above the din indicated drunkenness, coarse jests, oaths and threats, entanglements, sporadic fist-fights and other evidences of a growing dissipation.

Around the ballroom, the chandeliers careened wildly and with undeniable menace. Every light in the building flashed and flickered from the heavy stomping of feet. Collected around the building and standing in the snows were deer, squirrels, birds, and other small forest creatures, who peered into the rooms through windows rendered opaque by condensing steam. In their eyes glittered points of light that lost themselves within the carpet of stars stretching across the cloudless sky.

At the peak of the excitement the bride was seized, stripped of her gown and the rest of her clothing and dragged through the room onto the center of the floor. Now the revellers joined hands to form a dozen concentric rings around her. Circling in both directions they hurled obscenities upon her, combining spiteful taunts with unmistakable gestures. Horrified, the bride recognized her new husband among her loudest tormentors, his curses outdoing the others in ferocity.

The musicians paid not the least attention to anything happening around them, their muscles and nerves consumed, as within a destructive flame, by the music that rode them. Their luminous eyeballs, swollen and fixated, stared past the pages of their music to some malign power beyond the walls. They scarcely seemed to breathe, no sweat poured from their temples, their instruments groaning and reeling like drunk satyrs at an orgy.

Keeping time to the music's frenzied beat, his shoes twisting in the execution of quick and difficult steps, the bridegroom opened up a path through the rings of dancers towards the center of the floor. A crystal wineglass dangled from the fingers of his right hand, its purple nectar dribbling gouts over the immaculate cuffs of his shirt, leaving stains, dark like the blood of a butchered stag. His cheeks, flushed with exertion, pulsed like living hearts in his weak, dissolute face. Beneath eyes overflowing with malice gleamed the tips of sadistic teeth.

Advancing upon his bride, now his wife, he extended the goblet in her direction. She took it from his hand; dumb with terror, she sipped at its rim. With an upswelling of rage he tore it back again from her hands, drained off the remnants of the wine, and shattered it on the ground. Fragments of glass lay crushed beneath his heel, the rest scattering about the floor. Seizing her paralyzed, shivering body, he inflicted cruel bites on the pallid flesh of her breasts.

As if on cue, the festive community burst spontaneously into joyous song. Dissonant choruses of voices lifted to utterance of dimly recalled peasant lyrics outside all civilization, rooted in the old countryside. Scattered sounds of squalid couplings mingled with bestial grunts and cries of rape and incest.

On the instant the hellish orchestra ceased.

A sea of silence expanded in over-lapping waves from the innermost circle out to the far corners of the room. Slumped over their music stands, the corpses of the musicians looked as if they had never been meant to serve any function other than that of temporary habitation for the vanished demon horde. Neither bride nor bridegroom were anywhere to be seen.

Sobbing and shuddering, the circles of dancers edged gradually from the ballroom floor to rear up against the outer walls. There, at the center, where the bridal pair had stood now lay, split open from snout to rump, the stinking carcass of some vaguely identifiable savage beast, bear, wolf or boar. Through its exposed entrails, festering and hideous, crawled armies of vermin.

Sick with horror, the doomed mobs raced in panic through the opened doors of the hall. Yet: even from the moment of their crossing the threshold, there began their transformation into maggots, ants, spiders, cockroaches and other bugs, racing swiftly in every direction, losing themselves in cracks in the sidewalks and under the foundations of houses, down wells, the rest disappearing ultimately into the gaping mouths of huge flowers.

# II.

Was it really only yesterday that Eric stepped out of his apartment with Sylvia, his lovely fiancée, for a walk through our town? After a stroll along the river, and a visit to an unfamiliar neighborhood, they returned via a different route. Coming into the downtown they passed a complex of public buildings, including the municipal theater.

Men, women and children were running out through the doors in mad panic, pushing and trampling one another; some could also be seen leaping from the upper windows. Together with their human owners came pets, howling cats and yelping dogs, their wet tongues slavering over hot foaming lips.

Sylvia wanted to run away, but Eric told her not to be afraid. When all was said and done, the spectacle was more amusing than frightening. He pointed out the irony in the plight of an audience that, having paid so much to get in, should now be rioting to get out! They sat down together by the curb, bent double with laughter, Sylvia cradled in Eric's arms.

A gang of skinheads seized Sylvia by the arms and dragged her away down the street into the public square. Eric jumped up and started after them in pursuit; that is, until he observed his own father charging out of the building, arms waving in frenzy, hair standing on end, his face twisted from having witnessed some spectacle of unspeakable horror; and entirely naked!!

Thus rendered helpless, Eric could do nothing but watch the savage gang-rape of his Sylvia by brutes, a mob of onlookers gathered around them, wrestling for the best locations for enjoying the entertainment.

As time went on the persons fleeing the building began to be transformed into the incredible shapes of impossible beasts: antelopes with speckled horns and golden hooves; bears with strawberry complexions, talons of eagles, lion's whiskers and manes; goats with shaggy wolves' legs, horns curled up in vertical mollusk-shell towers, cusped with sparkling jewels, their metastasizing mammaries harboring many suckling whelps; hybrid creatures fashioned from the bloody limbs and organs of rabbits and dogs; long-legged crane-like bald-headed birds with long beaks like scythes, garlanded with multi-colored feathers jutting out from coats of mammalian fur.

A huge bull burst through the double doors. Swiveling its head like the cloud foam surrounding the eye of a hurricane, it lifted Eric's father up on the points of its horns and ran into the crowd, stamping and dancing about in diabolic rage. As spasms shot through Eric's body, his legs gave way beneath him. Yet as his father went into convulsions he had to rally. Averting his eyes he ran from the scene, the bull in full pursuit.

At the place where his Sylvia had been raped to extinction there remained only a black pool formed from hundreds of wriggling snakes. Sounds of wild organ music of psychotic propensities flooded out of the auditorium.

Looking back over his shoulder Eric saw the bull's hooves hammering away at the pool of snakes, scattering them in all directions, setting some on fire, the remainder crawling over its sleek loins, curling about its torso and neck until they reached Eric's hapless father, gasping for breath between hysterical screams. Later that evening he was either gored or poisoned to death.

Eric had run a considerable distance by that time, falling into a swamp and metamorphosing to a white water lily crowned with black stamens.

## III.

At last! Everything was ready to begin; at last! In the vestibule at the back of the church stood the glad young couple. The flower girl chatted nervously with the bride, while the best man straightened the lapels of the bridegroom's tuxedo. Waiting for their arrival at the altar the jowled minister, soft hands folded over paunch, practiced his perennially happy hypocritical smile.

The organist, a wizened man bent double by the years, squirmed before the keys of his instrument. For some time he'd been waiting, with mounting impatience, for the signal from the minister to begin the Wedding March. Tangled hair, wiry and long, fell down his back, completely covering neck and shoulders. A pulp nose and bright-eyed stare of grim defiance waded within a face rendered repulsive by a mind nourished for decades on morbid obsessions and malevolent schemes.

If one is to judge from the noise level of their conversations and their shuffling about in the pews, it seems that the congregation had also grown restless. On this morning the church was filled to capacity, with relatives from both families, friends of their relatives and all their children, well-wishers and friendly spectators from the outside. The minister had been compelled to call them to order more than once. Quiet was finally established only when the organist grazed the keyboard with his callused fingertips and music flooded the arches of the nave.

He played the Mendelssohn Wedding March with insistent malice, arrhythmically, hitting many wrong keys, yet with a diabolical authority of touch that contrasted strangely with his eccentric performance. One was hard put to know how to deal with the situation. All in all, it was still the Wedding March, wasn't it? The bridal procession could, by making an effort, synchronize its steps to the familiar old refrain. As for the majority of the other guests, those who weren't tone deaf had never learned to appreciate great music. Ultimately it mattered little how he played.

The bright sunlight entering through stained-glass windows streamed over the heads of the congregation and all things in its wake, wrapping crucifixes, candlesticks and decorative sculpture in comforting glazes, as hand in hand, the happy couple, he jolly and in high spirits (though nervous and unconfident), she demure and modest (blushing all the while), lurched down the aisle.

Suddenly it seemed as if the air resonated with witches howls, goblins' gibberings and the shrieks of ghouls. All hearts were gripped with panic as the music broke out in a hysterical cacophony, now devoid of all melody, harmony or form.

Pandemonium reigned through the church. The assembled multitude grabbed at anything within reach, coats, pocketbooks, umbrellas, cushions, hymnals, and hurled them at the procession. The noises coming from the organ amplified their din, the volume rising, in step with the satanic grin on the organist's hideous features, to drown out the prevailing mayhem.

Through the walls of the organ console and out of the pipes above the altar there flew swarms of bees, mosquitoes, flies, wasps and other winged insects that attacked the rioting crowd. The front doors were flung open and police brigades charged into the church. They rounded up and arrested the bride, bridegroom, flower girl, best man and all the wedding guests, not sparing the children.

Thence to remove them to the public square, to this end: that, to the solemn religious incantation of the minister and the growling of the hurdy-gurdy played by the organist they might be executed, every last one of them.

*Philadelphia, 1958*

# Sea Urchins

## I.

T was an early afternoon on a dry and sultry day in the last week of July, 1958. Two students sat on the edge of a metal frame cot in the small laboratory on the third floor of the Marine Biological Laboratories in Woods Hole, Massachusetts. On a table next to the cot books were stacked at random. A heap of stenographic tablets, hard-covered loose-leaf notebooks, data-sheets and assorted papers of all shapes and sizes climbed upwards from the floor to a height of four feet.

"Hey Clyde, its really great, us getting this chance to spend the summer here at the MBL, don't you think?"

"You bet, Jeff! You meet lots of famous scientists, that's for sure. Once in awhile you run into somebody working in your own field, even Nobel Prize winners who treat you like pals, just like ordinary human beings! It's such a terrific place to do biology. Good beaches, lots of sunshine, a fantastic library: you can't beat that."

The morning light entered the room through two large windows with low sills and bordered by dark frames. One stood at the far end of the cot; the other, set in the eastern face of the protruding southwest wing of the MBL building, gave access to an unimpeded view of the limitless vistas of the Atlantic Ocean.

Cartons of beer cans were piled one on top of the other at the foot of the cot. The cover on the uppermost had been torn open. Two emptied beer cans had already gone into the trash basket, and two new ones were cradled on their stomachs. The churchkey lying on the drainboard to the sink had been tossed there less than ten minutes before.

Now they leaned their backs against the wall. It was Clyde Cytochrome's first day in the famous marine biological research station at Woods Hole, the village of scientists at the southernmost tip of Cape Cod. His research grant had been sponsored by his thesis advisor Dr. Kurt Bergleson, professor in the biology department at Case Western University and a recognized authority on echinoderms. Bergleson was also on the faculty for the MBL summer school, and had so arranged things that his prize grad student would be there with him.

Jeff Benthic, still an undergraduate, had preceded Clyde in Woods Hole by a little less than a month. Now he was enrolled in the Invertebrate Zoology course being taught in the pair of frame buildings facing the main entrance to the MBL on the street named, appropriately if with little imagination, MBL Street. (It has since been replaced by the Swope center, a complex of dorms, cafeterias and conference rooms.)

Jeff's enthusiasm matched his friend's:

"Hey, Clyde, you bet! It's just—out of sight, being up here! Anyway you can describe your research to me?"

"Sure." Clyde took a swig of beer and choked.

"I'm sorry. Take your time." About a minute passed before Clyde replied:

"Sea urchins; obviously. That's why Bergleson wanted me here. Tube foot respiration in sea urchins."

"Yeah! That's some big field nowadays so they tell me. What's your take on respiration? Guess they gotta breathe, don't they, just like us?"

"Yeah—sure—they do. I'll be studying respiration under conditions of more or less air, basically."

Jeff looked about the room:

"What's that humongous do-hickey over there by the wall?"

He indicated an assemblage of instruments, containers and

accessories taking up most of the space of the wall separating the lab from the third-floor corridor. The light streaming across the room from the front window caused it to stand out in bold relief.

"My pride and joy, Jeff! Go on: take a good look at it. Better still, make a tour of inspection." As he stood up, Clyde continued talking: "It looks complicated, I admit. The fish tank has been prepared to reproduce as closely as possible the sea urchin's normal benthic environment, that is to say, sea water, sand and kelp under pressure. In the course of my experiments several basic gases in a pure state will be introduced in varying proportions and combinations. By manipulating pressure and temperature I'll be able to bring the global respiration of the population into stable equilibrium, then read the data off the different sorts of gauges surrounding the tank. It's simple, really. Think of it as somewhere between a frying pan and a pressure cooker."

"Yeah Clyde. Say, what's it called?"

"Oh," Clyde affected the stance of a modest individual ashamed of having to boast, "I've dubbed it the 'Cuisinart.'"

The Cuisinart was a tank of the sort used to house pet goldfish. Its approximate dimensions, in feet, were $1.5 \times 2 \times 4$. About three-quarters filled with water, its floor was seeded with pebbles, sand piles and nutrient seaweed. Six rubber hoses emerged through holes in its wooden cover, diverging to an equal number of tall gas storage tanks standing upright against the side wall. The outermost hose was green and labeled *Oxygen*. *Nitrogen* was on the red hose going to the tank to its left. From right to left there followed: yellow, *Carbon Dioxide*; brown, *Hydrogen*; blue, *Ammonia*; orange, *Methane*.

"How do sea urchins breathe?" Clyde intoned rhetorically, already mocking the gestures of the incipient professor: "That question is but a tiny scrap in the measureless storehouse of nature's undelivered secrets," (he scratched behind an ear) "yet innumerable monographs have been written on this one subject alone. There's lots of data around, all very inconclusive. No-one else to my mind has ever proposed anything like my experiments. The boss—Doc Bergleson that is, likes my ideas. Man!" (Clyde took a deep breath.) "If you ask me, this is God's country!"

He strode to the window and paused to look out across Water Street. A handsome well-trimmed lawn runs parallel to a stone breakwater fronting the ocean. A couple was coming out from the US Wildlife and Fisheries buildings. Clyde gazed at them for a full two minutes as they strolled along the breakwater to the obelisk, a sundial set on a broad octagonal base, with green copper vanes inset in its cubical head, the whole surmounted by a spherical knob like the pom-pom on a knitted winter cap. The couple sat down on a bench beside the sundial. As they spoke they distributed bread crumbs to the gulls and pigeons. The sunlight reflected off the metal fastenings on the masts of the research ship Atlantis made him squint. Presently moored in the docks of the Woods Hole Oceanographic Institution, it had returned only a few days before from a month of sonar mapping of the Deep Scattering Layer in the Pacific, that ambulatory continent of marine organisms that rises and falls in a daily cycle.

Jeff continued to regard the Cuisinart with unstinting admiration. A hose hanging over the lip of the sink drained off the excess water in a continuous stream. Another maintained a constant flow of water into the tank, combining in proper proportions with the sea water cycling through a coiled transparent vinyl tube hooked to a pipe running alongside the wall.

Jeff beamed:

"I always knew you were mighty handy, Clyde. That's one ingenious contraption you got there. What're you going to do with it?"

Clyde didn't reply right away. Some questions require deliberation: "As you see, there's nothing happening right now . . . normal atmospheric pressure, room temperature, so forth and so on. Once I start introducing the batches of sea urchins . . ."

"What's the species?"

"*Stronglyocentrosus droebachiensis*: the longest taxonomic label in biological classification! You can just call them 'green sea urchins.'"

"Good. I like the other name better but I'll never remember it. I didn't mean to interrupt—go on."

"Once the organisms are introduced, the valves attached to these nozzles will regulate the rates at which the gases are being infiltrated into the fish tank. Notice this row of pressure gauges; they enable me to adjust their relative proportions. Don't think I haven't done my homework. Take a look at these tables." He picked up a stack of chemical charts from the floor.

"$PV = kT$—and all that! Basic science every inch of the way!" Clyde pointed to another hose on the side of the tank to which a rubber suction sack and a pump were attached. "I can reduce the overall pressure in the tank with this suction pump. Then, if I remove this"—he indicated a cork 6 inches in diameter plugging a hole on the wooden cover—"all the gas flows out, and air at room temperature flows in. This apparatus should enable me to compile respiration statistics for various combinations of gases in differing proportions at any pressure desired. It's all hooked up to the Warburg respirometer."

A metal table stood at the side of the tank closest to the door. Upon it stood the gleaming black box of an instrument case from which protruded a dozen three-foot high lengths of glass tubing with rubber stoppers and valves, all secured within a metal frame.

"You did say something about raising and lowering the temperature. I'm not sure I understand how that's managed." Jeff finished off his beer and opened up another.

"It's right there, Jeff. That's my handle on $PV = kT$." Clyde directed his attention to an old-fashioned stove with four gas burners supporting a chassis on which the fish tank had been affixed by clamps and bolts.

"Holy smokes, Clyde! You'd better watch out!" Jeff gave a nervous laugh, "You don't want to boil all them respiring little critters before you've completed your experiment."

"Not to worry, Jeff... don't you worry about a thing! An adjustable thermostat is sitting on the floor of the tank. An alarm goes off if the heat exceeds my specifications." Clyde stroked the glass walls.

"Golly gosh!" Jeff commented, "It's just great being here! Say, can I get you another beer?" Jeff lifted the churchkey from the drainboard and applied it to a new can. As he handed it over they raised a toast:

"Cheers! Here's to..." Clyde thought a moment... "the Nobel Prize before I'm 30!" He went on: "The boss is really impressed with my ideas. He's promised me that I won't have to place my name under his in the published reports; I can keep all the credit! With luck I should be finished by the end of the summer."

"Where're you going to publish?"

"We talked about that. Bergleson advised me to come out with a preview in *Nature* or *Science*, just to see if anyone else is doing something similar. We've reviewed the literature and didn't find anything. Of course you can never be sure. Then we're thinking of sending it to the physiology editor of *Acta Echinodermata, Series Echinoidea*."

"I guess this is physiology, ain't it? I'm not even sure what the word means. I'm still stuck in first year course Invertebrate. Not doing too well I'm afraid."

"Aw, Jeff: I finished with the basics three years ago! That's kid stuff compared to what I'm doing now. Tell you one thing though: those introductory courses, they sure work you hard."

"They work you hard as a horse."

"Yeah—A biologist has to love hard work."

"You come by the labs any time of the day or night and you find the lights on. 3 AM, 4 AM—biologists never stop!"

"No joke! Oh, by the way: I didn't tell you, did I? This research has implications for space travel."

"Nope. Hey Clyde, that sounds really amazing! What's it got to do with space travel?"

"The idea comes from a suggestion from Dr. Heinrich. You know him, don't you? He heads up the Astrophysics department at Case Western. He gave a public lecture last year—part of the 'Vistas of Science' series, and he told us that the atmospheres of Saturn and Jupiter contain mostly Ammonia. He doesn't think life can survive under such conditions, but it appears that no-one's ever made the experiment. You see that tank standing by itself over in the corner? Look at the label."

Jeff turned over and inspected the tag on the blue hose: "Real interesting."

"I won't be spending too much time on that one. I'm more interested in finding out things about Nitrogen and Methane. Mom and Sis will be driving up from Ohio in a few days, and they're bringing an ultra-violet ray generator with them. After they get here I can begin work on some 'origins of life' experiments."

"The Origins of Life!"

"Absolutely. You've heard of Urey's experiment, haven't you? No? Well, Harold Urey passed electric discharges through a vacuum-sealed test tube in which Methane, Water and Nitrogen were circulating. The whole set-up was placed under a powerful beam of ultra-violet light. Those were the presumed conditions when life made its first appearance on earth."

"What happened next?"

"Some amino acids were produced."

"As a matter of fact I have heard of that experiment. Wasn't there an article about it a few years ago in Scientific American?"

"Yes: 1956. So okay; I though it might be interesting to investigate whether sea urchins can survive under the conditions of Urey's experiment."

"Why in God's name do you want to do that?" Jeff sputtered from a sudden intake of beer.

"Oh, I don't know. It's a common enough practice in science, looking at a problem from the other end of the telescope: how would life make out in the conditions under which life was created? Trust my Warburg to have all the answers!"

"Are you preparing an eyewitness account of how a green sea urchin dies a horrible death?"

Clyde chuckled, "Why not? I could even make up a separate data sheet for that one. Just preparing the data sheets for these experiments is going to involve an enormous amount of labor. For every gas there's going to be a whole set of related questions. For nitrogen: 'Does the sea urchin contract the bends?' For carbon dioxide: 'Is there chlorophyll in sea urchins?' For oxygen: 'Why is the blood of the sea urchin white?'"

"I didn't know they had any blood. I've always thought it was sea water. Something called the 'water vascular system,' isn't that right?"

"It might very well be. However it's always good to retest an old hypothesis. For hydrogen: 'What happens to sea urchins as they approach the sun?' That's the space travel angle again. All of these things have practical applications. For ammonia: 'Can echinoderms live on Saturn and Jupiter?' Finally for methane: 'The origins of life revisited.' That's six papers right there. Bringing in temperature, pressure and ultra-violet, I think we can contemplate something like a book in a few years: *Recent Advances in the Study of Metabolic Processes in Stronglyocentrosus droebachiensis*. Boy oh boy!" Clyde heaved a sigh of contentment, "Jeff, you can't begin to imagine how happy I am to be here!"

"Right on!"

"Yeah! Back in Woods Hole, doing cutting-edge research!"

"Yessiry! It sure is beautiful here. Right smack on the tip of Cape Cod. Good swimming on Nobska and Stony Beach. Students, biologists, tourists, villagers! You work all day till you drop, then head over to the Captain Kidd tavern by the drawbridge down on Water Street. That's where all the guys from the Oceanographic Institution hang out. Those guys can bang your ear all night long about hydrodynamics and weather maps."

"Don't forget the Gulf Stream! But hey, man: they work for

the Navy, strict 9 to 5 for them. We work day and night!"

"Yeah. They're just amateurs compared to us."

"Couldn't agree with you more, Jeff. We're the real scientists, over here at the MBL. Frankly I don't give those guys the time of day."

"Right, Clyde. And don't forget the parties we Invertebrates throw every night over on Stony Beach. Drinking and singing, and carrying on! Sometimes we just curl up in our blankets right there and sleep the night through."

"It's a great life, Jeff, no doubt about it."

Jeff leaned his back against the wall and continued to muse:

"If you ask me, Woods Hole is the next best thing to Paradise. Famous scientists everywhere: Albert St. György lives out on the Point. I saw Otto Loewi on the street just yesterday afternoon. George Wald, Linus Pauling, George Gamov, Crick and Watson, they all pass through here. Somebody told me Julian Huxley's expected here later this summer."

"Didn't know that. Never read anything of his."

"Me neither, but he's famous. I mean—uh—not like his brother."

"They've given him a desk in the library. He's supposed to be working on a book. I forget what it's about..." Jeff made an effort to try to remember what Julian Huxley's book was supposed to be about. "Well, they've always got famous people passing through here."

In this fashion did the afternoon slip away. The two students lounged about, their conversation filled with shop talk and banter, drinking more than was good for them. The consignment of sea urchins wasn't due until four, and Clyde had nothing to do until it came. His room had been organized in preparation for a siege. The cartons at the foot of the bed held about forty cans of beer. Cheese, bread and salami were kept in a small refrigerator by the door. Books, appliances and a few suitcases stood underneath the cot. Once Clyde got to work, he did not want to be interrupted. A sign intended for his door leaned on the drainboard of the sink surrounded by rows of pipettes, measuring cups, syringes and flasks: "Important Work. Do Not Disturb."

Scattered around the room lay debris, old newspapers, rope strands and slates of wood from the packing crates he'd shipped from Ohio. Science fiction magazines and biology textbooks were strewn haphazardly about the floor.

The cot had been confiscated from the MBL dormitories. Clyde had no intention of staying there in the bunk assigned to him. Right here, the lab, that was home. Back in the 50s the student dorms of the Marine Biological Laboratories overflowed within the confined space of a refurbished whaling depot called the Candle House, massively constructed from huge granite blocks. One finds a single reference to Woods Hole in *Moby Dick*. Ancient odors of whale oil and blubber seemed to cling to the premises, the atmosphere scarcely improved by having as many as 50 students crowded into a single two-and-a-half story building. What with papers, books, decaying specimens, formaldehyde, people and laundry, the climate did not encourage one to linger. Clyde had acted very sensibly in making his move to the labs.

Quite apart from such considerations was the fact that experiments like the ones he was contemplating required a sustained investment in time. Working through the nights would be the norm, not the exception. It had not been through caprice that the lab was liberally supplied with food, beer, science fiction magazines and paperbacks. He needed to be alone. Dr. Bergleson had indicated that he would be dropping around sometime that evening. Clyde intended to see to it that his visit was short.

Starting at four that afternoon, with a possible break for dinner in the MBL cafeteria over on Albatross Street, the schedule he'd worked out called for work through the night and into most of the next day. His mother and sister were expected in two days, bringing the ultra-violet apparatus and other supplies. The set of 'origins of life' experiments would fill up the next two days. What more could Science ask of him? He would probably collapse in their arms after that, but he would have laid the cornerstone for enduring fame.

As a follow-up he'd need a spell of lying out on the beaches, doing nothing for a while. Then once more back nose to the grindstone: all-nighters, collapse, rest, more work! It was the only way to accomplish anything in the field. Even as he spoke with Jeff, Clyde was mentally outlining the previews to appear in *Nature*.

Jeff stood up:

"Okay Clyde—I've got to be going. Sure wish I could spend more time with you here: I'd really like to be here when you pop those spiny creatures into the Cuisinart."

Clyde glanced at his wristwatch: "It's only 1:30. You've got to go already?"

"Yes; afraid so. Invertebrate class in half an hour and I'm not prepared for it. I wish you luck. You're pretty young to crack open the vaults of Nature's secrets, but you're the kind of guy who can do it."

He paused: "Actually, I've changed my mind; it's a waste of time to study. If I flunk, well—too bad. I can make it up next year. I'm going to get some of that sea breeze before class."

"Wait; I'm coming with you." Clyde took his jacket off the door, and together they took the elevator to the street floor and out into the daylight.

## II.

"Put them . . . right here. No . . . No . . . Careful . . . There . . . that's right! Good! Just leave them where they are. Thank you."

The two ten-gallon bottles, their sides covered by strips of black masking tape for protection against sunlight, were rolled into the room. Each was filled with a hundred sea urchins.

Delivered at the MBL's basement level and carried up on the freight elevator, they had been wheeled to the lab on a trolley through the third-floor corridors.

The delivery man was short, dressed in faded jeans and a tee shirt. Tough muscles on his exposed arms bulged like taut rope. On a squat neck was positioned a gourd-shaped head, its skin grizzled from oceanic weathering and exposure. His face, if not particularly intelligent, was friendly and expressive. He pulled a large, dirty rag from his pants pocket and wiped his brow:

"You know, fellow? Let me tell you something: I heard them things was poisonous! Am I right? I wouldn't touch them spines if I was you!"

"Not at all!" Clyde laughed. "Here, would you like a can of beer?" He opened a can and passed it over. Reaching into one of the bottles he pulled out a black ball of wriggling spines:

"You must have read something about *Diadema antillarum*. You don't want to run into *him* in the dark. His spines are a foot long! See? These are perfectly harmless. I'm holding him by the spines, but he doesn't do a thing to me. Here—you hold him."

The delivery man jumped away by reflex instinct:

"Hey no! Not me! Yes, I will have a can of beer." Clyde invited him to sit down in the one chair in the lab while he sat on the cot.

"I'm not going to take no chance like that! You scientists don't care what happens to you. You don't care what if your research kills you! I've lived on the Cape all my life and I've seen it happen. Me, hey! I look after number one. Thank you brother, but no! Say," his eyes roamed about the room, "get a load'uh that! This is a real nice set-up you got here! What's that fancy doodah you got sittin' over there in the corner?"

Goggle-eyed with fascination he walked over to the Cuisinart and inspected it.

"Nothing much. It's my experimental apparatus."

"Your experimental wazzis?"

"Apparatus. That's a fancy word for machine. Doodah is

okay too. It's for my research. I'm sorry," Clyde glanced at his watch, "I know you'd like to stay and watch what I'm doing but I can't allow myself to be disturbed while I'm working."

"That's okay, fellow. I don't know nothing about this modern science anyways! It frightens the hell out of me sometimes. Long as you believes in Jesus Christ, that's all that matters. What's your opinion?"

"I haven't got one. I'm a biologist. Biology doesn't deal with such questions."

"Biologist, huh? Like humans coming from monkeys? Stuff like that?"

"You've got it." Clyde was beginning to wish he would leave. Fortunately he changed the subject:

"Say, whad'ya think of the atomic bomb? You're not working on that, are you?"

"Close enough: Space travel."

"Space travel, huh? I gotta hand it to you, you're up there with the heavies! It ain't Top Secret, is it?"

"Well . . . yes and no. Nobody's supposed to know about it, but my papers are published in the journals." With a sad shake of the head Clyde confessed: "I've told too many people already, I'm afraid."

"Oh yea? In that case you better watch it or'n the F.B.I.'ll get on your tail. I've been around for a long time and I've seen it happen! Don't you worry I'm not gonna tell nobody! Space travel, huh? That's between you and me and them little bottled-up buggers. I keeps my mouth shut about what don't concern me nothin'. Don't you let nobody come around snoopin' though, or before you know it you'll be on television before a Congressional committee, wantin' to know whether your mother was some kinda Communist! I'd keep my head under my hat if I was you!"

"I'm not worried about that." Smiling, Clyde drummed on his empty can of beer, "My work doesn't have anything to do with national defense."

"No? I'm glad to hear it. Well, I hate to be going but I got

## SEA URCHINS

to be going. Thanks for that can of beer. And I wish you luck!"

"No trouble—no trouble at all! Wait a week and come again. So long!"

The delivery man left, leaving the door open behind him. Clyde deftly closed it, then walked to the front of the fish tank. He stood before it in absent-minded reverie debating what he ought to be doing next:

"Let's see," he mused, partly aloud and partly to himself:

"We've got lots of hard figuring to do, don't we? 200 sea urchins. How many experiments? Seven? Don't forget the control group. That makes eight. Oh . . . nearly forgot the ultra-violet. Nine. A batch just in case. Something always goes wrong. Ten . . . 10 into 200? That's 20 sea urchins per experiment . . . Will the tank hold that many?"

Clyde examined the fish tank and nodded.

"Looks okay. How many experiments did I say? Eight? Nine? Ten?" He picked up some scrap paper from his work table. "Should I use a stenographic tablet, lab notebook or a loose-leaf binder? I'm not sure . . . What did I say the problem was? Oh yes . . . Stenographic tablet or notebook? . . . Maybe I ought to go down to the supply store in the basement and buy me a few of those professional-looking computation notebooks, you know the kind used by investigators to write down data, make graphs, with brown covers and strong bindings . . . I'd better lie down and think about that . . . "

He lay on the cot with his back propped against the wall. Picking up a science fiction magazine, he started writing on the back of it.

"How many did I say? Ten? Twenty? That's right: ten groups of twenty urchins makes 200 . . . give or take a few, some might not make it . . .

"One thing I know for sure, each experiment has to have a separate data sheet. Ten experiments makes ten sheets. That's it!"

He jumped off the cot and strode to the work table:

"One of these will do." Clyde picked a stenographic tablet

off the top of the pile. With a large black felt magic pen he wrote *INVENTORY* on its pasteboard cover. For a few seconds he stared at the word in some perplexity. Then he crossed it out. Underneath he wrote *SEA URCHIN INVENTORY*. This also was studied from a number of different vantages. Then it too was crossed out.

"No, that's not right," he muttered. Crossing out *SEA URCHIN INVENTORY,* he wrote, simply, *INVENTORY* underneath it. Now the cover was filled with crossed-out words. Clyde swore:

"Damn! I'll have to use another tablet!" He put the first one down then picked up a second. This in its turn was labeled *INVENTORY.*

"But I can't just throw away the first one—it hasn't even been touched. I'll use it for making calculations ... How confused can you get! ... Just bad organization ... Well, I'm still learning. The truth is I'm very well organized, but it may not be in the manner appropriate to this investigation ... Let's see ... What was I saying?" He looked down at the tablet still gripped in his hand:

"Inventory ... Okay. Now, below that." He wrote:

### SEA URCHIN EXPERIMENT

Clyde crossed out the word *EXPERIMENT* and changed the second line to:

### EXPERIMENTS WITH SEA URCHINS EXPERIMENT

"Damnation!" he cursed under his breath, "All I had to do was put an 'S' at the end of 'Experiment.' When you do something wrong, it's better to do the whole thing all over again. Persistence: you get that drilled into you. Uh ... What's this? Oh yes ... " He read again:

### INVENTORY
### EXPERIMENTS WITH SEA URCHINS EXPERIMENT

"I don't like that crossed out word... Crossed out words look really bad. Future generations reading these lab notebooks might think I was some kind of amateur... Too many corrections just look bad... Gotta go on... The date? 'July 25th, 1958'... At least I've got that straight. Now for my name:"

### CLYDE CYTOCHROME

"Say... Should I include my thesis advisor's name?... I don't know." He drained off the remains of his beer. "What've I got?"

### INVENTORY
### EXPERIMENTS WITH SEA URCHINS ~~EXPERIMENT~~
### JULY 25TH 1958
### CLYDE CYTOCHROME

"Crap! I'm wasting valuable time, reading this stuff over and over again! This disorganization is driving me up the wall! Am I in some kind of rut, or what? Oh yes: 'Inventory' ... 'Experiments with Sea Urchins Experiment' ... That crossed out word doesn't seem so bad anymore... July 25th, 1958 ... 'Clyde Cytochrome' ... Hmmm ... Yes, I will put in the boss's name in ... 'Dr. Knut Bergleson' ... 'Case Western University' (?) ... No, that's not right."

He crossed it out and wrote:

### MBL WOODS HOLE, MA.

"But looking at it another way I am enrolled at Case Western... It's paying for my grant and equipment... Well, what should I do? What's the right thing?... All right, All right! Okay already! I'll put them both down."

Next to *Woods Hole, MA* he rewrote *Case Western University, Ohio.*

"That still doesn't look right. Hell! Why am I wasting my time on this nonsense! Nothing must stand in the way of scientific progress!"

With an angry imperious swipe he crossed out both *Woods Hole, MA* and *Case Western University, Ohio*.

"No address! Nothing! Just the date. Everybody knows this is Woods Hole, anyway. Time for a review, just to check if I've got it all down . . . BLAST!" He threw the tablet against the wall, retrieved it and sat down:

" . . . Take it easy . . . I won't get anywhere by losing my temper . . . Okay, okay . . . but let's get it over with quickly, There's too much to do. What have we got here?"

INVENTORY<br>
EXPERIMENTS WITH SEA URCHINS <s>EXPERIMENT</s><br>
JULY 25TH 1958<br>
CLYDE CYTOCHROME<br>
DR. KNUT BERGLESON

"I should write *Sponsor* after . . . no, before . . . *Dr. Bergleson* . . . it has to be before:

SPONSOR, DR. BERGLESON<br>
<s>CASE WESTERN UNIVERSITY</s><br>
<s>WOODS HOLE, MA</s><br>
<s>CASE WESTERN UNIVERSITY, OHIO</s>

"Pretty damn sloppy, if you ask me. Boy, what a mess! At least that phase is over."

Clyde was trembling. He wiped away the sweat pouring down his face.

"Hey; I worked pretty damned hard, didn't I! I deserve another can of beer." Opening one, he picked up a box of crackers and a Science Fiction magazine from the floor and lay back on his cot.

## III.

"I've got time enough to read one short story. Just one. This looks pretty good: *What Do You Do In A Jam?* Who's the author? It doesn't say. Oh yes: Izzy Azimuth! He's a top-notch sci-fi writer. I like all his stuff. Got to put aside this high pressure research for a bit, pull up my feet, and relax."

He removed his shoes, propped the pillow up against the wall and opened the magazine. In a short time he was completely engrossed in his reading:

"Hey: this is one really great story! There's this Martian monster, body of an insect—one thousand times earth size—intellect of a simian ape. The creature is a regression from advanced beings from past eons, whose science was a million years ahead of ours. It's a giant arthropod, really. Anyway, it's immobilized a space ship from the planet Earth between its six legs ... not bad ... All the crew members, the ones it hasn't eaten, are being held as prisoners. The creature wants the astronauts to teach its species our science, so they can set out once again to conquer the universe, which is what they'd started to do ages ago, before the earthquake depopulated the planet and the disease destroyed their intelligence ... Azimuth never writes cheap stuff ... No ray guns or anti-gravity or time machines ... No Venusian maidens, Saturnian torture chambers or Ganymedean prisons ... none of that obvious, cornball stuff! You sure read a lot of trash in these magazines, let me tell you ... "

"Uh-Oh! There's a complication!"

Excited, Clyde pulled himself up to a siting position: "The disease is contagious ... The captain of the spaceship has hidden the true nature of the emergency from the rest of the crew to spare them the horror of it. Now he's more worried that they might catch the disease than he is of anything else. That includes death, torture, or becoming the Martians' slaves ... What's he got up his sleeve? ... Apparently the captain's playing with some idea that hasn't occurred to anyone else . . . Say, this is a pretty long story . . . Oh boy! Oh yes! Damned ingenious, too . . . Azimuth to the rescue . . . He hypnotizes the giant insect with the spaceship's searchlights! Don't quite see how he manages to do that; the light beam can't be any bigger than a pencil to such a huge fly . . . Azimuth gets around that one too . . . There are a hundred facets in the fly's compound eye . . . Interference patterns . . . Hey! Did you ever hear of a cross-eyed fly? . . . Well, the spaceship escapes from old cross-eyes anyway . . . "

Clyde sat up, put the magazine away, and briefly pondered the surprising outcome of the tale.

" . . . That was a great story . . . time to get back to work!"

Clyde jumped off the cot to a standing position. Too abruptly: waves of dizziness assailed him.

"Wow! Have I been drinking, or have I been drinking? Six cans? Or seven? I don't remember anymore. Well, I've had enough. I'm sober at least." He picked up the steno tablet:

"What's this? Oh yes, 'Inventory' . . . Seems okay. The time has come to begin sketching outlines for all the experiments. That's the only way to deal with the confusion."

He flipped open the tablet: "What're we talking about here?" On the first page, in bold letters he wrote:

### TOTAL NUMBER OF SEA URCHINS: 200

" . . . I could just as well have written '#' . . . go on . . . "

| | |
|---|---|
| 1ST EXP | 20 |
| 2ND EXP | 20 |
| 3RD EXP | 20 |
| ⋮ | |
| 9TH EXP | 20 |
| 10TH EXP | 20 |
| TOTAL NUMBER | 200 |

"All I have to do is cross them off as I go along . . . " He hesitated, dissatisfied: " . . . I see what's wrong: am I sure I'll want to use the same number for each one of them? Something might come up. Animals do die, I might change my ideas about how to do this thing . . . Okay already!"

He tore out the first page and began afresh:

"*Total Number of Sea Urchins – 200* . . . Oh damn; I forgot to write '#' instead . . . Well, let it go:"

```
1ST EXP  . . . . . . . . . . . . . . . . . .  20
2ND EXP  . . . . . . . . . . . . . . . . . .  20
3RD EXP  . . . . . . . . . . . . . . . . . .  20
  ⋮
9TH EXP  . . . . . . . . . . . . . . . . . .  20
```

"Boy!" he laughed, taking a deep breath: "I sure am glad I didn't write *10th exp*. But I have to remember what the 9th is about."

Putting the tablet aside, Clyde bent over to relieve his throbbing headache. After a few minutes he sat up: "Oh yes . . . Boy, I was worried for a moment! The origins of life." He continued writing:

```
AMOUNT LEFT OVER  . . . . . . . . . . .  (?)
─────────────────────────────────────────────
TOTAL  . . . . . . . . . . . . . . . . .  200
```

"Then again I'm not sure I'll have the whole 200 when I'm finished . . . All right! There goes another one!" He tore out the page and hurled it across the lab. "Hell on earth! Blast it!! I can't stand it anymore! I've got to get out! I need a walk!" Once again he wrote:

# NUMBER OF SEA URCHINS

"'#' and 'NUMBER' mean the same thing. Okay! I'll cross it out!"

### # NUMBER OF SEA URCHINS

"You should have crossed out the word 'Number,' you boob! Oh boy . . ." He sat down, limp and exhausted.

"Let me get just this page finished, then I'll have to go out for a swim. I also need a can of beer . . . Too much nervous tension building up . . ."

He scrawled across the page:

$1^{ST}$ EXP . . . . . . . . . . . . . . . . . . 20

"Same mistake!"

$2^{ND}$ EXP . . . . . . . . . . . . . . . . . . 20

"Another!"

$3^{RD}$ EXP . . . . . . . . . . . . . . . . . . 20
⋮
$9^{TH}$ EXP . . . . . . . . . . . . . . . . . .

"No tenth experiment! No total! No nothing! My stomach's sick as hell! I need to piss like crazy! I've got to get out of here!" He threw the tablet up at the ceiling. It bounced across the room and landed in the water gushing into the sink from the fish tank.

"Let me out of here!"

Clyde wobbled about the room to the door and ran down the hall.

"Let me out of here!"

## IV.

Clyde spent the remainder of the afternoon on Stony Beach. Instead of returning to his lab he went back to the Candle House for a brief nap. Upon awakening he walked over to the MBL cafeteria which, at that time, was located down the road from the US Wildlife and Fisheries Service on Albatross Street.

After dinner he strolled up the walkway past the tennis courts, back to the entrance to the Lillie Laboratory, the larger of the two buildings making up the MBL. A low staircase of two 3-step ranges introduces a pair of solid doorways. At their crests rise semi-circular arches casting a protective shade over transom windows, gracefully decorated with wooden slats. Just above these stands a ledge with the name *LILLIE* carved in the ugly block letters one sees in most MBL official graffiti. This ledge supports a pair of bulky Doric pillars, on which there is another ledge with the incised message: *MARINE BIOLOGICAL LABORATORIES.*

The small lobby is located just before the principal lecture hall, the information *LILLIE AUDITORIUM* painted above its doors. Clyde had arranged to meet here with Jeff before going in together to attend that evening's lecture. Its title was: *On the Electrical Stimulation of Squid Eggs.* About the subject he knew nothing; about the lecturer he knew only that he was young and, by some people, presumed brilliant.

A pair of tables stands on each of the edges of the lobby. During the summer these may hold sample copies of recent publications by scientific publishers like McGraw-Hill, Birkhauser, Prentice Hall and so on. Before sitting down on one of a pair of low dark mahogany-stained benches, Clyde lifted a copy of a recent publication from McGraw-Hill from one of the tables, a treatise entitled: *Cyclical Breeding Patterns in Nematode Populations of Central America.* It was only sheer idleness that impelled him to leaf through its 967 pages, with sporadic flipping back and forth through the index for signs of familiar names or references.

In general Clyde was contemptuous of such narrowly focused research. It is however common practice among scholars to relieve boredom by the perusal of a boring book. Jeff finally showed up. The book was returned to its display table and they entered the lecture hall. It was already filled to capacity, yet they were able to find seats near the back, where they could converse in whispers without disturbing their neighbors.

"What's he going to talk about, Jeff? I only glanced at the notice."

"You know—I'm not sure? The guy is brilliant, no doubt about that. He practically runs the Biophysics unit in the Marine Research Institute at UC San Diego in La Jolla. He's built his reputation on delivering electric shocks to cultures of deep sea organisms' eggs. I actually went to the library this afternoon and looked up one of his papers. Frankly, I didn't understand a word of it. He's a lot more than just a biophysicist you know."

"Oh? What else does he do?"

"He's also got a Ph.D. in Electrical Engineering. Though technically a biophysicist he's done some impressive work in embryology. Seems to me I've heard he plays jazz piano in night clubs. They're all related, of course. That is, except for the night clubs."

"In science, Jeff, everything is related to everything else. You can't do cosmology without worrying about angiosperms."

"That's stretching it a bit, don't you think, Clyde?"

"Maybe. But everybody is going high tech. Mark my word. I was even considering requisitioning a spectrophotometer from Case Western before coming out here. I figured I had enough to do already. There always comes a point at which you've got to admit to yourself there's something you don't know."

"I'm not there yet, Clyde. Maybe that's because I don't know anything."

*You can say that again!* Clyde smirked to himself. Aloud he replied:

"Just keep coming to these lectures, Jeff. You learn an awful lot that way. It just sort of seeps through."

"Suppose you're right. I don't enjoy going to lectures I don't understand. Clyde—do you know anything about squid eggs?"

"Nothing in particular. Maybe he'll teach us something."

They turned their attention to the stage. The speaker, Professor Seymour Brine, walked onto the stage before the audience had fully quieted down and launched into a rapid-fire discourse:

"Five years ago, in the summer of 1952—" High-pitched screeches from the speaker system blocked out his voice. After a student technician came onto the stage and adjusted the microphone for feedback, Brine began again:

"In the past five years there has been notable work done in advancing our understanding of the havoc wrought by the electrical, chemical and radiactive abuse of the eggs of diverse species at various stages along the embryonic cycle. In matters of radioactive insult the salamander has been the favored animal. We now know a great deal about salamandric mutation, transmutation, regeneration, the effects of massive doses of radioactivity on its primary and secondary sexual characteristics, its coordination, balance, eating-habits, mating, intelligence, and so forth and so on.

"To paraphrase most of the conclusions in this field, the more juice you put into the beast, the more anomalies you can expect to find coming out at the other end. Gentlemen! We are in the business of manufacturing freaks of nature.

"Any of you present in the audience this evening who's spent as much time as I have zapping squid eggs with electric shocks will understand me when I say that the work is very frustrating and the rewards few and far between."

Laughter, cries of assent from the audience.

"I don't consider its methods terribly original. All one needs is some sort of equipment that manufactures high voltage discharges of electricity. Turn up the juice, watch the voltmeter, sacrifice the eggs, then study the effects under an electron microscope. Secretaries and librarians could do a much better job of it. Little more is involved than recording and transcribing data. It does however provide many opportunities for grad students churning out Ph.D. theses."

"When's he going to start talking about his own research, Jeff?"

"He's coming to that."

"Last summer here in Woods Hole I rejected all the standard methodologies in this field. I had to rethink everything from scratch."

"That's a real scientist for you!" Clyde exclaimed, "Strike out on your own and hang the consequences—that's scientific progress!"

"Routine procedures for zapping squid egg cultures with enormous voltages had always left an unpleasant taste in my mouth. In my opinion they are nothing more than disguised sadism. The people who do that sort of thing are second cousins to the sorts who write to prison wardens asking for permission to witness executions."

Clyde felt an upsurge of panic; in a moment he was going to be sick.

"The focus of my research for the past twenty years has been on the polarization of the squid egg, that is to say, the polarization of the lighter and heavier polar bodies. Since these always arise after fertilization, my lecture should have properly been entitled: *Electromagnetic Stimulation of the Fertilized Squid Egg.* In any case everybody knows what I'm talking about. This course of inquiry led me by a natural path to the study of the magnetic poles of the egg; if it has any. Don't scoff until you've thought about it—why shouldn't an egg have a magnetic field? Consider this: the solar system has a magnetic field. The sun has a magnetic field. The earth has a magnetic field. The egg . . . well, the egg wouldn't even exist if it wasn't for the solar system, the sun and the earth! It's a plausible hypothesis, you must grant me that much. Real progress in science, one must never forget, is made by asking the right questions.

"Finding the magnetic poles was another matter altogether. Imagine trying to inject a compass into a squid egg then searching the little pointer!"

A torrent of raucous laughter swept the auditorium. Clyde listened with unrelenting fascination:

"Practical considerations eliminated compasses from our list of options. Bar magnets, vanishingly small electric fields, iron filings: we tried them all! Nothing washed. It took a year for our instrumentation to achieve its final form. A magnetic field is produced by the passage of electricity through a wire coil. This coil is wrapped around a long cylindrical drum. The electrical field itself is created by the rapid rotation of the drum in the manner of the rotors of a power plant generator. The drum is 20 feet long, widening at its mouth to a radius of 10 feet, then tapering to a small instrument-packed box at the far end.

"The drum still exists: you'll find it in the basement of this building. We left it here last summer because it was too cumbersome to take back with us to California. Yesterday while preparing my lecture notes it occurred to me to go down there and make a tour of inspection. The drum was in the exact spot and position in which we'd left it! The janitor who looks after that part of the building told us he'd been saving it just in case we came back to claim it. He was very apologetic as he confessed that he sometimes crawls into the drum at night and uses it as a bedroom. He lives north of Hyannis, and it's often inconvenient to travel that distance late at night. Of course I made him a present of it on the spot. Admire the ingenuity of Man!"

Before going on, Brine paused for a moment in tribute to such ingenuity:

"The drum and coil were attached to a spindle hooked onto a powerful motor that rotated them at a top speed of 10,273 revolutions per minute. I don't remember why we chose that upper limit. A current was thereby induced via the agency of hundreds of little metal whisk-brooms. The technology is fairly complicated and there's no need to go into it here. Then we souped it up to 20,000 volts. You'll be seeing the results in a moment. The box at the far end supported a devilish arrangement of mirrors, with a deftly placed camera in their midst. Pictures could thereby be taken at any speed."

"Hey, Clyde, that sounds like real stuff, doesn't it?"

"Yeah Jeff, you better believe it: real science. Not like most of the research you hear about, where some cranky old professor throws together a few test-tube racks, shakes some amino acids in them, then writes a paper on the color changes per shake, or something like that."

"Yes sir; this is the real thing." While they were whispering back and forth Brine was occupied in pulling a strange-looking object out of a wooden case.

"We called this the—uh—'gun.'"

Brine held up a 3 foot long metal rod. A tube jutting from its middle was fashioned to slide into a wooden stand affixed to the floor. One end of the rod had been outfitted with a trigger. The other branched out into the form of a spatula, roughly the shape and size of a Petri dish.

"Descriptions of the gun's construction and modus operandi fill eight pages of the June 1956 issue of the Ballistics Bulletin. It's designed to shoot culture dishes into the maw of the revolving drum. This meant that the eggs would not have to be killed before subjugation to our experiment. An unpleasant trade-off had to be accepted: an accumulation of large amounts of broken glass at the far end. This couldn't be helped: it was essential that the fertilized eggs be kept alive. Dead eggs may lose their magnetic fields.

"The eggs could not however be expected to survive collision with the walls of the box. This was not a problem, since the superb engineering that went into the installation of the camera guaranteed the capture of images of the spinning culture dish while yet in flight.

"The photographs in this next slide," he signaled the operator, "have been enlarged 100 times. In them the orientations of the polar bodies are clearly seen. I will interpret the data in a moment. But first: a brief pause, to honor the rapid advance of science in our time, along with all the brilliant discoveries and inventions that have brought Electrical Engineering! Electrodynamics! Electro-magnetism! Electronics! Photography! Embryology! Optics! Mechanical Engineering! Metallurgy and Ballistics! together in a single experiment."

The chaos of a thunderstorm would have been drowned out by the waves of adulatory applause that swept over the auditorium. Another slide flashed onto the screen as the room was plunged into darkness.

"This is a picture of the experimental apparatus." Brine indicated its salient features with a blackboard pointer:

"The mouth of the siphon points in the direction of the south magnetic pole; likewise, the far end points to the north magnetic pole. The rotation of the drum is counter-clockwise. You can see the motor off to the left. Because of the telescopic sighting device on the gun stand, we were able to aim dead center into the box at the far end.

"It was not possible to predict the exact moment when the culture dish entered the box. Instead, the camera was set to take exposures at the rate of 50 frames per second from half a minute before the dish of eggs entered the drum until half a minute or so after crashing. The next slide please."

A graph flashed onto the screen.

"The line on this graph portrays the total magnetic force acting on the flying dish at greater and lesser speeds of the dish, that is, the x-axis, in terms of greater and lesser angular momenta of the rotating drum, that is to say, the y-axis."

"Isn't there a mistake somewhere, Jeff?"

"Why no, Clyde. Where do you see a mistake?"

"Well: if one axis gives the acceleration of the drum, and the other gives the velocity of the dish, where is the axis giving the effective magnetic force on the squid eggs?"

"I don't think that matters, Clyde. He's big in his field, so he must know what he's talking about. If it doesn't make any sense now, it will later on. I don't see anything wrong myself.

Let's just listen: he's showing the next slide."

A split-second exposure of a flying Petri dish jumped onto the screen.

"Here we see the dish with its magnetically oriented squid eggs flying through the instrument box. In the next slide we show a millimeter square section of the former slide enlarged 50 times. As indicated by the arrows, the eggs are all oriented in a North-South direction. The heavier pole usually points north, whereas the lighter pole, that little black mark, almost always points south. After examining hundreds of such photographs, we applied a variety of standard statistical measures until we found one that uncovered a tendency for the heavier polar body to assume a northern orientation, of about 7%. This must be considered statistically significant. We were thus led to the conclusion that the heavier pole, being attracted to the north, has a south magnetization, while the lighter pole has a north magnetization. The final slide," he pointed to the screen, "shows the debris of several shattered Petri dishes inside the box. That broken glass really doesn't look so bad after all, does it? Now for some concluding remarks."

Blinking eyes re-adjusted as the lights were turned on.

"Certain questions remain. Influencing our results to an extent, that is, predisposing them in a certain way, one might say, is the fact that the heavy polar body was at the heavier end of the egg, while the light polar body was at the lighter end. Ignoring the effects of friction may have been an unwarranted over-simplification. That will be the subject of our next series of experiments.

"All the same, I encourage everyone here to contemplate the far-reaching consequences of these findings. It is not going to far to say that the very future of biology as a science is at stake. The relationship of magnetism to life has perplexed scientists since the 16th century. What indeed is this relationship? How? Why? When? Since the magnetic field is at right angles to the electric field, so, perhaps life itself is at right angles to . . . who can say? Who dares say?! What depths of horror lie at the heart of the living phenomenon? What unsuspected grandeur? What black cloud hovers over our existence? Life triumphant! Life ever onwards! Eternally mysterious! The biologist's quarry, repulsive of his boldest assaults, stubbornly resisting extermination! And with these thoughts, I leave you."

Brine quit the stage amidst deafening applause.

## V.

As Clyde re-entered the lab he was immobilized by a feeling of despair.

"I can't bear to look at it ... beer cans all over the place ... piles of paper all over the floor ... sci-fi magazines everywhere underfoot ... This place was cleaned up when I started work this morning." He began putting the room back into shape.

"Going to that lecture was a good idea. Now I'm all fired up with ideas ... There, that's better ... Where was I this afternoon just before I walked out ... " He picked up the stenographic tablet that had been left open to dry on his work table.

"Oh yes ... 'Inventory.' I've already done the first page, haven't I? ... What's it look like? Okay. I don't like it, but it'll do. So, what next?" He sat down on his bed and lowered his head into his hands. He had absolutely no idea of what he should do next.

"Let's shape up that next experiment, how about it? ... Use the loose-leaf notebook for that one ... " The sight of the steno tablet filled him with loathing. He slammed it onto the worktable and pulled a blue loose-leaf binder out from a box under the cot.

"What's happening? Yes! Oxygen, for the first one."

As a kind of commentary on his decision, Clyde stood up and took a long, healthy breath. " ... To be followed by combinations of oxygen with nitrogen . . . . What proportions should I use? Don't know: how do they occur naturally? . . . nitrogen 20%, oxygen 80%. That's my control experiment. Altogether 5 experiments: nitrogen 0% 20% 40% 60% 80% 100% . . . Oops! I meant six. Okay . . . Just do the same for all the other gases. How many? Count . . . oxygen and carbon dioxide, 6; oxygen and ammonia, 6; oxygen and nitrogen, 6; oxygen and methane, 6 . . . That's 30 experiments to begin with and I haven't even begun to exhaust the combinations. Anyway I may want to mix them all up, 3, 4, 5, 6 of them together! It's obvious, isn't it? Just use the most significant mixtures, out of a total of . . . " (he did some calculations) "73 possibilities, without getting into mixing their proportions, which puts the number into the many thousands! . . . No reason to get upset . . . My problem is, therefore, to reduce this mess to no more than 20 or 30 experiments . . . Start with the 6 pure gases, naturally, at increasing pressures . . . Then oxygen, carbon dioxide, and nitrogen . . . Hell! What did I say the proportions were? Something like this: . . . "

| OXYGEN | CARBON DIOXIDE | NITROGEN |
|---|---|---|
| 0 | 20 | 80 |
| 0 | 40 | 60 |
| 0 | 60 | 40 |
| 0 | 80 | 20 |
| 0 | 100 | 0 |
| 20 | 0 | 80 |

etc. . . .

"Hey! That's 25 right there, even before we start thinking about varying the temperature, pressure, volume . . . Damnation! 'Why does nature overwhelm us with its complexity?' . . . I need a can of beer . . . ."

As Clyde sat there debating the most efficient course of action, who should walk in but Dr. Knut Bergleson!

# VI

"Oh, hi boss! I've been waiting for you. Come in. Here, have a can of beer."

"Clyde, how are you? We expect great things from you, you know. Yessir! We're really counting on you, my boy! Show me what you've been up to. What've you done?"

"Dr. Bergleson—"

"No excuses now! You've got to show me everything. Down to the fine tuning, is it? Ha, ha! All the pipes in C, are they? Yes, I will have a can of beer. Thank you, my boy. Clyde, I want to confess something to you . . ." Though balding and prominently bulged around the middle, Bergleson normally radiated an aura of vigorous health. Now he suddenly appeared old and worn:

"You're really like a son to me." He removed his glasses and dried his eyes.

"My son never wanted to have anything to do with science. He thinks it's all his old dad's nonsense. Ah me," he made a gesture of disparagement, it not being clear who or what was being disparaged, "Stewart drives a Cadillac; wears nothing but Brooks Brothers suits! Custom-tailored shirts! If that's all he wants out of life, he's welcome to it.

"I've never had any talent for business. Research has been my passion all my life! Did you know, Clyde: I got my start right here in Woods Hole, just like you're doing? I still remember the title of my first published paper." He leaned his head back and intoned: " 'The Effects of Epinephrine on the Circadian Rhythm of the North Atlantic Crayfish.' It was a presumptuous paper for sure: title and all! I'm glad to see you've chosen simple names for yours. Not that I'm not still very proud of that first paper. How I slaved to get that written! Ah me . . ." He mopped his brow, then replaced his handkerchief in his pants pocket.

"Say, young man. That's a mighty good beer you've got.

What's it called?"

"Jack's Guts. It's a local brew, from a place near Menemsha on Martha's Vineyard. It's real cheap, too."

"Fair enough. Never let it be said that a student of mine ever had bad taste in anything." Berglesson turned the can slowly in the light of the ceiling lamp, "Only it's a little warm. When you find time, unpack those cartons and put the cans in the refrigerator . . . That reminds me. I see you've hooked up the Warburg."

Berglesson stood up and ambled over to the Cuisinart. He lifted the wooden lid and peered inside the fish tank:

"Make sure you keep the cork in tight, or you'll ruin everything."

He examined the apparatus carefully, humming to himself. Then he turned around to face Clyde:

"There was something I wanted to ask you . . . Oh yes: I didn't notice any heat source. You wanted to make some temperature experiments, didn't you? I remember your saying something to that effect."

"Yep. It's right there." Clyde proudly pointed to the gas range beneath the tank.

"Wha—what's that??!"

"That's my heat source. Don't you like it?"

"Don't I like it? Why, I'm at a loss for words! It's utterly incredible! What do you want to do, fry them? What's for dinner, folks? Shall we have *Entrecôte Phyllacantus parvispinus?* Perhaps a garnish of *Asthenosoma intermedium?* Make sure the chef doesn't try to slip you some *Toxopneustes pileolus!* Oh the poor dears!"

"Boss . . . it was the best thing I could come up with on such short notice," Clyde faltered, helplessly, "it's ingenious, don't you think?"

"Don't make any temperature experiments! Leave that part out! And whatever you do, I don't want you using that gas range!"

"All right, but—"

"I'm coming back tomorrow, Clyde. I hope, for your sake, to see things in better shape. Take that thing to the dump! I don't want you ruining everything! Okay, I've got to go now." Bergleson opened the door.

"Clyde, I expect better from you. Don't use that gas range!"

He walked out, slamming the door behind him.

Depression descended over Clyde's spirit in thick blankets of gloom. He drained off the remnant of beer. Chewing idly on a leftover sandwich, he thought through the situation:

"It took a lot of work, bolting the fish tank onto the gas range. I don't think the boss fully appreciates the effort it's cost me . . . " Clyde's expression registered defiance, "All right, I'll use it but he won't know about it. It's too late in the game to change everything. But, Jesus Christ! Sometimes I think the boss is no different from a cop! You never know when he takes it into his head to act up . . . What's he expect from me? I'm just a first year grad student in biology, trying to find a way for myself, really, just trying to find myself like anybody else my age!" He emitted something between a sigh and a belch:

"I need to sit down and rest, after what I've just been through," he reached for the loose-leaf binder and a pen, "Where are we, by the way? . . . "

"Oh yes . . . now I remember . . . I'm looking for 20 to 30 significant experiments out of thousands . . . No, I've done it all wrong . . . just 73 . . . it all depends on how you look at it . . . I think I said the first one requires a 25-place table . . . That's too much. Maybe, maybe not. I don't know." He tore out the page from the binder and crumpled it in his hand preparatory to throwing it across the room. Almost immediately he unfolded it and flattened it on the table:

"Damn it all to hell! Crap! I needed that! Why can't I get anything off the ground? It's all very simple, really. Just make a selection out of the 25. How many? 5? All right. That's final! Thank God! That's settled! All right . . . How many . . . Just five  . . . Write that down before you forget it! Which five? . . . No problem with the first three. Here you go:"

| Oxygen | Carbon Dioxide | Nitrogen |
|---|---|---|
| 0 | 0 | 100 |
| 0 | 100 | 0 |
| 100 | 0 | 0 |

"What about the other two . . . Should we make it six. No! Just five!! All right! Six then! It's horrible being a perfectionist! Best write the whole thing out:"

| Oxygen | Carbon Dioxide | Nitrogen |
|---|---|---|
| 0 | 0 | 100 |
| 0 | 100 | 0 |
| 100 | 0 | 0 |
| 0 | 50 | 50 |
| 50 | 0 | 50 |
| 50 | 50 | 0 |

"Actually, that's already six experiments. And I'm certainly going to need 3 more . . . Make it nine then . . . but not ten! That's the limit! 'The integer n < 10', like the mathematicians say . . . Okee-dokee . . . what are the other three? . . . Damn! I've already used up four sheets of paper and torn out three. Maybe the complete table needs to be written out all over again on another page . . . Damn! Damn! Damn! I could have done all this computation this morning, instead of wasting time chewing the fat with Jeff. He'll never make it as a scientist," he shook his head in commiseration, "hasn't got what it takes, I'm afraid . . . "

| Oxygen | Carbon Dioxide | Nitrogen |
|---|---|---|
| 0 | 0 | 100 |
| 0 | 100 | 0 |
| 0 | 50 | 50 |
| 50 | 50 | 0 |
| 0 | 0 | 50 |
| 20 | 40 | 40 |
| 40 | 40 | 20 |
| 40 | 20 | 40 |

"Good enough. Finally:"

CONTROL  80  2  18

"Hey!" he held the table at arm's length, admiring his penmanship: "That's really clever! It's over and done with, thank God. Now at last I can turn to the origins of life. That work may even get me the Nobel Prize! What'm I gonna' need?... ultra-violet light for that one... but that's the most interesting experiment anyway, so it's worth the extra complication:"

| Water | Methane | Nitrogen |
|---|---|---|
| 20 | 40 | 40 |
| 40 | 20 | 40 |
| 40 | 40 | 20 |

"... No. Something's wrong here. That 40% water... it's too small. Okay. Looks like I've got to make another table." Clyde's curses had roared into the infra-red. He stood up and wobbled about the room. Then he reached for another can of beer:

"You know something? I've forgotten all the details of Urey's experiment. I don't even remember how the results were interpreted."

He seated himself at his work table. For 15 minutes he tried to recall the basic features of Urey's 'origins of life' experiment. He gave up, shaking his head:

"There's no hope for it . . . I have to head over to the library and dig up that article from the Scientific American . . . right in the middle of all this intensive labor!" As he stood up again he cried aloud:

"Everything's on hold!"

As he scanned the chart of the oxygen experiments he allowed himself a brief descent into pessimism: "And I haven't even begun thinking about the others. Hundreds of charts just like this one will have to be done before I'm finished! I won't have a scrap of blank paper left by morning. Not counting the origins of life! And space travel! What have I gotten myself into?"

He picked up the new can of beer, an untouched steno tablet and a few ball-point pens.

"Off to the library! Sooner or later I'm going to have to digest all the literature. There are lots of holes in my reading, and it'll take years to catch up on what's current in the field. I can't think about that now, my mind's cluttered up enough as it is." Closing the door behind him he headed down the corridor.

## VII.

When Clyde entered the deserted library it was 2 A.M. The library's two reading rooms and three floors of stacks take up half the space of the Lillie building. For the rest of Woods Hole's scientific community (the Oceanographic Institute, the US Wildlife and Fisheries, the Geodetic Service and so forth) the MBL library is its most valued resource. Until recently its four stories of stacks were at their disposal 24 hours a day. (In the 90s the MBL library began issuing magnetized plastic key cards. It still allows open access during normal working hours.)

The informal reference room holds two round tables about six feet in diameter, with space around each of them for about four chairs. Predictably the decor, including the upholstery, the carpet and the floor to ceiling window curtains (garnished with prints of marine plants and organisms), is seaweed green. Four high-backed chairs and a sofa take up the central section of the room. A few portraits of former MBL directors hang on the walls.

The far more spacious reading room, approximately 50 by 20 feet, has been magnificently designed for serious work in comfort. Entering it one immediately notices the circuit of magazine racks around three of the four walls, holding well over a thousand professional journals. Nine round polished wood tables sweep across the room, each large enough to accommodate six or more persons. Salmon-tinted carpets muffle footsteps. The seven great windows, covered by white shades and framed by regal hydrangea-printed green curtains, open up the western and northern containing walls to bright sunlight, air and, at night, the sea-saturated freshness of an inky sky.

From inside the reading room one enters the stacks through a door to the right. Before they were replaced by computers, the indexed card catalogues were located near this entrance. Clyde strode over to them and pulled out a drawer at random. He held it in his hand, mutely gazing, inert and in total perplexity:

"What did I say I'm looking for . . . Linus Pauling? (Pardon me, I mean Urey.) I've forgotten his last name (I mean his first name) . . . A real scientist would be looking up Urey's original papers through the journals . . . I'll do that later, when I compile the bibliography . . . Hell with it for now, I've got too much to worry about . . . What's the first thing that comes into my mind? Of course!" he snapped his fingers, "the origins of life! Should I browse under *Origins?* Or *Life?* Why not both?"

Under the keyword *Life* he found nothing, not all that strange for a biology library, 'life' being the ultimate taboo word in that field. Under *Origins* he discovered a reference to an article written by the Nobel prize winner George Wald in 1956, then reprinted in a compilation of Scientific American articles on the origins of life controversy.

"That's good enough. It's bound to contain references to Linus Pauling's—I mean Urey's! Damn! What planet am I on?—original papers."

The book was quickly located. He yanked out another 10 on related topics and re-entered the brightly illuminated reading room. Sitting down at a table near an opened casement, he began outlining the article by George Wald.

" . . . Fascinating, that's the only word for it . . . Statistical models for the factors operative at the time of the appearance of living forms on this planet . . . 'more likely' as against 'less likely' . . . I don't know a thing about statistics except that I hate it . . . I do like graphs, but not when there are so many numbers attached to them . . . Louisiana a likely site for the beginning of life . . . Marshy, sandy bayous . . . What if I throw mud into the fish tank? That should do it. A good scientist knows how to improvise . . . Weak cloud cover, ultra-violet light pouring in from all sides . . . Thunder, Lightning . . . Methane . . . Nitrogen . . . I'M GOING TO DO THIS EXPERIMENT TONIGHT! TONIGHT! It'll take too long to sort through the thousands of options in my other experiments. Anyway, this is the most important of all of them! . . . Plenty of time to worry about the others later . . . You can only do one thing at a time . . . But, what about the ultra-violet? Mom won't be arriving for another two days . . . Stuff the ultra-violet; the gas range is good enough. And that's that!"

He cradled the pile of books in his arms and started out the door.

"These are going back to the lab with me . . . maybe I ought to fill out the filing cards, it'll just take a minute . . . On second thought... Boy do I hate to fill out library cards! I lose patience, and it takes forever... I make so many mistakes filling out library cards, then the librarians say they can't read my writing... Why bother?... Return the books when you've finished with them.... That's why I avoid libraries... You'll find very few scientists in libraries, they're all in their labs... Yes, but suppose somebody else needs them in the meantime?... I can't be worried about that; I've got a job to do!"

Clyde stumbled out the door and down the corridor, his arms and hands encumbered by books, papers and the unfinished can of beer.

# VIII

He walked the length of the corridor and up to the third floor. Upon arrival at his lab he posted the "Important Work. Do Not Disturb" sign outside the door. The ceiling light was switched off and replaced by the dim illumination of a small desk lamp. Then he locked himself in.

"Now, where am I?... Oh yes... Hell, I never did get those proportions... They must be somewhere in these books...

"Don't bother to look them up right now, it'll just distract me... I'm going to do this experiment! Get it over with! And that's that!!... I can't spend the rest of my life haggling over petty details. Everything's terribly cluttered up already. Between you, me, and the local population of horseshoe crabs, any old proportions will do... Any advance is a good advance... How about 40, 40, 20?..." He reached out for a scrap of paper and hastily scribbled a new chart:

| WATER | METHANE | NITROGEN | HEAT (RANGE) |
|---|---|---|---|
| 40% | 20% | 40% | 100 F |

"At last! Now for 20 little squiggly urchins!" Clyde reached into one of the jars and pulled out a handful and dropped them into a large bowl.

"I'll never use them all anyway; why not take forty? One step at a time . . . another beer." With trembling fingers he opened a new can and guzzled its contents at a fearsome rate. Then he scooped up another 20 urchins.

"I've got to control my nerves, otherwise I won't get anything done . . . Wait a minute . . . I can't bear the thought of dropping living creatures into ice cold water! First heat up the tank."

Clyde struck a match. The glow in the semi-darkness highlighted his haggard features. "'He fumbled for a match,' just like the sci-fi stories. They're all crap, if you ask me. Come on."

Fragile flames danced over the two front burners of the gas range. Slowly Clyde picked up the sea urchins, one at a time, and dropped them into the saline waters of the fish tank. Closing the lid, he plugged in the cork and squeezed it until it was as tight as he could make it.

"Open the valves. Full steam ahead!" Faint streams of Methane and Nitrogen could be seen invading the interior of the tank. As they bubbled into the water he earnestly watched the gauges on the compression tanks, the nozzles and the various instruments.

"There'll be some computations to do later. You know: $PV = kT$, etcetera . . . What's $k$ by the way? . . . That's Physical Chemistry, not my field. Don't get sidetracked."

The thermostat was supposed to work but didn't. Nothing happened until the heated water began giving off bubbles. Then he quickly turned off the two burners and stopped the flow of the two gases.

"All I need to do now is wait 15 minutes, read off the figures on the respirometer and call it a night. Good!" He heaved a sigh of relief. "I didn't know it would be so easy. I'll write down the figures later, then calculate the proportions from the amounts left in the gas tanks."

Clyde lay back on his cot and rested his head on the pillow.

"It must really be something to be a great scientist." He closed his eyes and fell asleep instantly. When he awoke again it was 6 AM. He sprang off the cot:

"Check the instruments, pronto! What's the reading on the Warburg?" He studied the long glass tubes and read the dials. They registered: nothing. He peered into the tank. Desperately he tapped the walls. Nothing happened.

All the sea urchins were dead.

# IX

An article with accompanying photograph appeared on the front page of the Falmouth Enterprise of July 27th, 1958. It revealed that on the evening of the previous day Clyde Cytochrome, a 22-year old graduate student at Case Western University engaged in research at the Marine Biological Laboratories in Woods Hole, had been discovered in his lab, lying in a coma. An ambulance rushed him to the emergency room of the Cape Cod Hospital in Hyannis. His condition was reported as being stable, however he had not yet regained consciousness. The doctor in charge stated that Cytochrome had succumbed to toxic alcohol overdose sometime between 10 AM and noon. Dr. Knut Bergleson, eminent zoologist at Case Western and Cytochrome's thesis advisor, could give no reason for this grim turn of events.

More than 40 empty beer cans were counted. The student's laboratory was described as being in a terrible disarray, with beer cans, papers, glassware, specimens, instruments and electronic equipment scattered every which way. Fragments of shattered glass tubing looked as if they had been wrenched from their supports and broken across his knee.

Scraps of paper ripped out from steno tablets and looseleaf binders littered the room. They were thickly written over with ludicrous doodles, charts, mathematical calculations and random notations. Apart from some suggested connection with physiology, not a single one of the scientists at the MBL could make any sense out of them. Science Fiction magazines and paperbacks were also thrown about at random. Bergleson surmised that such junk literature may have exacerbated the depression of a young man he described as his "prized student."

Bergleson stated that he'd visited with Cytochrome the night before, and had found the room orderly and in good condition. The reporter was skeptical: scientists, he observed, live in a dream world peculiar to themselves, and what is neat and tidy to them need not be neat and tidy to anyone else. In his opinion Cytochrome had been hiding out there for months, terrified, afraid to step out of his refuge from the world.

A large water cooler bottle and the remnants of another were found on the premises. Bergleson identified them as the containers designed to hold the sea urchins ("spiny animals like little porcupines") used in Cytochrome's research. The first was empty and had been smashed against the wall, the second was still filled with about a hundred of these peculiar creatures. According to Bergleson they were all dead. They should have been dropped into salt water immediately upon arrival. They'd all suffocated within a few hours after delivery. Bergleson admitted that he'd been so shocked when he'd learned what Cytochrome intended to do with his gas range that he'd not noticed this detail.

The missing sea urchins were soon discovered clogging up an odd Rube Goldberg apparatus bustling with pipes, hoses, gauges and valves. Most of its accessories were busted. It was believed that in his delirium Cytochrome had dumped the whole bottle of sea urchins into the tank, then turned the valves and burners on and off at random. At the peak of his frenzy he'd drunk himself into oblivion because (it was surmised by a senior investigator under guarantees of anonymity) he believed he'd permanently ruined his future chances for tenure at any name university. Bergleson confided that he was both confused and depressed from what had happened. He described Cytochrome as a promising scientist, full of ideas, a little wild of course, but that was because he was very young, or so he'd thought all along. He'd expected great things from him. Now he wasn't so sure. He intended to adopt a wait-and-see policy.

Cytochrome's buddy, Jeff Benthic, also a student enrolled at the MBL summer school, testified that he was mystified by the mishap that had befallen his friend. He'd always though of Clyde as the calmest, most collected, most ambitious person he'd ever known. Jeff was summed up as a type one often runs into in the scientific world, bug-eyed and horn-rimmed, a "typical nerd."

The article concluded with a brief description of Woods Hole, its international fame as a marine biological research center, and reminding readers that it is the docking terminal for ferries to Martha's Vineyard. As a vacation venue in its own right it came highly recommended.

*Philadelphia, 1959*

# The Revelation of Doctor Snew

## Dedication

**T**HIS essay is dedicated to all those stentorian bores who have informed the on-going dialogue of civilization by their delineation of the grand themes linking the science, art and history of this century with the deathless truths of the past, that in tones of dire prophecy caution us about the potential threat to the survival of Western Civilization posed by the glorious achievements of the Scientific Method. The British Isles seems to have led the way in their adumbration of this indispensable intellectual duty, sheltering sages of the stature of Malcolm Muggeridge, Jacob Bronowski, Lancelot Law Whyte, C.P. Snow, Kenneth Clark and the incomparable Sir Peter Medawar. Nor have we been chary in our contributions, having given to the world Buckminster Fuller, Gerard Piel, Kenneth Boulding, Harold Bloom, Jonathan Schell, Walter Kaufmann . . . Theirs bewail the "Legacy of Empire." Ours promote the "Demise of the American Dream."

The bond that links all of them, so distinct in politics, intelligence and imagination, is a perverse unquenchable affection for the ponderous. C.P. Snow, as one of the most boring, that is to say, successful, practitioners of the art, is here presented as the exemplum for all the others, although aspects of several of them appear in this portrait of Ignatius Y. Snew; yet still with a great deal left out, else he would be unbearable.

These elders are not New Age prophets. They are worthy of my satire. I would not waste my time ridiculing the "New Age."

# Prologue

The narrator, a college dropout from Mushposh University, still lives in its college town, Lamely, South Carolina. In 1980 he is privileged to meet and converse with visiting scholar and artist in residence, Dr. Ignatius Y. Snew, whose very original ideas on the Two Cultures Dilemma bear a surprising resemblance to those of Dr. C.P. Snow.

> *In the moral [life], [scientists] are by and large the soundest group of intellectuals we have . . .*
>
> —*The Two Cultures*, C.P. Snow

> *Industrialisation is the only hope of the poor. I use the word "hope" in a crude and prosaic sense.*
>
> —Ibid., op.cit.

> *Although I believe that the acceptability of transcendent answers must be valued by the degree to which they bring peace of mind, I believe I was mistaken in thinking that empirical congruence—that is, the correspondence of explanation with real life which is the distinguishing mark of scientific explanations—can be left altogether out of account, for whatever else we may expect of transcendent answers, we also expect that they should not be outrageously incongruent with the world of experience and common sense—for if the incongruence is flagrant and barefaced, we shall lose peace of mind.*
>
> —*The Limits of Science*, Sir Peter Medawar

*I once said in an interview on the BBC that I had had a marvelous life because I'd always been paid to do what I liked—just like a prostitute . . . But, of course, technicians love what they are doing, and therefore, for instance, it is quite certain that all those people who worked in Los Alamos were going to blow that bomb; you couldn't stop them . . .*

—*Magic, Science and Civilization*, J. Bronowski

*The liberal mind, effective everywhere, whether in power or in opposition, particularly so during this period of American world domination, systematically, stage by stage, dismantling our Western way of life, depreciating and deprecating all its values so that the whole social structure is now tumbling down, dethroning its God, undermining all its certainties, and fully mobilizing a Praetorian Guard of ribald students, maintained at the public expense, and ready at the drop of a hat to go into action, not only against their own weak-kneed, bemused academic authorities, but also against any institution or organ for the maintenance of law and order still capable of functioning, especially the police.*

—*The Great Liberal Death Wish* (1970),
Malcolm Muggeridge

*"Man," I cried, "how ignorant art thou in thy pride of wisdom! Cease; you know not what it is you say!"*

—*Frankenstein*, Mary Shelley

❋ ❋ ❋

TEND to look upon the decades of my life spent in the college town of Lamely, South Carolina, seat of Mushposh University, as largely wasted, yet there were compensations. Among these I must include the encounters with distinguished thinkers, many from abroad, who came for engagements of a year or more. None was more memorable for me than the visit, during the school year of 1979-1980, of the internationally acclaimed philosopher, scientist, novelist, social critic, cultural historian . . . and so forth and so on: Ignatius Y. Snew.

Snew's sojourn at Mushposh was far more than a compliment to us, it could better be called arrant flattery! It remains a mystery to me that someone at his level of intellectual distinction would bother to linger in Lamely even a day. His emolument was drawn from 1810 Endowment, set up in the year of the death of the founder of Mushposh, Vladimir Huxley.

Huxley's name is a household word in our town, the only Lamelyite to achieve recognition in the outside world. Although he is well known to scholars of the Enlightenment, his reputation has not reached the educated majority, and his name does not appear in any encyclopedia. I therefore append a brief sketch of his life and works:

Vladimir Huxley to Lamely is like Benjamin Franklin to Philadelphia. He came to this part of the world in 1753, an immigrant to the thirteen North American British colonies from northern Novaya Zemlya, the uppermost of a pair of islands (Severny) off the coast of Siberia in the Barents Sea. Not much of his life is known before he came here. He was born in St. Petersburg in the 1730s in an aristocratic household, joined an archaeological expedition to the island as a college student, and once there decided to stay. He could not have been out of his twenties when he came to Lamely, for him to accomplish everything that he did.

Historians have ferreted out an indirect connection between him and the family of British writers and scientists. Authorities on both sides of the Atlantic have reached a consensus that

Vladimir Huxley is the closest relation to the English Huxleys from the Russian branch of the family. However, *Huxley* is not a Russian name; nor is *Huxleyski*, or *Huxleyvitch*, nor any variant thereof. *Huxley* is the closest approximation in English spelling to a word in archaic Finno-Ugric, an honorific that means something like "diabolical medicine man." He undoubtedly earned this title through his activities with the indigenous nomadic tribes of Eskimos and Lapps.

The reason I know all this is because stories of Vladimir Huxley's life and deeds are drilled into the minds of Lamely's schoolchildren in a kind of high-pitched sing-song from an early age. When we get to high school (not before), we also learn that his hasty departure from the island was connected to a scandal in which an English actress, one of the members of a Shakespearean troupe vagabonding through Siberia under the invitation of the Empress Elizabeth, was somehow implicated. This is not the version Huxley gives in the biographical fragment, written in English, found among his papers after his death. There he states that he was driven off Severny into the Matochkin Shar (the one and a half mile strait separating the upper and lower islands) by a mob of superstitious Lapps whom he'd terrified by his investigations into *"ye ellektric realitie of ye lightnings shaftt."*\*

Yet Vladimir Huxley never did become fluent in English, even after many years in the colonies, and contemporary Huxley scholarship tends to argue that the word *ellektric* is actually a misnomer. There is no word for electricity in archaic Finno-Ugric, and it is likely that Huxley used it as a substitute for some cognate notion he did not know how to put into English. Since all words in the languages of the natives of Novaya Zemlya derive from observations of natural phenomena, there may even be a metaphor at work in the word *shaftt*!

---

\*It is instructive to compare this date, 1752, with that of the researches of Franklin and d'Alibard.

Well! Going under the reasonable assumption that this fickle Ophelia did have something to do with bringing the family of the great English Huxleys into existence, to her also belongs the credit for the transmission of all of Vladimir Huxley's higher genes. For the Russian Huxley was the incarnation, if not the re-incarnation, the standard bearer, the quintessential representative, even the exemplum, nay the very paragon, of the cultivated *two-new cultured mind*: artist; scientist; artistic in his science, scientific in his art; sometimes artist, sometimes scientist; sometimes both artist and scientist; *when* scientist then assuredly artist; *if* artist then indubitably scientist; veritably poly-artist and multi-scientist in ones, twos, threes, fours, and manifolds besides.

Huxley prepared a catalogue of his inventions and supervised its publication; it fills several old vellum tomes. We can at most make a selection from among the most remarkable of them:

☞ He designed a steam engine safety valve which roasted a side of mutton when opened.

☞ He installed a pipe organ in his own home which did double service as a blast furnace.

☞ He built an ingenious cuckoo clock: the door on the face of the clock opens at midnight to reveal a transparent fertilized cuckoo egg. Every hour on the hour it opens again and announces its progress through the stages of cleavage and differentiation. At 10 PM it produces a complete foetus. At 11 the new-born chick breaks its shell. The door opens every five minutes after that to mark the growth of the bird to a mature cuckoo. At five minutes to midnight it disappears, leaving a new egg in its place.

☞ He drew up blueprints for a fiendishly sharp razor, dubbed by him the "Occam's Razor," for excising *ad hoc* hypotheses from scientific texts. There is documentary evidence to suggest that Joseph Priestley availed himself of this instrument to help him in reading books and papers in chemistry that promoted the phlogiston hypothesis.

☞ He concocted a miraculous poison, a death-delivering potion which so works upon the brain of its victim that in his dying moments he sees Christ's Passion projected before the mind's eye with awful vividness, thereby assuring him of eternal salvation. Like most of the enlightened scientists of his day, Huxley was either a Deist or a Mason. Certainly he subscribed to no conventional religious hocus-pocus. It was owing to reasons of humanity alone that he invented this poison, to relieve the hearts of devout Christians looking for some way out of this earthly misery without having to worry about spending time in Hell.

Every penny of the fortune Huxley accumulated from his inventions was sunk into the establishment, in 1786, of Mushposh University. Although it has since become as opportunistic, hypocritical and irrelevant as universities everywhere, Mushposh was, for the times, both far-sighted and courageous. In the founding document it is stated that Mushposh was to be dedicated:

*"TOO YE FURTHERENSE OF YE CONKATENATION OF ALL & YVRY SPIESIES OF YNTELLECTUELLE AKTIVITIE!"*

Rarely has the world witnessed more boldness of educational philosophy! All candidates for a teaching post at Mushposh were required to deliver a public lecture about some subject in their field in the language, concepts and style of some remote, or even completely unrelated discipline. The earliest issues of the Mushposh Annals, founded in 1795, carry much delightful material. One finds, for example, the text of a two-hour peroration by a musicologist which presented an overview of 18th century Estonian piano music in the terminology of Lamarckian biology. He depicts Neapolitan chords as "acquiring characteristics" through association with other chords over time. The sonatas by Latvia's leading composers are analyzed with reference to their digestive tracts and circulatory systems, and he develops a model, based on parasite-host symbiosis, of the relationship of the performer to the score . . . and much more of the same.

These learned dissertations were published in the *Mushposh Annals*, the *Transactions of the Mushposh Academy* (circa 1825) and in *Lamely Postscripts* (1836 to the present). It was expressly stated in their contracts that all faculty members had to contribute to these journals on a regular basis: Vladimir Huxley was the first American college presidents to enunciate, without beating around the bush, the doctrine of publish or perish.

Standards were higher then, judgments more absolute, penalties more severe. It is amusing to read in the *Transactions* of a certain vulgar fraud who was not only refused a post at Mushposh, but was snubbed out of Lamely altogether for having the effrontery to deliver a lecture on violin playing in the language of anatomy, entitled *Sensitivity of the Gut*.

Another presumptuous sophist delivered a talk whose title was, in essence: *Human Psychology Described by Newton's Laws of Motion, with Applications to Alienist Practice*.

Someone in the audience took the trouble to compute the numerical value of his fundamental equation:

$$\text{PROFUNDITY} = \frac{\text{MOMENTA OF ATOMIC SENSE IMPRESSIONS}}{\text{INTERSTITIAL SIGNIFICANCES OF MEANING DYADS}}$$

and discovered that he had divided by zero! This fraud was tarred and feathered, then run out of town on a rail. Oh, they were tough in those days!

Vladimir Huxley died in 1810. The Huxley Memorial Endowment follows the terms laid down in his will. It underwrites the residence, for a year at a time, of creative intellectuals who, in the world's estimation, have made substantial contributions to experimental aesthetics, artistic research, or theoretical culture. Recipients receive the stipend of a full professor, access to all facilities, and, apart from their slight contractual obligations, endless free time in which to follow their fancies in their unique quandry of disciplines. In exchange, a VHM Endowment fellow delivers two public lectures in each of the terms of his residence, and maintains at least 5 office hours a week for students during the school year.

❋ ❋ ❋

> *Granted that the foregoing teleological theorem of the cause and process of genius articulation is acceptable for understanding what Einstein means by man's "doings" being motivated by either fear or longing; granted that genius is responsible for the progressive inventions by man; and granted that the genius, like all others, has to eat (economics), it becomes of interest, in a study of the vital motifs and trends underlying man's history to trace the patronage of the artist throughout the ages of our particular civilization.*
>
> —Nine Chains to the Moon, Buckminster Fuller

From the moment that Dr. Snew moved into his suite in the faculty quad the question "What's new in Lamely?" could not only, for the first time in 200 years, be given a positive response, it became redundant!*

The town's only newspaper, a rag read by nobody, named *The Lamely Weekly*, printed its first headline since the Civil War. A dozen new faces were sighted on the streets of the downtown area. They did not stay for very long. Lamely's last hotel went out of business in 1730, 10 years before the arrival of its patron genius.

---

*Our little jokes. Provincial way-stations like dear old Lamely cultivate a kind of humor that may not be very sophisticated, yet leaves a fond aftertaste of nostalgia in the hearts even of those fortunate enough to kick its dust from their shoes, never to return.

Dr. Snew brought several unusual items with him, gathered from diverse regions of the globe for his manifold research interests. They provided much material for public curiosity and rumor in the diners, barbershops and poolrooms where public opinion is made. Included among them were: a painted, ornamented and jewel-bedizened octopus tentacle in a tank of formaldehyde; an hourglass with sands that spontaneously and unpredictably flowed uphill, evidence for the fluctuations in the 2nd Law of Thermodynamics predicted by Ludwig Boltzmann; an antimatter Geiger counter; the eraser from a pencil used by Albert Einstein in writing the drafts of his first paper on relativity: a project that had engaged Dr. Snew's attention for many years was the deciphering of the fragmentary bits of equations embedded in its eraser; a book that was locked up in the Mushposh Library's Limited Access Collection on the day of his arrival, a pornographic novel banned in all civilized nations that, in graphic detail, catalogued all the conceivable positions of coition to the points on the boundary of the Mandlebrot Set!

He also had in his possession an egg that grows real human hair!

Dr. Snew set a high value on this object. In his first Vladimir Huxley Memorial Lecture, he told the audience that its purpose was to refute the "egg-head" stereotype that the ignorant apply to intellectuals. "Behold!" he exclaimed, raising it above the podium and pointing to it with his right index finger: " An egg is not necessarily bald; and a bald man—unless he be Humpty-Dumpty, a figment of the imagination invented by my late lamented colleague, Dr. Dodgson—is not an egghead!"

I knew that I wanted to consult with him privately about the difficulties I'd encountered in my long academic career. I soon realized, however, that he was very popular with both students and faculty, and that it would be impossible to see him for more than a few minutes during his posted office hours. When not required to be on hand, Snew shunned the campus like an embarrassing relative. I suspect that much of his time in North

America was spent going to bookstores in the US and Canada to promote the sales of his novels. This led me to the devising of a scheme for dropping in on him unexpectedly in his quarters. Six months passed before it could be put into effect.

In the end it turned out to be remarkably simple. The night watchman of the faculty high-rise apartment building at the south-eastern rim of the Mushposh campus was known to belong to a familiar species of alcoholic, characterized by sociability and garrulousness. At the cost of a fifth of Scotch and an hour and a half of putting up with a stream of largely incomprehensible babble, I had the run of the building by midnight.

Dr. Snew was not in his suite, but the door was open and he'd left the lights on in his living-room; he was probably somewhere in the building. I began a search on all the floors which led to my discovery of him at work in a warehousing area taking up the north end of the basement. He was deeply engrossed in his work. Every square foot of this large expanse had been converted to serve some aspect of his multi-disciplinary research. Dr. Snew was seated on a high laboratory stool before a long vinyl-topped worktable overladen with books, glassware, electronics and other equipment. Leaning his paunch against the table, he was peering through his plate-glass spectacles, by the dim light of a neon fixture loosely dangling from the ceiling, into the objective of a microscope. Though advanced in years, his brow deeply furrowed, almost bald with a bit of grey around the temples, and decidedly overweight, Dr. Snew remained active and alert, from what I could judge, altogether in excellent health. A delicately trimmed goatee, groomed sideburns and floppy blue beret rakishly cocked over his left ear gave him the appearance of an Impressionist painter.

Hearing the sound of footsteps entering the room Dr. Snew started up out of his seat. Surprise quickly gave way to annoyance when he turned around to confront me. My presence was acknowledged with a shrug and a deep sigh. He knew, of course, why I'd come.

"I must say," he grumbled. lifting himself off his stool, "Your sort has persistence!"

I emitted the silly, self-deprecating laugh that is one of my recognizable characteristics.

"I will grant you a *very* brief interview," he went on. glancing compulsively at his watch, "on the condition however that you promise me that you will not encourage any other friends of yours to disturb me after midnight."

Feeling very much like an intruder, I turned around as if to leave. But he raised his voice, calling me back:

"Please don't go away! You're here already! For the moment I must admit I'm rather relieved to have somebody with whom I can have a chat. The work I am doing," he rubbed at his eye sockets and yanked his jowls, "is very strenuous."

He waved me onto a high stool identical to his own, at the right side of the worktable. From my new vantage I could now distinguish the individual items around the room. It was cluttered without being disorderly, intimate without being cramped, with additional elements of excitement provided by the sounds of trains and river boats, the noise of distant traffic and the night's impenetrable opacity entering in through the rows of rectangular windows along the sides and at the far end of the basement. Although the racket produced by steam and hot water burbling through the pipes made me feel we were under machine gun fire, I soon ceased to notice it.

At the upper left hand corner of the room stood a writing desk. In various places I discerned a large freezer, a desk computer, an oscilloscope, a Warburg spectrometer, the antimatter Geiger counter, a refrigerator, a large bottle of distilled water, a tuba, a harpsichord, a bazooka, a scrambled pile of the kind of junk one might pick up at a garage sale, numerous gadgets whose function I could not identify, and rows of opened and unopened boxes. Barely visible in the dense shadows around the back wall I recognized the outline of an electron microscope. The wall to my left was completely covered from floor to ceiling with files, books, journals, reprints and papers.

My curiosity was aroused by the presence of a strong and repellent odor, quite unlike anything I've ever encountered before or since. To feign ignorance of this horrible odor was impossible. Dr. Snew, the epitome of refined academic courtesy at its height, observed my discomfiture at once and quickly identified its source.

"Oh, I *am* terribly sorry." Snew walked to the front of the room and soon returned, bearing the jewel-encrusted octopus arm, now in an advanced state of decay. I nearly fainted with the stench. With the adroitness of much experience he wrapped it in aluminum foil, then put the package into the freezer.

"I'd forgotten that visitors aren't used to the smell. I don't notice it anymore."

"Does that tentacle figure in one of your experiments, sir?"

"Indeed it does, young man: I'm investigating the decomposition of a work of art!"

As he spoke, I realized that Dr. Snew was glaring at me with a fascination amounting to obsession. Springing with alacrity off his stool, he quickly walked over to me. What he did next mystifies me to this day. Using the thumb and forefinger of his left hand he grasped me on the scalp and below the nose. Then he circled about me a quarter turn and squeezed my temples between his right-hand fingers. Twisting my head to the left, Snew stared into my eyes for an intolerable length of time. Letting go with the left hand, he started tapping on the apex of my skull with the middle finger's foreknuckle. The reverberation resembled that of a struck wood block. He kept repeating this operation.

With each tap of his knuckle on my scalp, a smile spread broadly across his face. Finally he released my head, thereby earning my gratitude, as my neck was nearly broken. After which he walked, rather he waltzed back to his side of the table, with something excessively smug spread, like cream cheese on a bagel, over his features, chuckling softly to himself as from some private joke. He climbed back onto his perch and resumed his intent and embarrassing, though I would say not unfriendly stare. From his confused mumbling and giggling I was able to extract a reference every now and then to "... *457 cycles*..." Whatever the meaning of that odd remark, I'd passed the test; or so I imagined. As I watched him with some anxiety, it seemed as if a black cloud of doubt at the back of his eyes had crossed over from the right side to the left side of the brain.

"I must ask you this in all seriousness."

The venerable Dr. Ignatius Y. Snow placed a forefinger to his lips to indicate silence. A quiver rolled through his wise and beady eyes, and an isolated strand of hair at the top of his head unraveled and fell over to the right. He leaned backwards on his stool, pressing his spine against the edge of the table while continuing to regard me fixedly in a haughty manner. The execution of a quick 180° maneuver left me with a full view of his back and nothing else. Slowly he twisted his head to the left and, like a guerrilla peeping out of the jungle, glared at me over his shoulder.

Once again emitting an exclamation of delight, Snow twirled around and around on his stool while clapping his hands, as if he'd found the merriest sport known to man! Then he stopped abruptly and looked me square in the face. With his right hand he covered his mouth and scratched his sideburn with its thumb. Then he said:

"What I must absolutely know is this: Are you a Philistine?"

Again the upraised finger to the lips!

"You're going to have to answer my questions. I won't talk to you if you're a Philistine. To begin with, you've got to tell me all that you know about the parity non-conservation experiment of Lee and Yang."

My state of panic was complete:

"Ha, ha!" I cried, "Ho, ho ho! Well, sir, as they say: parity begins at home! ... and take my word for it, non-conservation may be bad for the economy, but I don't scare easily! I'm ready for anything!" (followed by a fit of laughter) "And that goes around twice for microcosms! If you ask me, people who don't know a boson from a fermion shouldn't be in the civil service!

Not in this high tech world, with competition from the Japanese! Am I right now? And between you, me and the cyclotron, I don't care it if was Lee and Yang, or Crick and Watson, or Abbot and Costello! Basic science is a discipline, my honest fellow! A discipline! Not a circus act! Ha, ha, ha!!!"

I crumpled forwards on my stool. Sweat poured from my brow and my limbs trembled. My fear of giving the wrong answer had spent my forces, and I lay across the table, gasping for breath. Dr. Snew went on placidly observing me with a mixture of curiosity, suspicion and amusement, like some fascinating species of bug.

"That reply . . . will do," he said at last, with a separate emphasis on each word, "You may in fact not be a Philistine after all. Tell me . . . you're not the kind who's likely to be steeped in Wagnerian opera, are you? In that case, let me remind you that in the first act of *Siegfried*, Mime must give correct answers to each of Wotan's three questions. Do you know why?"

"No," I whined in a pitiable whisper.

"To save his head!" As an after-thought he added, "He fails, of course."

There was something so sinister in this remark, particularly in the way the hiss preceding the final syllable combined with the flinty gleam in Snew's eyes, that I gripped the lapels of my jacket with both hands and steeled myself to fight for my life, if necessary. Oblivious to my distress, Snew went on:

"My next question is this: Trace the evolution of the interior monologue in the modern novel, from Marcel Proust's *Du Coté de Chez Swann* to the magical realism of Carlos Fuentes in, say, Part II of *Terra Nostra*. Or you can use Part I, I don't care. Don't Mime your words! Wotan knows! Tra-La-La!"

"There is no interior monologue," I howled, "Interior and exterior designate the alternatives of a false dichotomy in an incompletely formalized metatheory! There is likewise no exterior monologue either! Between monologue and dialogue there is little choice; even less is there to be found any real difference between C.P. Snow and Humphrey Bogart!"

This last observation threw the elderly savant into a dither.

"That's radical thought!" he muttered, "Radical... 457 cycles... exterior monologue... interior monologue no exterior, no interior... monologue, dialogue... Bogart, Snow, my word; what would Sir Peter Medawar say to all this?"

Snew stumbled off his stool and shambled to his desk; whereupon he threw himself into a swivel chair, opened a journal and began, in a wild frenzy of creativity, whirling in dervishlike fashion, to write. He head bobbed up and down like someone drowning, and he shouted:

"You're going to be in a book of mine! C.P. Snow is no different from Humphrey Bogart! That's priceless! Magnificent! My God, sir... that's stupendous!"

Over the next hour Snew's pen did not once stop moving. I fidgeted in my seat, spellbound, afraid to move or utter a word. At last his inspiration peaked. He lowered his arms to his side and bowed his head, drained of energy; nothing remained to be said. Removing his reading glasses, he wiped them with a piece of silicon tissue and put them away. With a fatherly sigh he heaved his pachydermous bulk out of the swivel chair and tottered back to his laboratory stool.

"Is that how you write all your books?" I asked him, after he was again seated.

"That's right. I write up conversations like ours in my notebooks. Then I shuffle the sketches together in a pile, call the whole thing a novel and contact my publisher."

"How would you characterize your method? As a form of improvisation?"

"Why of course, young man! Isn't that the avant-garde trend? That's how I really think of myself: as an avant-garde artist! *Chance must rule: Reason can at most supervise.* Remember that! Remember that, young man! It may be the most valuable thing I can teach you!"

I.Y. Snew then turned his back to me and, as if I no longer existed, resumed looking through the microscope. Like a dense fog that, without warning but from conditions already present in the atmosphere, arises to blot out the sun, a reactive cloud of confusion had been stirred up by his hour of compulsive writing. It manifested itself in the aimless manner in which he shuffled his papers, as well as in the performance of an incredible number of small superfluous gestures. Every bodily motion came pre-embalmed in its aura of purposelessness. He was having such trouble concentrating, that the thought crossed my mind that it might help him if I showed an interest in his work. Meekly I muttered:

"Dr. Snew: can I see what you've got under the microscope?"

Honestly, the eminent doctor shot bolt upright as if his bottom had hit a tack! Through my indiscretion his morass of befuddlement had merely been replaced by a fixation on some horrible thought. He sat immobile, bobbing his head in Lissajous figures, staring wildly into space.

I waited for him to return to an awareness of his surroundings; which he did, eventually, with something of a crash, slamming his elbows onto the table and burying his overwrought brow in his hands. For a long time he held this posture, his body rocking in mute anguish.

Suddenly I realized that without my noticing it he had locked his head in the crook of his left elbow and that his swollen eyes were glowering at me from the center of his face. Never had I seen anything so baleful!

"You appear to have forgotten, darling, that you haven't answered my third question!"

Dr. Snew raised his head, pulled himself erect, gesticulated erratically in the air with the fingers of both hands like a drunk conductor and sighed, as if his unique burden of cares rendered him the most miserable of men:

"I will not talk with a Philistine. Any person who hasn't heard of the Lee and Yang parity non-conservation experiment is a Philistine.

"If you can't carry on a discussion with me about the Second Law of Thermodynamics, you're a total wash-up in my book. Any member of our God-forsaken species who cannot explain upon cross-examination the difference between the interior monologues of Virginia Woolf and James Joyce is a Philistine. Your final remarks, sir, were most perplexing: for if Humphrey Bogart be no different from C.P. Snow, then how, I ask you, is Ignatius Y. Snew different from . . . well . . . Kermit the Frog!! How indeed!!" he groaned aloud.

Just watching him moved me almost to tears. The poor man groped about the books on his worktable, coughing, moaning, shaking his head to the sound of somebody's Requiem in his inner ear.

"Dr Snew!" I yelled, "get a grip on yourself! You're a famous man! If you belittle yourself, take some thought for the world that reveres you! Can you imagine Leonardo da Vinci carrying on like you're doing? Pythagoras? Blaise Pascal? Benjamin Franklin? Vladimir Huxley? For shame, sir! Why, what you're doing is cowardice! That's all it is, sir: arrant cowardice! It is your part to lug the burden of fame on your shoulders every day of your life; do it like a man!"

This reproach brought him to his senses. His eyes twinkled and color returned to his cheeks. Perky as ever, he pulled himself upright on his laboratory stool.

"Are you now ready, young man," he asked, "for my third question?"

I'd thought he'd forgotten all about that. My blood froze.

"My third question is this: How may we best supplant the pseudo-aestheticism infecting the spiritual consciousness of the West, emanating for the most part from the stew-pots of the Parisian Left Bank, by edifying Analytic Empiricism, while at the same time avoiding the Socialist Realism bugaboo of the Marxist-Bolshevists?"

Asking me about my politics gets my hackles up. Seeing my resistance stiffen, Dr. Snew wagged his right forefinger in my face like a puppy-dog's tail:

"I might as well let you know that I'm constantly being plagued by unwelcome interruptions from Philistines. Philistines! Parlour Pinks! Trots! Green Revolutionists! Ban the Bomb fanatics! Pseudo-aesthetes! Do-gooders of every stripe and complexion! Just so much wretched rabble, sir, who accumulate on my doorsteps like the cans of garbage during a dustman's strike! Answer me! Answer me, young man, or," he winked, "by Wotan: I'll have your head! Tra-La-La!"

A thrill of pure terror coursed unalloyed through vein, lymph node and synapse. One and only one answer would do. That I was sure of. That and nothing else.

By good fortune it was my very state of gawking muteness that saved me. With paralyzed tongue and mouth open, staring moronically at his lips I began, through an automatic locking of kinematic responses, to emit the same phonemes as he did.

"... *iPTTEhhh* ..."

Dr. Snew leaned into to my face to coax the sound from my glottal depths:

"............ *ECCHHhhh* ......" His "ech" sounded more like "eschhh."

"......... *NNNAHHHHHHHH* ..." In my insensibly terrorized state it seemed as if I would never let go of this nasal hum. However, Snew himself broke the feedback overload by screaming out the rest of the word:

"... SOPHY!"

My jaws shut down with such force that they locked. Snew helped me pry them apart with a serving spoon.

"That's right, darling! That's right my good man! Hurrah! Bravo!"

The sagacious Dr. Snew did a little hornpipe, chewing like a ghoul on the piece of elastic which served to connect the arms of his glasses around the back of his skull:

"TECHNOSOPHY! TECHNOSOPHY! TECHNOSOPHY! The salvation of the world!"

Snew brought his dance to an end and returned to his stool. His manner had once again become friendly:

"Isn't it about time you told me your name? I find you particularly apt. If you care to listen, I can teach you something of the greatest importance. I very much doubt I'm going to find anyone else in this educational shantytown who could begin to understand it."

"My name's Modus Ponens."

"Your middle name?"

"That's been excluded."

"Obviously." We both chuckled.

"Very well, Modus, tell me something about yourself."

"Dr. Snew: I'm what they call a burnt-out case. Within the last two decades I've majored in almost every degree program offered at Mushposh; no mean accomplishment since, as you know, every course is obliged to incorporate two or more unconnected disciplines.

"My studies began in 1963 when I enrolled in Cybernetic Choreography; within a year I'd changed my major to Algebraic Politics. I flunked out at the end of that year and went to work as a poolroom attendant. In 1967 I re-enrolled, determined to excel in Linguistic Sculpture. I soon got sidetracked into Phonemic Lithography, which, despite superficial resemblances, is a completely different subject. In the Spring Term I took a leave of absence to avoid flunking out a second time. This pattern has been repeated, with only minor variations, half a dozen times since then. Not only don't I have a degree after all this time, none of my credits can be applied to any degree I may want to acquire in the future.

"All my education's done for me is to make me unemployable. I'm unable to relate anymore to the people I used to work with in drugstores, poolrooms, five and dimes, greasy diners and so on: we've got nothing to talk about and I'm totally intolerant of their mores. Yet I've got no training for doing anything else.

"Nor can I strike out on my own: I know a little bit about a whole lot of things and can't apply any of it. I'm doomed, Dr. Snew—doomed! I'm going to remain on South Carolina's welfare rolls for the rest of my life!"

Even as I spoke, the smile on Ignatius Y. Snew's face grew until it lay in his face like a jolly crescent moon above the sands of the Gobi Desert. Evidently he was proud of my dismal history of failure!

"Good!" Snew cried, "Very good! Very, very good indeed! Modus: I do believe, more and more, that you're the only person I'm going to encounter during my stay here who will prove not to be a total waste of my (that is to say mankind's) valuable time. I'm going to explain to you why you aren't a failure. Modus! Listen to me! You aren't even an . . . er . . . "burnt-out case," a quaint Americanism, I dare say. Yes sir! Yes indeed . . . That poor man, Modus Ponens, is, unknowingly, merely the victim of the staggering burden of the dire *two cultures dilemma\** now confronting Modern Man . . . threatening him with extinction itself, lest he mend his ways!"

Dr. Snew remarked that he was feeling a bit hungry. He gave me some money and sent me out across campus to the New York Deli a few blocks away to pick up sodas for both of us and a cornbeef sandwich for himself. This errand consumed the better part of an hour.

※ ※ ※

When I returned it was to find the learned Snew once again hunched intently over his microscope. So absorbed was he in his work that he didn't hear my footsteps when I entered the room. Nor did he notice that I had resumed my place on the high stool to his left. His reaction of shock when he lifted his head and saw me sitting there took me completely by surprise. With his right index finger he pushed his glasses up onto the bridge of his nose; then he squinted at me with suspicion. His tone of voice was hostile and vaguely confused:

---

\*Editor's Note: The "two cultures," as defined by C.P. Snow, are the arts and science, though he is really talking about literary people and physicists. The "two cultures dilemma" is the apparent lack of communication between them.

"Who might YOU be?"

Had he tried to strangle me with the octopus tentacle, I could not have been more astonished.

"Surely you remember me, Dr. Snew! Weren't we having a conversation here less than an hour ago?"

"What's that? An hour ago? That's irrelevant! "Time" isn't one of my scientific interests, young man! An hour; a year; a century! So what? Empires can crumble in half an hour! Monsters can be conceived," I distinctly saw him shudder, "in a few short minutes! I haven't the foggiest notion of who you are! Furthermore, I consider it most impertinent for you to be disturbing me at this late hour while I'm engaged in research of vital importance to civilization's survival into the next century!"

"Dr. Snew!" I implored, "Surely you remember you sent me out to get you a cornbeef sandwich?"

"Well? Where is it? Give it to me!" Snew's outstretched fingers reached greedily for the package, which he yanked out of my hands and tore apart with animal savagery. Even as he stuffed the sandwich down his throat, the flow of his conversation continued uninterrupted:

"Sir! You don't seem to realize that, granted you were conversing with me within this past hour (which I very much doubt) and supposing, in theory, that I did send you out on some sort of errand, which may even have been to get this sandwich . . . why, hang it, man! All this is besides the point, don't you see? You conjure up no mental image, I don't know you from Hammurabi! I observe somewhat lazy and dissipated features, vaguely hominid if I may say so; I've the impression you're a harmless sort, and so on. But you may very well be quite different from the person you claim to be—for all the difference that would make!"

"What person are you referring to, Dr. Snew?"

"Weren't we just talking about him?" He sat there and stared at me, momentarily perplexed.

"Well; never mind. Just give me your name and I'll report you to Public Safety." I slouched against the wall, realizing once again the impossibility of getting out from under the authorities of Mushposh. My sense of defeat was total.

"Your name, sir? Your name! Come on, out with it."

"Modus Ponens."

Snew tossed his pencil into the air. It flew across the room and embedded itself in the scalp of the hairy egghead: "Modus Ponens! Why the hell didn't you say so in the first place?"

"Picture yourself being stuck on the *Pons Asinorum*."

"Very good, sir, very good. Here. Take the pickle; I never eat it." Snew enlisted my admiration by picking up our conversation where we'd left off:

"Vladimir Huxley is of indisputable greatness. The fact remains that there is no longer any correspondence between his ideas and those of the world we live in—nor has there been for a century or more. Modern Man simply doesn't employ those things they used to call *ideas* in his thinking anymore. The modern equivalent to an idea could be called something like an—er—*schizophrenia*. We must applaud Vladimir Huxley's noble effort to bring unity into the thought of the Enlightenment; our desperate need today is for a *unification of the schizophrenias*."

I reached for a pen and paper:

"Dr. Snew; do you mind if I start taking this down? I might be able to get an article into the student newspaper."

"Go right ahead. Only if you want to quote from my books you've got to contact my publishers. Let's go on. Where was I?"

"You were talking about Huxley's inappropriateness to the modern day."

"Yes—good—thank you. Mushposh reached its apogee in or around 1859, the year of the publication of Darwin's *Origin of the Species*. In those days, it smacked of genius to require every teaching candidate to deliver a long-winded lecture on his subject in the language of another subject.

"We've come a long way since then, baby! Modern avant-garde thinking has depreciated the market value of antiquated views like Huxley's to virtually nil. Today we're dealing with notions such as *arming for war; prosperity through spending; balancing the budget through lower taxes; minus matter bubbles in empty space; exotic statistics; negative capability; unconscious pain; wave-particles; dictatorship of the proletariat; criminal justice; substance abuse; feasible deniability* . . . you know what I mean.

"Hang it, man! Mushposh doesn't live in reality! One has a right to expect much more from today's professoriat than what was required in the 18th century! This is how it ought to be done: anyone applying for a university faculty position will have to be able to deliver a paper in his discipline *as if he in fact believes it to be a paper in some totally unrelated discipline*!

"My novels are a good example: I don't give a hoot when some critic disparages their artistic merit, knowing as I do that what I'm writing is really science. And what difference can it make to me if their veracity is thoroughly debunked? Works of art are not required to be historically accurate! If you want to criticize me seriously, you must attack the integrity of my schizophrenic delusion that I'm producing art while in fact I'm really doing science . . . or the contrapositive! D'you get my drift?"

I nodded in dumb amazement. Never had I hoped to encounter an intellect of such dazzling brilliance.

"Modus! Master the art/science of technosophy! Technosophy is . . . (I take note of your astonishment; you're in good company. I obtained much the same reaction when I walked about the high table at Cambridge asking the so-called scientists if they had anything to say about the historic role of T. E. Hulme in the creation of Imagist verse . . . ) a neologism, an oxymoron, a portmanteau, a coinage of my own crafting, combining *manufacture* with, that is to say, wisdom.

"You're witnessing an example of technosophy at work. You've no doubt figured out, my boy, what I'd doing with this microscope?"

"Microbiology . . . or could it be 'Bacterial Epistemology'?"

"Nonsense, old chap! Have you really noticed nothing at all since coming into my studio? What about this?" Snew crooked a finger up towards his floppy beret, "Or these? Ho, ho!" He tugged at his goatee and frisked his sideburns.

I shook my head in mute incomprehension. Snew stretched forth his hands in a gesture of eloquence and cried:

"I'M PAINTING! In the new way, the avant-garde way, the only really modern way to paint! Modus; come over here and take a look."

Snew pushed aside a stack of calculations and graphs to make it easier for me to look through his microscope. He alighted from his stool and I climbed up onto it. Staring into the eyepiece for several minutes I could discover nothing more than mobs of bacilli squirming about in some nutrient medium. The look of sheepish despair with which I turned to Dr. Snew brought forth a gale of laughter.

"Well, what is it, Modus Ponens? What is it? Come on! Out with it!"

I shrugged obsequiously: "Dr. Snew: I've no idea how painting comes into what I've seen you doing."

"Well, it's useful, isn't it?"

"I suppose so, but . . . "

"Then it's far in advance of painting, let me tell you! Research like mine would have done more to reduce the infant mortality rate of the 18th century than any pursuit hitherto designated as painting!"

"But, sir, speaking with all due respect, that doesn't make it . . . "

"Now, now Modus: this *is* painting, radically modern painting. Your confusion stems from pre-conceived notions of the true goals of Art. You still believe that people paint (or compose music, or write poetry, or whatever) because they want to produce an object called a painting, a symphony, a sonnet, and so forth. That kind of thinking, I'm very much afraid, is fundamentally flawed. The *real* purpose of these pursuits is to enable the person who does them to IMAGINE himself a 'painter,' 'composer,' 'poet,' and the like."

Like a Bacchic gnome, Snew raised two fingers on each hand to indicate quotation marks.

"*Quel malheur!* Such activities in the past had never been of any use to anyone. This is the VERY ESSENCE of the Two Cultures Dilemma! Just imagine it, Modus: if Rembrandt had used those magnificent eyes God gave him to peer through van Leeuwenhook's magnifying lenses, instead of wasting humanity's time in the production of useless paintings, merely because of his immature need to say to his friends, 'I am a painter!' . . . When I think of those millions of wretches dying of tuberculosis, merely so that this one man could gratify his ego fantasies!!!" Snew blubbered: a mixture of agony and mucus clogged his windpipe.

"Pardon me, Modus." Snew dashed to the other end of the room and vomited into the sink. I went over to assist him but he pushed me away. "No need. Modus! No need," he muttered, "It must have been the cole slaw."

He got back up on his seat and sat there for awhile, abstracted and dazed. Then he picked up where he'd left off:

"The great beauty, Modus, of applied technosophy is that normal human beings can derive all the ego-gratification required to maintain themselves in a state of happiness, while at the same time doing something that's of some real value to the human race, finding a cure for cancer, building bridges, draining swamps: things like that. The enlightened two-cultured being of the future world utopia will believe that Mathematics is Poetry, Computer Programming is Dance, Biology Painting, Chemistry Music, Engineering Sculpture . . . "

"My God, Snew!" I cried, "That sounds like the extinction of all the arts!"

"Not the extinction, darling! Far from it! The fulfillment! Your name may be Modus, but your ideas are terribly outmoded. Just imagine: if Tennyson had believed that high finance was a form of poetry, the balance of payments quandary would have been laid to rest more than a century ago! No World War I — no World War II — Universal Bliss!"

Snew gave me a genial wink, as if to indicate that I was not at all the failure I imagined myself to be, merely a talented soul who'd fallen victim to the evils of bureaucracy.

"Now you see, Modus, why you've flunked out of Mushposh time and again. The educational philosophy of this once great institution derives from utter ignorance of the great truths of technosophy. What was that subject you were telling me about? Cybernetic Choreography? I sat in on a few classes in that subject shortly after my arrival. Finally I got up and walked out, sadly shaking my head. As it's taught at Mushposh, it appears to be an attempt to apply Norbert Wiener's (yet another unfortunate victim of the two-cultures divide, I'm afraid. A regular fellow by the way; we've often chug-a-lugged together)—cybernetics to ballet and modern dance.

"That's thoroughly wrong-headed! What the truly cultivated man of today needs to do *is to convince himself that, even though he is working for an insurance company as a computer scientist, he is every bit as much of a dancer as Baryshnikov!* The sweeping socio-economic revolution proclaimed by technosophy may be summarized as follows:

"*All engineering schools should be labeled art schools; all art schools should train engineers. All medical schools should call themselves conservatories; all conservatories should be teaching their students to become medical technicians. All* . . . but you get my meaning."

"Your ideas are bound to encounter considerable opposition at Mushposh; after you graduate from here you're not able to do anything."

"Yes, I'm well aware of that. I've already been the recipient of more than my share of dim-witted prejudice. Mushposh University is the ultimate case history of an academic backwater. Mind you, some wonderful work has been done here, and still is being done. None of it addresses the requirements for a modern society. Let's stick with the example of Cybernetic Choreography: for the first two years, students translate all of the classic choreographies from Labanotation into Fortran.

# THE REVELATION OF DOCTOR SNEW

Then computers cut them up and paste the pieces into myriad permutations and combinations, subject to constraints based on the current fashions in aesthetics. One can be certain that any choreography deconstructed and reconstructed by these means will never be accepted as a thesis unless it is completely undanceable by any human being, past, present or future."

"I'm beginning to understand you, Dr. Snew. You believe that the students in Cybernetic Choreography ought to be producing dances that *can* be performed!"

"Nonsense, my boy! You haven't understood a thing I've said: *everything* about Cybernetic Choreography reeks of the Ivory Tower. The realistic approach to this subject is this: the teacher takes the class down to a computer center with a program for processing air pollution statistics in some major city over the last 25 years. As the computer crunches the numbers, the entire class dances *Appalachian Spring* in front of it!"

"Don't you think *The Golden Calf* would be more appropriate?"

"Golden Calf? Golden Calf? Are you talking about Arnold Schoenberg's modernist rubbish? What's it got to do with this? What the deuce are you talking about, young man? You know, Modus, the way your generation thinks remains a complete mystery to me! . . . Well: what d'ya think of my ideas?"

"Dr. Snew; they are breath-taking! I feel as if I'm on the cutting-edge of knowledge. They're bound to be immensely helpful to me. Before I go I want you to know how grateful . . ."

"Oh, Modus! Please don't go! Not just yet. I work so hard and there are so few people I can talk to. You're probably finding all this talk about such weighty matters of philosophy just a bit boring. I agree! Even a great artistic mind* like mine wearies from too much dedication to its mission in life. Let's make—small talk! Nothing in the world so refreshes me as academic gossip. Tell me about some of your local scandals."

---

*ho,ho!—raised index finger

160

This request from the learned doctor took me completely by surprise.

"Well, Dr. Snew: hardly anything ever happens in Lamely. There's only been one really big scandal here in the last two hundred years: Vladimir Huxley's lightning experiment. Even that happened over in Siberia before coming here."

"That sounds fine. I don't know a thing about it. Tell me more."

"Vladimir Huxley came to Lamely from Novaya Zemlya in 1753 . . ."

"That much I already know. Go on."

"It's commonly believed that the real cause of his exile was some impropriety involving a young actress."

Snew's face dropped a foot: "An actress? What kind of actress? Where was she from?"

"The biographies state that her home was in London . . ."

"English!" he rasped. "No! That's impossible!" In his excitement Dr. Snew knocked over the microscope, spilling the Petri dish and all its contents onto the floor.

"That has to be impossible! But Modus . . . tell me: what sorts of roles did she play?"

"The way the story goes, she was celebrated for her performances as Ophelia."

Dr. Ignatius Y. Snew emitted a blood-curdling wail that froze me to my seat:

"Then it's true!" he cried. He tore off his glasses, jumped off the stool and stumbled erratically about the room, colliding into pillars, chairs, the freezer, the electron microscope, falling into the harpsichord, kicking at the boxes and the piles of junk. Collapsing over the worktable he sobbed:

"There's no hope . . . absolutely no hope at all . . ."

As I had not the slightest idea of what had occasioned this new fit, I could do nothing but allow it, as with all the others, to pass over in its own time. Snew raised his tear-streaked face from the tabletop and turned to me, begging for mercy:

"Modus, you've got to help me! Please! . . ."

# THE REVELATION OF DOCTOR SNEW

"You must tell me what's the matter, Dr. Snew. Couldn't it just be a figment of your imagination?"

"Out of the question! It all fits in too perfectly. The truth must be known. THE TRUTH MUST BE KNOWN, MODUS PONENS, AND THE TRUTH SHALL BE KNOWN!"

Dr. Snew stood up and strode over to me. Seizing me by the lapels of my jacket he screamed into my ear:

"VLADIMIR HUXLEY IS MY GREAT-GREAT-GREAT-*GREAT-GRANDFATHER!!!*"

I fell back into my chair, stunned. Not because of his revelation; I was afraid he'd broken my right eardrum. When I realized I wasn't injured, I feebly croaked: "That's ridiculous, Snew! Vladimir Huxley is the closest relative to the famous English Huxleys on the Russian side of the family."

"Young man," Snew barked, professorially jabbing his octopus-slime-encrusted index finger at my eyes:

"Vladimir Huxley is the most direct ancestor of the Snews on the *Eskimo* side of the family! I've only just now learned it from you. I'll explain everything."

Snew walked to the refrigerator and threw open the door. After a certain amount of digging about inside he returned with a wide-bellied bottle that he held up to the light. Within, preserved in formaldehyde, lay a foetus. Snew held the bottle up to the light and tapped it with a blackboard pointer:

"*This!*" he cried, glowering in morbid triumph, "*This* is the child of Vladimir Huxley by that English actress!"

I pressed my temples between my hands. The room was spinning around me:

"Dr. Snew! You must explain everything to me before I go mad!"

He spoke to me in a low voice, in tones of strictest confidence, interrupting his discourse at frequent intervals to compel me to an oath of confidentiality.*

---

*Under the circumstances, I have seen fit to break this trust.

While he spoke the bottle rested upon his knee. At key moments, when his discourse became unusually animated, the bottle's contents were shaken with such vehemence that the limbs and body of the ancient corpse did a kind of minuet around the fluid. How fortunate that it was he, and not I, who had eaten the greasy cornbeef sandwich!

"Very few persons," he began, "know the real reason for Vladimir Huxley's sudden departure from the idyllic life he'd made for himself among the Eskimos of Novaya Zemlya: that 'lightning experiment' is a real corker of a euphemism! Huxley lorded it over the natives for many years as an all-powerful medicine man, thereby providing himself with the wealth and leisure required for the tranquil pursuit of the life of an artist/scientist. The great project on which he worked unremittingly for 10 years *was the artificial creation, through a combination of scientific, artistic and magical means, of a living being*!

"A year or so before he fled," Snew rattled the foetus with such violence that my stomach turned over, "he had perfected the complex technology required for the *in vitro* creation of a humanoid entity. Yet *Vladi'mir Hux' ley*," (he lay emphasis on every syllable) "a scientist to the manner born if there ever was one, momentarily hesitated before the realization of his dreams."

Ignatius Y. Snew bent over and whispered in my ear: "He needed *a control!*"

The blood drained from my face. The horror of that moment has not left me to this day.

"A child created *within a living womb* using the methods he'd developed, to compare to his other, autonomously conceived creature! From what you've just told me, it was this English actress who conspired with him in the production of this control experiment. Alas! Alas!!! Huxley was forced to flee Novaya Zemlya before he could realize the fruits of her labor! He was never to learn that his control experiment never went further than this bottle which I am holding up to you in my hands at this very moment. It was not, therefore, his liaison with the

## THE REVELATION OF DOCTOR SNEW

actress that was the cause of his being hounded from the island, but the existence of his artificially created Frankenstein monster, christened Yevgeny.

"Yevgeny was human in shape only, and that but a caricature. The old chronicles state that his gaze alone sufficed to cause miscarriages and cardiac arrest. Yet he was of a superior intelligence, owing to genes installed in him by his maker, the so-called *two-cultures genes*. So great among the Eskimos was the awe in which Huxley was held that it was only after *he had kidnapped a woman of the tribe and forced her to submit to Yevgeny*—(Ah! the scientific integrity of that great man!)—that a mob of enraged hunters drove him onto an ice raft in the Matochkin Shar, with only a plank torn from the floor of his laboratory to use as a paddle. The child of this union—that of Yevgeny and the tribeswoman—was passably human, and was adopted by the English actress who took her back home with her when the troupe set sail in the late spring.

"I am the direct descendent of the son of Yevgeny. The name Huxley was Anglicized to Huxlew, then later shortened to Slew. Somewhere in the 19th century it became Snew."

All of this sounded so incredible to me that, unless he were making fun of me, he had to be raving mad.

"Very well, Dr. Snew; but then how do you account for all those other Huxleys: Thomas, Leonard, Aldous, Julian and so on?"

"That's it! That's the whole point Modus!" he cried out pitifully, "Don't you see?"

" I'm sorry, Snew, but what you're saying makes no sense to me whatsoever."

"Don't you see? This actress figures in the genealogical tree of the English Huxleys. Yet, since this pickled foetus is also unquestionably hers, and it is well established that I am Yevgeny's direct descendent, then it must be the case that they are descended from . . . from . . . from . . . "

"FROM WHOM, DR. SNEW? FROM WHOM?"

"FROM VLACHESLAV! Vlacheslav Vladimirovitch Huxley! But he died! He must have died! Unless . . . she brought him to England . . . and the records were destroyed . . . and . . . and . . . But don't you understand, Modus? . . . THEY, TOO, HAVE THE GENES!!"

Snew's rantings were beginning to fall into place:

"You mean, Dr. Snew, that Vladimir Huxley also created, either directly in the laboratory, or indirectly through Yevgeny, another proto-human named Vlacheslav, who, until this very moment, you believed had not survived but who, you are now convinced, was in fact the true original, ancestor of the famous English Huxleys . . ."

"It must be so. But that means that . . . that . . ."

"That what, Snew?"

"THAT I AM NOT THE ONLY PERSON IN THE WORLD TO POSSESS THE TWO-CULTURES GENES!! Without which one cannot be a true artist/scientist! Or understand how Lee and Yang's non-parity experiment is connected to the interior monologue of James Joyce! Or how technosophy will save the world! Lacking which the Second Law of Thermodynamics ceases to be a cultural paradigm! MY genes, squandered on the Huxleys! Rivals to my transcendence! SHARERS OF THE BLOOD OF THE MASTER RACE!!!"

Blinded by rage, his mind in chaos, Dr. Snew roamed at large about the basement. He pulled the fire-ax from the wall and started to advance wickedly in my direction. I jumped up onto his worktable and hurled myself through the windowpane. My last memory before losing consciousness was of the sound of shattering glass.

※ ※ ※

Two weeks later I emerged from my coma to find myself lying in a bed in Lamely General Hospital. Four months passed before I remembered that I had visited with Dr. Ignatius Y. Snew and began to recall parts of our conversation. He'd gone back to

## THE REVELATION OF DOCTOR SNEW

England by that time and I don't expect I'll be seeing him again. I consider this something of a personal loss, for I have a number of questions I'd very much like to ask him.

- ☞ Why have the family of Snew (Slew, Huxlew) preserved the stillborn remains of Vladimir Huxley's only *in vivo* experiment in a pickle bottle through almost three centuries?
- ☞ Can anyone not possessed of the two-cultures genes hope to practice technosophy successfully?
- ☞ Did Vladimir Huxley create yet another creature right here in Lamely?
- ☞ If so, couldn't there be members of the master race of two-cultures genes people now living in North America, or South Carolina, or even here in Lamely itself?
- ☞ *AND THEREIN LIES THE TRUE HORROR!* Might it not be the case that ALL of us who dwell here in Lamely, South Carolina, on the banks of the Wheeze, are but the sons and daughters of (who can say how many?) monsters forged in the furnace of Vladimir Huxley's foaming genius?

*Philadelphia, 1963*

# Recent Advances in the Measurement of π

Dr. Roy Lisker
Precision Measurements Lab
University of Colorado, Boulder, CO

## ABSTRACT

ISSATISFACTION *with conflicting mathematical theories as to the correct value of π have led us to an empirical method for deciding this matter. Recent innovations in technology have enabled us to solve a problem that was known already to the ancient Greeks. Our method gives π to 40 places. Quantum effects prohibit any greater accuracy; this fact alone suffices to demonstrate the incorrectness of calculations made on the basis of so-called pure mathematics.*

## INTRODUCTION

This report describes joint work with Torvald Schmidt, Aram Chang and Srinivasa O'Banion at the Stark Laboratories for Precision Measurements. It has long been recognized that mathematical methods are, in and of themselves, insufficient for the determination of the exact value of $\pi$. Any number which is in such heavy demand from practical applications in so many domains of technology can only be ascertained by empirical means.

Mathematics is dubious at best. To take one of the best known examples, the celebrated "Last Theorem" of Pierre de Fermat has still not been proven, although it was stated as long ago as 1637. Yet hundreds of proofs of this theorem, some of them by otherwise famous mathematicians, have been advanced. Dr. Andrew Wiles of Princeton now claims to have a proof, but not many people agree with him. That so few admit to understanding what he has done is, in itself, sufficient evidence for the suspicious character of his boasts.

As a matter of fact, we do not even need a mathematical theory in order to measure $\pi$ accurately. We can measure it anytime we run across a circle or a sphere that is more perfect than we dare hope. The perfection of circles and spheres cannot, however, exceed the quantum limit. Our best theoretical projections tell us that any calculation of $\pi$ must break down after about 40 places.

# STRATEGY

Our experiments were carried out over a six-week period from April 1st to May 16, 1995. Blobs of molten iron were tossed into the field of a wide but weak magnet that poised them mid-way between the apparatus and the floor.

The blobs were then molded into the form of perfect spheres by the action of dozens of banked lasers focused on the object's center of gravity.

The weight $W$ of the ball was then determined by measuring the magnetic field strength needed to keep it hovering above the floor. The diameter $D$ was obtained through the use of a CAT-scan. Since the density, $\Delta$, of normal iron at room temperature is known, the volume $V$ of the ball could be calculated from the well-known formula:

$$V = W/\Delta = (4/3)\pi R^3 = \pi D^3/6$$

from which we obtain, finally:

$$\pi = 6V/D$$

# REPORT ON THE EXPERIMENT

The execution of the experiment was delayed for about a year, as it was necessary to engage in a considerable amount of political lobbying beforehand. In fact, the city of Boulder had already entered into an agreement with a private contractor, Doyle & Brs., to throw up a 60-story skyscraper a few blocks away from the Stark Labs. Had such a venture been allowed to proceed the local gravitational constant would have been significantly altered, so much so that all our intricate computer calculations, which had already used up most of our NSF grant, would have become worthless.

By dint of our persistence, we were able to persuade the NSF to pressure the Justice Department to mount an investigation into corruption and fraud in the construction industry in Boulder, Colorado. Our cause was given a further boost through a traveling audio-visual presentation tour shown to physics departments on 50 campuses. The mayor's office quickly caved in after that: the skyscraper has been moved out of town about two miles.

Our next challenge was to locate someone experienced with tossing colloidal globs into the air. After a protracted search we ended up hiring a chef, Jeff Slocum, from the International House of Pancakes in Colorado Springs. Altogether, Jeff scooped up and tossed over 2,000 pre-spheroid globs into the magnetic field. His extraordinary services to Science have been commended by a plaque that hangs on the door of the men's room in the International House of Pancakes where he works.

A major miscalculation made at the beginning of the experiment set back our plans another six months. When we started out, no-one knew the relative field strengths of gravitational and magnetic fields, and we foolishly placed the conversion factor between Newtons and the inductive coercivity of the magnetic field on the wrong side of the equation. When the apparatus was switched on, the power of this field was such that every metallic object within a city block radius was sucked through the walls of the frame house into the room. Not only were the Stark Labs severely damaged, but Srinivasa O'Banion spent a year in the hospital. It took courage on our part to petition the NSF for another grant and, it must honestly be said, courage for them to give us one, but we were able to resume our operations in the last weeks of December, 1994.

Srinivasa's hospitalization in fact ultimately worked in our favor. His many skull fractures necessitated his being passed through the CAT-scan cylinder almost every day. As, lying face upward on the conveyor belt, he was moved under the scanners, he (with the blissful smile of someone who is releasing a pigeon to freedom) held aloft one of the iron balls from the experiment. These were brought onto his ward hidden in flower pots.

The hospital is now suing us to recover the fees they claimed to have lost because we hadn't told them what we were up to. We managed to measure the diameters of 639 balls before they caught on. It must be admitted that one of the reasons that he was put through so many CAT-scans was because the doctors could not figure out the provenance of the enormous tumor that kept on showing up on the computer monitors. The case is now in its third month in federal court, and is certain to bankrupt myself, all my co-workers, and the Stark Labs as well, which were limping along in any case because of so many recent federal cuts.

After averaging calculations over these 639 virtually perfect iron spheres, the following figure was obtained for $\pi$:

$$\pi = 3.\underline{28}1592653589793234\underline{4}626433832795028\underline{89}1971$$

The underlined figures are those which differ from those obtained through current mathematical schemes. The correlation is rather close: a difference in only 4 figures out of a total of 41. Observe, however, that a 10% difference must be considered significant. This demonstrates quite well, we believe, how far off-base generally accepted methods have been in the calculation of this important constant of nature.

Anyone wishing to send contributions to our legal defense fund, or with suggestions about ways of improving our methods, are encouraged to contact:

Dr. Roy Lisker
Precision Measurements Lab
University of Colorado, Boulder, CO

*Hudson Valley, 1997*

*RECENT ADVANCES IN THE MEASUREMENT OF* π

# The Hotel Quagmire

*When in doubt, go to the best hotel.*
Isadora Duncan

OU are in charge of the branch office of an American publishing house in some foreign country, France for convenience sake though it could just as well be anywhere. When you came here fourteen months ago, you spent a few months just shopping around until you rented a 4-room suite in the Hotel Grothendieck. When you first moved in you didn't realize you would be staying so long; you might have gotten a lower rate by contracting for the year.

Forethought and intelligence were apparent in your choice of location, on the Rue Mormoiron, away from the bustle of the big city yet within walking distance of the attractions of the downtown. You knew the city well and avoided the tourist traps, the flea bags, the haunts for disreputable activities. It's a colorful street, this part of the rue Mormoiron in the *XVième Arrondissement*, with its mix of shops, little restaurants, café-tabac, bureaucrats, foreigners, loving couples, street characters, clochards. The traffic can be noisy; your suite being up on the 5th floor, you are not unduly disturbed by it.

The bathroom is acceptable by modern standards, linens and towels provided, the rooms cleaned and bed made up at regular intervals. Even here, the insidious influence of Americanization is present: the Grothendieck provides bars of soap! The management is collective: owners, grandmother, brothers, a sister, cousins; all one family. It is not some faceless bureaucracy that is charged with your well-being, not some distant corporation deciding your fate. Humanity overrules the profit *motif*—you're among friends.

Do you have some problems we haven't heard about? Come into the office and talk them over. Would you like an expresso? Courtesy of the establishment. Jacques, my older brother is away for the afternoon. I can perhaps be of service? You're one of our best customers! Don't think you're going to be pushed out onto the street if you fall behind in your payments for a few weeks—even a month! No, the rent is not about to go up. If and when it does you'll be told months in advance. We can always work out something.

You've been there a year, and everything's been satisfactory. You receive a paycheck in the mail about once each week. If for some reason it's held up, the next check covers the full two weeks. You weren't sure at first that you could trust the postal service. Now you realize that, provided it or some relevant division of the Civil Service isn't on strike (a big proviso), it functions better than the US Post Office. Most delays and mix-ups are caused by the mishandling of mail over there.

You've settled in; perhaps too much: hard yet challenging work, good friends, restaurants, bookstores; concerts, plays, strolls through the parks; frequent trips to the countryside and the beach; vacations in Italy, Spain, Morocco, Greece. You entertain, hold small parties. You make a serious effort to improve your command of the language. Life is good.

The first intimations of trouble surface gently, like the moist breezes that, circling like wizard's wands, presage a distant storm.

No check comes during the first week in November. You dip into your savings. The next week's check is less than the full amount for two weeks. The check after that is insufficient to make up the difference. A pattern of irregularity sets in that will plague the rest of the winter. Only in late February do you make the calculations that reveal that you've given the Grothendieck well over thousand dollars that has yet to be reimbursed by the company.

You're a practical man at heart, quite different from the glint-eyed daydreamer inventing you, and you arrange at once to have a talk with the hotel management. You meet with the father himself; he's one who makes the final decisions. You start to discuss taking a cheaper apartment. At this stage you've no intention of moving out, but that, also, should be considered an eventual option.

*Nonsense, my friend! We like you here. We want you to stay! You don't keep late hours, you don't make noise, nobody ever comes to us with complaints about you. You pay your bills on time, it's people like you who attract a higher class of clientele.*

—*Here, use the telephone.* He picks up the receiver, dials the code for international long distance, and hands it over.

—*Call the company at home. The hotel will pick up the bill.*

Because of the time difference you reach your supervisor just as he is about to go off for the day. You explain the situation. He tells you not to worry. There's been some oversight. How much was the amount? $2,000? That's not much, that's less than a month's salary. He promises to instruct the accounting office the next morning to send a check to cover the deficit.

We are in mid-March. Still no supplementary check. Another two weeks; even your regular paychecks aren't coming! A frantic call to headquarters. There is less confidence in the supervisor's tone of voice. A new word, *restructuring*, is swimming around in the conversation. Let's put it this way, there's been some playing of musical chairs in the upper administration, even some layoffs of vice presidents and other top level executives. Go pick up a copy of the Herald Tribune and study the stock market reports. No one's honest enough yet to use the words *financial crisis*, but to be frank the company is in some sort of trouble. There is *absolutely* no cause for alarm: your job is *secure*. Someone will *always* be needed to run the French office. Is it too much to ask to wait another two weeks? If you don't hear anything by then, *call again.*

With many variations, and increasing turbulence, this format will continue through the next 3 months. Paychecks do arrive: on time, a week, or at most two weeks, late. Somehow the company never does seem to end up paying you your full salary. And, too, you have gradually built up a debt with the hotel. Now you owe a full month's back rent.

You balk at dipping into your tight reserves at the bank: the future has suddenly begun to look bleak. It is undeniable that the mood at the reception desk has perceptibly chilled. The younger sister greets you with a cryptic "bonjour," then tells you that they would very much appreciate it if you would have something to show them by the end of July.

Desperate calls to headquarters are now being made on the average of once a week. A new voice over the line; you don't recognize it. Not hostile, not very friendly; all business, lots of jargon. For the very first time you're hearing that the company's been bought out in a merger! There have been numerous demotions, layoffs, firings. Your former supervisor was one of the first to get the ax. One good piece of news: *your* job is safe! Your paycheck was sent out—(*just a moment while I make a call down to accounting*)—*hello, are you still there?*—two days ago. Tell the hotel that the debt will be cleared up once things settle down.

Jubilation! The letter arrives, as promised. The desk clerk shakes your hand while passing it over to you. You go upstairs to your rooms, sit on your couch and open it. Horror clutches you at the entrails: you have been placed on half-time! Henceforth the Paris office will be open only in the mornings, and then only by appointment.

The slip of paper you hold in your hand is the last full-time paycheck you'll be receiving. One more thing—the new corporate owners do not intend to pay you the $10,000 owed you by your former contract. You are welcome to sue the company, but you ought to recognize that a lawsuit is bound to cost you much more than the sums, if any, you might regain.

A few days later you are rushed to the American Hospital in Neuilly for an emergency operation. The remainder of your savings go up in smoke. There is, in addition, a new burden of debt. But you are not easily ruffled.

Back in your suite the next week, over coffee and croissants, you calmly review the options. They're really very simple: you must move to another hotel.

## Entering the Hotel Quagmire

All courses of action depend upon a frank exposition of your situation to the hotel management. You assemble some papers, take the lift down to the first floor and ask to speak with the owner. He tells you to wait while he calls in the rest of the family. His manner is distrustful, suspicious. Among the rest of them you arouse varying degrees of sympathy, but you know that they will not go against him.

He is adamant on one point: you will not be allowed to move until at least $2,500 of the $3,000 you owe them is paid. How long has it been since you began leading them down the garden path? Six months? A year? Why should they believe you now, when you've disappointed their expectations so many times? You show him the bill from the hospital. That's not his concern, he says. The younger brother, always friendly to you, asks his father to show a little heart: a ruptured appendix isn't your fault. You show them the letter from your company, instructing you to close down your office.

The ancient grandmother rises up on her two canes, and with a free hand disdainfully pushes it back in your face: it's written in a foreign language, they wouldn't understand a word of it! You could tell them anything, and how could they know if it were true or not! She's had a long, hard life. She can tell you what it's like, washing cold paving stones on your knees from dawn to dusk. She's learned never to trust foreigners: Germans, Americans, Algerians, Spanish. All the same!

After some discussion between them, it is decided that no legal action will be taken against you and you will be allowed to stay, provided you keep up your regular weekly payments on the room. Don't forget that the debt will have to be paid soon!

You have now entered the community of untold thousands of beings throughout history: the longer you stay the more you owe; the more you owe the harder it is to leave. The only way to make the money to pay your bill is to go elsewhere, but the management will not let you do this. Each day the bill goes up; but it is the bill that is keeping you there.

The hotel quagmire is not so much an economic difficulty as an emotional condition. The experience of being trapped in a room beyond your means, because you can't make good on what you already owe, must be lived to be understood. Reactions are of two kinds: the desperation response, the response of despair.

Mere desperation tends to stimulate the tenant to raise the money by any means at his disposal, not stopping short of bank robbery. Despair, coming from the conviction that he is trapped and his cause hopeless, can lead to seemingly irrational behavior: since there's nothing he can do to escape his dungeon, what prevents him from going out and spending his last penny on a good time?

I, sadly enough, tend to be in the latter encampment. My exceptional insights into the elaborate mechanisms of ploy and counter-ploy that can emerge when the situation has degenerated into its final stages, has all been derived from first-hand experience.

# Tenant's Options

1. Windfall of money that pays off the debt. (The Marx Brothers in *Room Service*.)

2. Jumping the rent when the desperation pressure, $\Delta \times P(t)$, rises above a threshold known as the "lower critical platform," LCP, or $\nu_{max}$. This is the occasion of the first stirrings of desperation in the mind of the tenant. It can be several weeks away from the $\Gamma$-point. (See below.)

3. Keeping the desperation pressure below the "modulus of initiative activation," MIA, or $\zeta$. This is the first critical state of perceived tension between tenant and landlord at which management may consider take several of the steps listed under the landlord's options.

4. Calling in Legal Aid, tenant's unions, rent control boards, etc., to delay or forestall eviction proceedings. Political sex appeal, which the character in our story doesn't have, helps.

5. Having landlord warned or arrested for aggravated threats and/or violence.

6. Moving luggage in small amounts to storage lockers in the nearby train station. An example of how this might be done will appear someday in the memoirs of Lisker, R. A variant is to store all valuables with a sympathetic friend who lives in the same hotel.

7. Calculation of the $\Gamma$-point, or *point of no return*. This is the date beyond which there exists no further option other than jumping the rent, otherwise known as flight. It is primarily a function of the ADC, or "absolute debt ceiling," $\psi$, the largest amount the landlord will allow you to owe to the hotel. Other factors may also intervene. Knowing this date makes one more effective in all one's eventual strategems.

8. Throwing luggage from the windows at 3 A.M. some night and clambering down from the fifth floor on a knotted sheet.

(These things only happen in the movies, though I have read that Richard Wagner pulled off something almost as dramatic in Vienna with a waiting horse-cart.)

9. Refusing to leave the room, even when it is locked from the outside. (The painter-novelist Frederick Rolfe (Baron Corvo) tried this. The landlord and his wife picked up the bed with him in it and dragged it out into the street.)
10. Marrying the landlord's daughter, thereby becoming part of management. His troubles now move to the landlord's list.
11. A providential earthquake that destroys the hotel, thereby absolving the debt. This is sometimes known as the $\delta.\epsilon.\mu.$ *factor*, or "deus ex machina." A war can accomplish the same thing. Wars can be a blessing for certain kinds of homeless people, particularly if they are lucky enough to wear some kind of uniform. (It is instructive to see what the novelist Hugh MacLennan does with this in *Barometer Rising*.)

## Landlord's Options

1. Harass tenant, make him feel he's not welcome until the rent is paid up.
2. The reverse strategy: Treat him like an honored guest lest he contemplate any of the possibilities in the above list.
3. After several warnings, store his luggage and all personal items in the attic and put locks on the door. There is always the risk that the tenant may anticipate this move and empty out the room, an item at a time, over the last few weeks.
4. Issue no warnings, just put locks on the doors. Make sure that the tenant has not already contacted a lawyer. Even in France there are some laws against this sort of thing, though you'll never see them printed on a card hanging over the bed.
5. Do nothing until he tries to bolt, then have him arrested. Americans can always find money.

6. Ignore it: life is too short to have nervous breakdowns.
7. Take him to court.
8. Tell the tenant to clear out immediately and cancel the debt.
9. Calculate the landlord's $\Gamma$-point, which may be different from the tenant's $\Gamma$-point, then forget about the whole thing until the moment arrives. This gives peace of mind beforehand, and assists decisive action afterwards.
10. Declare bankruptcy and move out, leaving the tenant alone to handle taxes, fuel, electricity, repairs, tenant's complaints, unpaid bills and overdue rents, legal actions, visits from the board of health, fines for fire violations, pay-offs to politicians, cops and gangsters, fluctuations in property values, your screaming mother-in-law, and the vagaries of the tourist trade.
11. Invite the tenant out for a long night on the town. You both get drunk and thrash out your differences.

# The Mathematics of the Hotel Quagmire

The normal assumption is that the rent rises linearly. Hotels may lower their rates if rooms are rented by the month or year, but one can still compute a daily rent rate, $\rho$. The amount of rent that is expected by day $t$ is therefore $\rho t$. The total debt is then:

$$A(t) = \rho t - \int_0^t \omega(s)\tau(s)ds + K$$

where:

$\rho$ is the *predetermined incremental multiplier* (PIM), otherwise known as the rent.

$\tau(s)$, sometimes called the *reactive density* or *reactivity*, is the amount of money paid out to the hotel on day $s$.

$\omega(s)$ is a weight-factor which is a function of the ratio of the exchange rates between the tenant's country of origins and present country of residence.

Calculations are greatly simplified by letting

$$\mu(s) = \omega(s)\tau(s)$$

since the weight factor and the reactivity density always occur together. $\mu$ is known as the *lump-sum consideration*, or *lsc*.

$K$ is the amount owed to the hotel before the tenant fell into the hotel quagmire. When the debt goes below this amount, the tenant will be allowed to leave.

We define two *cross-section constants* $b$ and $c$. $b$ is commonly referred to as the *jump discriminant*, while $c$ has often been called the *coefficient of inhibition*. $bA$ is that part of the pressure on the tenant coming from the total accumulated debt that impels him to quit the hotel by any possible means, while $cA$ expresses the sum of all paralyzing forces such as the tenant's perception of the strength of the landlord's refusal to allow him to leave, the difficulties of knotting a sheet or hiring a horse-cart, etc.

The constant $\beta = b - a$ measures the *net debt pressure parameter*, or NDPP.

We wish to calculate the TDP, *total desperation pressure*, $\Delta \times P$ on the tenant. We assume that if $\Delta \times P$ goes above the critical $\zeta$ (see above), the tenant will try to sneak away, but that if it remains below this value, he will stay. $\Delta \times P$ consists of two parts: the NDPP, *coupled with a term that is proportional to the rate at which the debt is increasing*, $dA/dt$. is often called the *panic factor* (PF). Thus

$$\Delta \times P = (PF)dA/dt + (NDPP)A, \text{ or}$$

$$\Delta \times P = \alpha \frac{dA}{dt} + \beta A$$

$$= \alpha \frac{d(\rho t - \mu(t) + K)}{dt} + \beta(\rho t + \mu(t) + K)$$

$$= -\alpha\omega(t)\tau(t) - \beta\mu(t) + \beta\rho t + \theta, \text{ where}$$

$$\theta = \alpha\rho + \beta K$$

The constant $\theta$ can be adjusted to zero, it being observed that desperation pressure is always relative to the ground level from whence it springs. This gives an expression for $K$:

$$K = -\frac{\alpha\rho}{K}$$

*The total accumulated debt is equal to the net debt pressure times the duration, minus the lump-sum consideration, plus the initiator.*

*The desperation pressure is equal to: minus the panic factor times the product of the weighting factor and the reactivity, plus the net debt pressure times the total accumulated debt.*

*The net debt pressure is equal to the jump factor minus the of inhibition.*

*The initiator is equal to minus the net debt pressure parameter times the predetermined incremental multiplier, divided by the net debt pressure parameter.*

❄ ❄ ❄

Imagine that a friend of the tenant, a mathematician in residence for a year at the *Institut des Hautes Études Scientifiques*, has been summoned to advise him. Like any medical doctor, his first concern is to stabilize the condition of the patient. He therefore wishes to keep the desperation pressure constant at a certain level, say $\lambda$. He solves the differential equation:

$$[E] : \alpha\frac{dA}{dt} + \beta A = \lambda$$

where the constants $\alpha$, $\beta$ and $\lambda$ may be taken from the initial conditions. The solution to $[E]$ can be found in any textbook on first-order differential equations, and is given by

$$[F] : A = Re^{-\frac{\beta t}{\alpha}} + \frac{\lambda}{\beta}$$

where $R$ is an arbitrary maneuverable constant.

Since
$$A = \rho t = \mu(t) + K$$
we can solve for the *lsc*, $\mu$, to get:
$$\mu(t) = \rho t - Re^{-\frac{\beta t}{\alpha}} - \delta, \text{ where}$$

$$\delta = \{\frac{(\alpha\rho + \lambda)}{\beta}\}$$

One sometimes sees the term *latent reactive potential* (*lrp*), used for the constant, $\delta$.

If the *lsc* is equal to, or greater than this function, the desperation pressure on the tenant will either remain the same or fall. The arbitrariness of the factor $R$ is striking. It means that there is a margin of choice: either the reactivity can be taken to be very small in the beginning, in which case it is compelled to rise rapidly; or it can start fairly close to $\rho t$, then be augmented by small amounts. If the tenant is clever enough, he can arrange so that he is always paying in just slightly less than the predetermined incremental multiplier, while still lowering the desperation pressure.

There is a school of thought which claims that the primary factor in the desperation pressure is the rate $dA/dt$ at which the debt is mounting, and that the actual accumulation $A$ is of only secondary importance. Certain landlords will be appeased, at least temporarily, if they see a greater amount coming in each week than the previous, and not notice right away that the total debt is rising. The formula that has been proposed is:

$$\Delta \times P = \frac{dA}{dt}(\iota A^2 - \epsilon A)$$

where $\iota$ is the climb slope and $\epsilon$ is a modified coefficient of inhibition.

This formula has been derived empirically: it had been observed by clinical social psychologists at the Medical School of the University of Michigan that whenever the rate at which medical bills rose was doubled, the increase in the number of heart attacks also doubled. They concluded that $dA/dt$ ought to be a multiplicative factor. The second part of the right hand side of the formula was derived by treating the debt itself as a kind of amplitude. The desperation pressure can be interpreted as an intensity, which varies as the square of the amplitude.

This formula was extensively tested on rats. They were punished for poor performances in negotiating labyrinths by being kept cooped up in their cages for long periods, during which time their noses were tweaked by electric prods. The dosages, in watts, were proportional to the square of their misconduct. Then their physical and psychological reactions were measured with an electroencephalogram. The results were very close to the predicted values, after several dozen irrelevant factors were eliminated.

Setting the desperation pressure once more equal to some reasonable value, $\lambda$, we find that

$$[G]: \frac{\iota}{3}\Lambda^3 \quad \frac{\epsilon}{2}\Lambda^2 = \lambda t \mid h$$

$h$ being an arbitrary constant that relates somehow to the general state of disarray of the tenant before checking in at the hotel. This equation gives hope, for we see that if the debt rises slowly, as the cube root of the time, then the stronger panic factor $dA/dt$ will visibly decrease. In fact, $\Delta \times P$ will eventually level out to a steady state. All of this can be summarized as:

*If the payment structure falls off from the rent as the cube root of the time, the coefficient of proportionality being equal to 3 times the critical desperation pressure $\zeta$ divided by the coefficient of inhibition, then the debt can mount up indefinitely and the tenant can neither escape nor be evicted.*

The proof of the above is left as an exercise for the reader.

# THE HOTEL QUAGMIRE

ALAS!! Even under this model, there will always be an *Absolute Debt Ceiling*, ADC, or $\psi$, above which, despite the lack of psychological tension, the management will either

1. Put locks on the doors;
2. Go to small claims court; or even
3. Have the tenant arrested.

A clever tenant will therefore know the value of $\psi$, and use it to calculate how long he can stay on before the inevitable $\Gamma$-point.

1. The coefficient of inhibition, $\epsilon$.
2. The ADC, $\psi$, usually a rigid or fixed idea in the mind of the hotel ownership.
3. The critical desperation pressure, $\zeta$.

Ingenuity must ultimately exhaust itself. These situations have been around for thousands of years and people still seem to be unable to find any way out of them. The real world is not comprehensible by the unaided intellect, for it remains true, even in the last decade of the 20th century, when we can send people to the moon and store information at the quantum level, that a human being lacking a piece of green paper with a 20 printed on it can die in the streets of hypothermia. This is not the fault of landlords; nor of tenants. The blame lies rather with the incorrigible Evil festering in the bone marrow of the soul.

*Hudson Valley, 1997*

# The Governments of Chelm

## Introduction

IN the Yiddish folklore of Eastern Europe, the Polish town of Chelm is the traditional village of fools. Some perspective on the relationship of this literary convention to the history of the real Chelm (city and province) is provided by the following entries from the Encyclopedia Britannica, 1986:

> Chelm: *województwo* (province), eastern Poland, established 1975, comprising an area of 1, 492 sq. mi. (3,865 km). On the east, it borders the Soviet Union; on the south, Zamos'c' province; on the West, Lublin; and on the north Biala-Podlaska province. Chelm, one of the least densely populated provinces, has extensive meadows among fields of potatoes, rye, and sugar beets. The Bug, which constitutes the Soviet border, is the largest river; others in the province are the Wieprz, the Udal, and the Siennica. The Wieprz-Krzna drainage canal crosses both the northwestern and the southwestern corners of the province. During World War II the Nazis established the Sobibór (q.v.) extermination camp in the village of that name near the Bug River (the Ukrainian border) south of Wlodowa, then in

Lublin province but now in Chelm. Some 250,000 Jews died there. Pop (1982 est.) 232,800.

Chelm: city, capital of Chelm, *województwo* (province), eastern Poland. The city is located on the Uherka River, a tributary of the Bug, 15 mi. (24 km) west of the Soviet border. It received town rights in 1233, passed to Poland in 1377, and fell to Austria (1795) and then to Russia (1815). During World War II, 90,000 people died in two German prisoner-of-war camps in the town. The Polish republic was proclaimed in Chelm in 1944. The city is a rail junction and commercial centre, with an economy that includes mineral extraction, wood processing, flour milling, brewing and the manufacture of cement (a quarter of Poland's annual production) and machinery. Pop. (1982 est.) 54,900.

Legendary Chelm is a *shtedl* located somewhere between the Russian *Pale of Settlement* and the north-eastern provinces of Poland. To image a *shtedl* think of *Fiddler on the Roof*, or the stories of Sholem Aleichem on which the musical is based: part market-town, part peasant village. Apart from a small number of successful businessmen, living on the outskirts and more concerned with their affairs in Lublin, Moscow or Warsaw than with life in this dilapidated hamlet, everyone is desperately poor. Indeed, Chelm is so poor that most of its inhabitants make a living by "clawing their way up the walls."

Although the rest of the world, Jews and non-Jews alike, laugh at their folly, Chelm's inhabitants are proud of their great tradition of wisdom, embodied in the persons of the dozen or so rabbis, of distinguished genealogy and credentials, who form the Council of the Wise Elders. This Council meets irregularly though frequently, at times of major political or economic crises, to put their stamp of authority on resolutions of religious controversies, to debate thorny legal matters, or to sit around telling each other stories.

Owing to its peculiar status as a *legendary* shtedl, Chelm is always able to produce on demand at least one representative of every stock figure of Ashkenazic life: *rabbis*; *shadchans* (match-makers); *chazzans* (cantors); *moels* (circumcisers); *melameds* (wandering tutors); *maggids* (revivalist preachers); *shochets* (kosher butchers); *yentas* (female busybodies); *schnorrers* (beggars); *goniffs* (thieves); *schlemiels* (clumsy fools); *schlemazls* (luckless fools); and so on. Several of these appear in the pages of this story. There are even some scientists in Chelm, the evidence for which is given by this classic account:

> It had been assumed for so many centuries that a dropped slice of toast always lands butter-side-down, that this conclusion had come to be taken for granted. During the Enlightenment everything was called into question, and this was no exception. From his studies at the University of Cracow a student had learned about Galileo's experiment, when the great physicist dropped objects of various weights from the Leaning Tower of Pisa to demonstrate that all things travel at the same speed in free fall. The student suggested to the Council that the buttered toast theory be tested in a similar fashion.
>
> Witnesses to the experiment included two rabbis, one a skeptic, the other a believer. The student buttered a slice of toast, lifted it off the table and released it. Sure enough, when it collided with the floor, the buttered side was down.
>
> "I rest my case," said the rabbi who had never doubted the wisdom of the old saying.
>
> "Aha!" retorted the sceptic: "He buttered the wrong side!"

THE GOVERNMENTS OF CHELM

# The Council of the Wise Elders

On a morning around the turn of the century—the exact century being immaterial—the wise elders of Chelm met in the assembly rooms above the Talmud Torah to determine the form of government most suitable for Chelm. Chelm, if one can imagine it, didn't even have a mayor; without a mayor, Chelm wasn't a city, wasn't a town, wasn't a village: it wasn't even Chelm! And, since one couldn't expect the mayor to come from elsewhere, he had to be a resident, didn't he? Accordingly when a local well-to-do businessman, one Chiam the cattle merchant, offered himself for the post, he was as good as inducted on the spot.

Just before the vote was taken that would have confirmed him, an objection occurred to Rabbi Lefkowitz:

"If Chiam is a citizen of Chelm, and at the same time its mayor, to my mind there's a conflict of interests. Others he obliges to obey his laws; but if he doesn't want to obey his own law? *Nu*; so he changes it!

"A room filled with such learned sages can easily understand that it is no more possible for a citizen to be his own ruler than it is for a servant to be his own master. Let's not get lost in abstractions: although Chiam the mayor can punish Moishe the *nebish* for stealing *blintzes*, who punishes Chiam for watering milk?"

Nobody spoke for quite some time. Then Rabbi Yonkel said, "I have a solution. Chelm needs two mayors, someone who also rules Chiam. I propose that we appoint another rich man, Yitzhak, owner of the shoe factory."

"But Reb Yonkel, how can a master of erudition like yourself propose such a thing? Who rules Yitzhak?"

"Chiam! Who else?"

The decision to appoint Chiam as mayor was therefore postponed until the next meeting, when the proposal to appoint Yitzhak as well could be properly debated.

# A Question of Logic

At the next convening of the Council, Rabbi Sobel arose to announce that he had discovered a fallacy in Rabbi Yonkel's logic:

"That's all very well and good," he observed, "but if one of our ordinary citizens has a complaint, to whom does he go: Chiam or Yitzhak?"

The wise elders gave the matter their serious consideration. Eventually they decided that people with complaints would go to Chiam.

"And what if someone wants to complain against Chiam?"

"He should go to Yitzhak."

"That's all very well and good," countered Rabbi Sobel, who was always using that expression, "but suppose Yitzhak himself has a complaint. To whom does he go? Answer me that one!"

"That's such a simple question," retorted Rabbi Yonkel, "that I marvel at the ignorance of someone who would raise it. Look: if somebody has a complaint which doesn't involve Chiam, he goes to Chiam. If he wants to complain *about* Chiam, he goes to Yitzhak. And if Yitzhak himself has a complaint, well ... well ... well: he comes to us!!"

# The Cowherd's Complaint

At the next Council meeting, a citizen who wasn't Chiam, and wasn't Yitzhak either, a landless peasant and cowherd, showed up with a grievance:

"Learned rabbis," he said, "I got a complaint against *both* Yitzhak and Chiam!"

He was given the floor and allowed to speak.

"Here in Chelm—what can I say? Chiam? So, it's common knowledge, Chiam is the mayor. He's mayor, not somebody else? Not me, not you? Good! Why is he the mayor? Well—it's because he's got a big cattle business and owns a dozen farms up in the hills. *Nu?* So; Chiam's mayor: good. If it's God's will, even a broom can shoot.

"Yitzhak? Well; he's mayor, too! This is Chelm, and because it's Chelm, we do things differently from everywhere else in the universe. So we got *two* mayors! Why is that? *You* say, somebody's got to be Chiam's mayor. But *I* say, it's because he's a rich shoe manufacturer, what has a factory with maybe 30 employees that slave for him like the Israelites under Pharoah from dawn to dusk and can't take so much as a prayer break. About some other fool, every fool's an expert.

"Now, *you* say there ain't no conflict of interest. Yet in fact, Chiam and Yitzhak are, both of them, traders in cow flesh: Chiam's cows graze on all the surrounding meadows, and some of them become shoe leather for Yitzhak.

"Let's deal with Chiam first: what's he do the minute he gets into office? He raises the price of beef! Give a chair to a dog, he'll want to get on the table. Between you and me and the Almighty (Praise the Lord!) he would have succeeded, too, if he was the only mayor. I gotta hand it to you; you wise men outsmarted him! You made Yitzhak *his* mayor, so he don't get away with it! I'd take my hat off to you, but this is a holy place. *Mazel Tov.*

"Next: Yitzhak raises the cost of a pair of shoes! In my own family even, we ain't got four shoes between the five of us. All the same, he does it and thinks he can get away with it, because he's mayor. But! Praises be to the God of Abraham, Isaac and Jacob for giving us such a Council of eminent rabbis! Chiam sees to it that this didn't happen.

"What more is there to say? What won't a Jew do for a living? These two *goniffs* put their heads together, and when they're finished talking, they issue a joint decree lowering wages for many categories of workers, starting with *nebishes* like myself, cowherds that take care of the cattle from which they make all their money, may it rot in their pockets before they get to spend a *groschen* of it!

"Already my family has to dig the ground for roots after the harvest is over. Who is it does all their dirty work and never receives more than a kick in the ass for his pains? (Begging your pardon, eminent sirs!)

"*Der oisher hat nit kein yoisher*! The rich have no sense of justice. Give us a bit of justice, and there'll be peace."

The vigorous debate that followed threatened to turn into an uproar. Rabbi Lefkowitz stood up and requested silence. He had a notion:

"Since cows seems to be the common interest of our two mayors, our system of government cannot function unless they also have a mayor!"

Accordingly Horowitz, a well-to-do landlord, was invited to serve as mayor for the cows of Chelm. He was contacted in due time, raised no objections to the proposal, and was sworn into office.

"Now everything is perfect!" commented Rabbi Silverstein: "Say someone has a complaint about Chiam, Yitzhak, or cows: send him to Horowitz!"

## The Tenant's Complaint

A villager presented himself at the next Council meeting:

"Gentlemen!" he said, "I want to lodge a complaint against Horowitz."

"*Nu?* Out with it!"

"It's like this: suppose Horowitz gets it in his head to do something he knows neither Chiam nor Yitzhak are going agree to, like what he did last month when he doubled the rent on all his tenants. Well, Horowitz goes to Yitzhak and says:

" 'You don't want that dog, Chiam, to raise the price of shoe leather, do you?'

" 'I should say not!'

"'I'll see to it that Chiam keeps down cattle prices.'
"Then Horowitz goes to Chiam and says,
"'Do you want to stop Yitzhak from raising the price of shoes?'
"'Of course!'
"'I'll stand by you in making sure that shoes stay cheap.'
"Then Horowitz again leaves. Well, you see it's this way: Horowitz knows that Chiam is always trying to raise the price of cattle. He also knows that Yitzhak won't stop trying to find a way to raise the price of a pair of shoes. Therefore it must be his *duty* to get them to stop trying to cheat the good people of Chelm. By some kind of *schmegegy* logic, he concludes that this gives him the right to raise the rents!

"And by the time he gets through explaining his reasoning to Chiam and Yitzhak, they're so confused they don't know what to think."

Angry voices broke out all around the room:

"Fire Horowitz!" someone cried.

"But what about peasant discontent? What about the cattle market?"

"Then fire Chiam and Yitzhak!"

"So! We should keep Horowitz then?"

"Is a thief honest just because he can't steal? Fire them all!"

"What do you want? Anarchy?"

It was a problem which called for much deep thinking and study of the Talmud. After dissolving the civil administration they had put together with such pains, the Council adjourned for two weeks.

At their next meeting, Rabbi Yonkel was the first to arise. He had brought with him a proposal for an amendment to the town constitution:

"The Talmud never wearies in reminding us that the study of the Law is higher than all other pursuits and occupations. Did not the Rabbi Yochanan state that a *schnorrer* with education is superior to a wealthy rabbi who also happens to be a nincompoop?

"Esteemed sages, far be if for me to vaunt my own learning to you, knowing full well as I do the words of the great Rabbi Hillel who said:

> *He who wears the crown of learning for personal gain shall surely perish.*

"And, this is, indeed, what we see coming to pass: all of the failures in our institutions of government to date have come about through the greed of those who would place their own mercantile self-interest above the word of God.

"Yitzhak and Chiam are like the fox and the snake in the story of the . . . of the . . . well, I don't remember the story. And Horowitz! Whoever lies down to sleep with a dog gets up with fleas! Truly it was with such a person in mind that Solomon states that *He who seeketh mischief, it shall come unto him.*"

Rabbi Yonkel removed his spectacles, looked around the assembly room, and commented: "It's because of people like him that we've had to place the synagogue's donation box so close to the ceiling that nobody can reach it."

He coughed, adjusted his spectacles and once again consulted his notes: "To my mind there is only one way out of this dilemma. To avoid a conflict of interest, we must require that a mayor of Chelm be without any occupation whatsoever."

"But Reb Yonkel," cried Rabbi Sobel, "That is all very well and good, but whom are we going to find without an occupation? Do you expect Chiam and Yitzhak to go out of business? Will Horowitz rent rooms for nothing?"

"Reb Sobel, you are an idiot—a *Chelmer chochem*!" snapped Rabbi Yonkel, "and I wonder sometimes why you are allowed to remain on the Council. I have no intention of asking Chiam or Yitzhak or Horowitz to give up their thriving concerns. From this time forth, the mayor of Chelm will be the town *schnorrer*!"

And it was entered into the records that the town beggar would be required to serve as mayor in Chelm.

# THE GOVERNMENTS OF CHELM

## The Schnorrer's Tale

For several months there was a gratifying smoothness to the spinning of the wheels of government. People with proposals, grievances about the government, or conflicts requiring mediation went to Bogow, the lazy disreputable beggar of Chelm, a derelict to whom it appeared not to make the slightest difference whether he were mayor or not. If somebody wanted to lodge a complain against Bogow he could, in theory, put in a word at meetings of the learned Council. Yet for two months the elders heard no news of any further disturbances of the public order. Pleased with this lull in the affairs of Chelm, and as a reward to itself for its own cleverness, the Council voted itself a month's vacation.

Upon its resumption, a citizen came with a grievance to be presented to the assembly of the wise. It was Bogow.

"Gen'lmen," he said, making a determined effort to behave in a dignified manner: "Zis *vitz*, zis joik hez got to shtop. I'm no more cut out to be ze mayor zen zis louse." He held up the one he'd extracted from behind an ear and crushed it to death between thumb and forefinger.

"It is your civic obligation!" Rabbi Lefkowitz barked at him, "Let me remind you, Mr. Bogow, that the Torah makes no distinction between civil and religious duties!"

"Duties! Schmooties!" Bogow retorted, "Ferst—vat ken I tell you? It's a disgrace to haf somevon like me as mayor; a nogoodnik, a *Trombenik*! You ken't fill a seck mit hoils. In all my life I ain't earned so much as von bent kopek! I ain't got *kadoches*! But—let it go. Your disease don't gif me no fever. Ze Talmud says? . . . the Talmud says . . . vat I know about ze Talmud?

"I'm lyink under a tree—sleepink—*shlof ist a goniff*—I gotta empty stomach vat makes a noise like a oild *chazzan*. Vy does poverty vistle? . . . Beggink your pardons, learned *rebbes*, I'm mindink my own business . . . when *zese two schlemiels!*, Hyman Rebinovitz unt Lev Goldshtein, people vat in ze real voirld vouldn't gif me ze time of day, come runnink up to me—because—like you say—I'm supposed to be some kind mayor—eskink me for—vat else? zey vant justice!

"Let me tell you frenkly, vize *rebbes*, I ain't got ze least idea vat is justice: 'Who judges ze judge?' It's in ze Talmud. But—I'm ze mayor? . . . I'm ze mayor. Unt, because I'm ze mayor I promise at least to listen. Keep your mouth shut, and people vill call you *chochem* —a vise man. Of course: zey won't get nothin' vrom me widout they pay me—and vell, too! Zen I esk Rebinovitz:

"'You got *tsuris*?' *Oy Gevolt*! Learned rebbes!—Right avay it's skreamink! Und yellink! *A groisse tummel*! Mit shakink ze fists, right in my face, mind you! Threats! Curses! A ruckus like I ain't never hert in oil my days! So I shout:

"'*Hak mir nit kein chineck!* Don't bang ze tea kettle!' Zen I say to Rebinovitz:

"'You ferst, *nudnik*!' So he spins me a long, ridikilous yarn, a *gantze bubba meysha*, not von verd—belief me—is true:

"'Reverend mayor,' he begins. I vant go *kochsen* mit zis 'Reverend mayor' *meshegass*, 'Reverend mayor, I own a business.'

"And, I esk you, learned *rebbes*: vat I got to do mit his business, me, vat nefer earned so much as a kick-in-ze-pents for cartink vood? But . . . I'm ze mayor? . . . I'm ze mayor . . . *Nu*? Even a broiken vatch is right tvice in ze day. So talk already! He begins:

"'Well, your honor: My son is a good-for-nothing wastrel, a *grauber yung* who does nothing all day long but play cards and drink up my money. Since he's the youngest of my three heirs, I have taken steps to put this son of mine, this *farshvender* I've created, out of my will.'"

Bogow paused, then commented:

"Between you unt me, learned *rebbes*, I know his son. From a goose you can't buy oats. Vell, he goes on:

"'Lev Goldstein, here, on the other hand, has a daughter who, God's ways being mysterious, is in love with my *momser*!'"

"Mr. Bogow," interrupted Rabbi Abramovitch, "I would

remind you that we are a dignified body, and do not tolerate the use of expressions of that sort . . . "

"I apoligize, to itch and ef'ry von uf you, although it ain't me vat said it, it vas Rebinovitz. Beggink your pardons, he continues:

"'Goldstein's daughter wants to marry my son. What can I say about Goldstein's daughter? They bury prettier girls. But all right; Goldstein's daughter. Goldstein informs her that she won't see a penny of any dowry unless my son gets put back into my will. Which, he can wait until the coming of the Messiah, won't happen.

"'Secretly, without either of us knowing about it, this pair of *pishers* run off to the neighboring village, wake up the magistrate—a man without scruples who can turn any law or custom to suit his pocketbook, who agrees (under Polish law but against all Jewish tradition) to marry them on the spot: an elopement! That by itself wouldn't be so bad, *kinohoira*, except that the very next day there she is, Goldstein's daughter, knocking on my door, demanding my son's inheritance! Now what kind of a *schlemiel* do I have for a son!?'

"Zat's vere he ought'a hev shtopped. But zis Hyman Rebinovitz! It vas all *yatata-yatata! Oich uh dray kop!* Mit all my fingers shtuffed in my ears, he vouldn't shtop talkink! Vat I care about him, his *gelt* or his *verschlugene* son, neither? *Noch a mol!* Zere zey go egain: Goldshtein breaks in mit yellink:

"'Liar! Swindler! Mangy dog! Reverend mayor, that's not the way it happened! You see, I can explain . . .'

"'*Geh in drerd arein . . . drop dead!*' I svore: shut up! Zen I points to Goldshtein, nod my head and say '*Nu?* You deaf or vat? Spick!'

"'Reverend Mayor: Hyman Rabinowitz is a liar! As the Talmud says, there are four enemies of mankind: a liar, a slanderer, a flatterer, and a deceiver. Rabinowitz, and I take King Solomon as my witness, is all of these things!

"'In the first place he's a liar: because didn't he lie to you just now? Then he's the worst sort of slanderer, because he's been slandering my good name in front of you. Then, begging your pardon your honor, he's a flatterer, too: wasn't he trying to flatter you right now so that he could cheat my daughter out of her rightful property? Last of all, he's a deceiver! Because he deceives me, my daughter, and even you, honored sir.'"

"'Spare me the *mishegass!*' I'd hed enough. 'Crep or get off ze pot!'

"'Your honor: like Hyman said, his son is a worthless, no good, low-life, a *paskudnyak*, it's true. His accomplishments, if we can call them that—are limited to sleeping through the day, gambling, and sponging off innocent young women. So this worthless *schlepp*, who doesn't even know how to pronounce "Torah" if you know what I mean, comes to me and says, "Sir. I've come to demand your daughter's hand in marriage."

"'What do I do? Of course: I throw him out! The very next day his father, this *schvindler* standing next to me, this *shnuck*, this *oisvorf*, Hyman Rabinowitz! comes to my house and pleads: "Please," he whines, "let my son marry your daughter! I'd do anything to get him off my hands. I promise you, he'll get 50% of my fortune, even before I kick the bucket."

"'And how did I receive this, your honor? I say, and I can find you a hundred witnesses to prove it, I say to him: "Not until the coming of Elijah, not until the oceans dry up and the sun drops out of the sky, will I allow you to marry my daughter, fortune or no fortune!"

"'Then Rabinowitz leaves my house hurling curses at my head, and I slam the door in his face. But then what does this— *moujik*—(may he be burned to a crisp!)—do next? He tells his son: "It's all arranged. You get your inheritance on the day of your marriage to Goldstein's daughter." And then, *perfidies of all perfidies*, worse than Haman he is, he goes to my daughter, *my daughter* mind you, and says:

"'"Your father just told me you'll get a big fat dowry when you marry my son."

"'So secretly he arranges the marriage. But the very next

day, his *shikker* son is knocking on my door, demanding the dowry!

"'Am I *meshuga* or what? For one whole week I tear out my hair—I beat my breast—I wear sackcloth and ashes! However, sooner or later, you have to accept that what is done is done. Without a hand you can't make a fist. That young idiot won't see a penny of any dowry, because I know that in two weeks it'll all be gone. But a little money from Rabinowitz's estate may do my daughter some good, and I'm determined to get it from him.

"'And do you know what this *goniff* said when I went to talk to him? He told me "There's nothing in writing!"'

"'Liar! Thief!' Rebinovitz skreams. Unt before you ken say *Baruch Ato Adonai*, it's vonce egen ze whoil *gantze megillah* mit shoutink unt curses! Learned and esteemed rabbis, may I drop dead if in von second I didn't age a hundert years!"

"Mr Bogow . . . er, your honor . . ." Rabbi Yonkel suggested, "Must you draw out the story with such tediousness? All we really need are the facts."

"Venerable sages! *Ravs*! *Lamdens*! Hoily *darshens*! endless apoligies to itch and ef' ry von of you; I'm almost finished. Efter zey calm down, I let zem know I don't belief von tink vrom vat zey been tellink me. *A naye geshicta*!

"'If you esk me,' I say, 'it's you vat are ze scoundrels vrom ze Talmud. Correct me if I'm wrong, but here's vat heppened:

"'Hyman Rebinovitz, I bet you got your reasons vy you vant cut out your *boychik* vrom ze vill. Unt you, Goldshtein, you also got your reasons you don't vant pay no dowry.

"'In fect it vas Goldshtein, not Rebinovitz, vat arranges ze weddink. Von day, zis lazy bum son of a Rebinovitz, whom Goldshtein don't know vrom ze *shammas* ov Boiberik, shows up, dressed like a professor, and hints—maybe—he vants open up some kind business, unt—also—he's smitten by Goldshtein's *techter*. Goldshtein esks to see ze business before he shows ze daughter. Menkint veeps but Got lefs. For ze first time ze son mentions his *tatte*'s name iz Rebinovitz. Now Goldshtein find ze idea more int'restink, he vants talk mit ze *tatte*.

"'Vat Rebinovitz vants is to get his son off his hends. So, he goes visit Goldshtein and togezer zey cooks up a big pot *tsimmas*: a conspiracy! He don't say nott'en ebout no vill, but he don't say his son ain't no more in ze vill neither! Even in Lublin zey know Rebinovitz is von shmart operator: *a dreyer*!

"'So, gentlemen, vy I tellink you all zis? You know ze rest! You shek hends, ze weddink is arranged, vitsh ain't no sicret neizer, because you reserve ze biggest hall in Chelm, hire ze best caterers and put up ze the notices at ze synagogue a month in advance.

"'At ze weddink—right unter der *chupah!*—Goldshtein gives Rebinovitz' son ze *nadan* in a lump sum—vitch in a veek's time it's gone: down to ze lest *groschen*.

"'All of a sudden, you, Lev Goldshtein, realize what kind fool you've been. It's too late, ze marriage ken't be chenged, but—you ain't shtopped being shtupid. Now you tink maybe you ken mek Rebinovitz pay back ze *nadan*. Enyvay, iz possible, he hopes, he can disgrace Rebinovitz so much zat he iz writink his son's name back in his vill, mit sometink put aside for ze *techter*.

"'Zat's vay you vant me: if I buy Rebinovitz' *bubba meysha*, his cock-unt-bull story, Goldshtein don't get nott'en. But, if mine judgment goes mit Goldshtein, my guess is he goes home, sits arount unt vaits until Hyman Rebinovitz drops dead so's ze *techter* ken collect.

"'Gen'lemen! I vant help you, belief me! I ain't ze *Rashi*, but I ain't from *Schnipitchuk* neither! *Rachmones!* May your hearts be far from trouble. I've considered your problems; unt here's my edvice:

"'You're a real pair *schlemiels*, both of you. You got lots of *chutzpah*, I'll grent you. Gen'lemen, I got only the highest respect for zat *eydler mensch*, Rebinovitz's son. He's ze von honest man in ze whoil *machloikes*. You *grosse machers*, you hot shots, are all *chazers*: you vant lif like lazy bums, but mit respectability.

"'Since Rebinovitz's son is ze hero, he deserves ze heppy endink, *Nu? Mazel Tov!* My vish is zat Rebinovitz's son vill go on makink you bot look like fools—and gets rich too! If I vas him, I'd do exactly like he does—*kinohoira*, I ain't got his telents! *Zai gesint!* Good day to you, gen'lemen!'

"Honorable, vise, distinguished, learned and sagacious *rebbes*! I vas flabbergasted at zer reactions! Zat zey vouldn't like vat I say, zat I know already; but I didn't expect zey vould greb me, cover me mit curses, spit on me, shek and rettle me till all ze teeth fall out! Zey empty out my pockets unt tek beck all zer *gelt*. (It von't do zem no good: brains you ken't pay for.) *Oi Vey*, zey slep me around! Vat ken I tell you? On ze vay hoim they dropped me into a big pile horse *dreck*!

"I got just von more tink to say: Chelm is too respectable to hef a men like me for its mayor. *Ich zol azoy vissen fun tsuris*: ebout how to be a mayor, I should know as much about misfortune! *I QVIT!*"

The wise elders of Chelm were struck dumb by this new revelation.

"That's all very well and good," Rabbi Sobel wondered aloud, "but how can a mayor be respectable if he hasn't got an occupation?"

"But isn't he working at being mayor?" Rabbi Rubin asked.

"But who's going to pay him?" asked Rabbit Yonkel, to whom the thought had not previously occurred.

"The citizens of Chelm, who else? Let him raise taxes!"

"But for what?"

"What do you mean, for what? For his professional capacities!"

"But what does the mayor do?"

To this there was no answer. Nobody could state what the mayor of Chelm was supposed to do.

# A Discourse on Government

For the next meeting of the Council Rabbi Yonkel showed up early with a position statement on the functions of government. It had been composed after long nights studying relevant passages in the Bible, Torah, Talmud, Mishnah, Gemorah and other commentaries. Nor had he stopped there, but had continued his readings in the treatises of Greek philosophers, notably Plato's Republic, Machiavelli's Prince, the writings of Ibn Khaldun, Rousseau, Montesquieu, the Federalist Papers and the Declaration of Independence, the Wealth of Nations and the Zohar. It may come as a surprise to some that so much scholarship was being invested into the matter of finding a proper government for an insignificant settlement like Chelm. As with all municipalities everywhere, from New York to Tokyo to Paris, to Pamplona, Spain, Camden, New Jersey or Middletown, Connecticut, Chelm is convinced that it is at the center of the universe. No amount of effort was deemed excessive in figuring out the best system for its administration.

Rabbi Yonkel exchanged greetings and shook hands with each elder as they filed into the assembly room. When they were all seated, he rose to speak, document in hand:

"Eminent seers," he began, "worthy sages, scions of knowledge and founts of erudition, heirs to the ancient prophets, purveyors of eternal light and wisdom, blessed with the most profound sagacity." He stroked his long white beard and scratched under his *yarmulka*:

"Since the days of Moses and Abraham—and before, since the beginnings of recorded history—and before, since the expulsion of Adam and Eve from the garden of Eden—and indeed even before that, since the 7 days of the Creation—earthly government has always had two, and not more than two, essential functions. The first obligation of any government is to provide security for the lives of the governed. The second obligation is to make them happy. Now, whether it is the *purpose* of rule to promote happiness, or whether it is *possible* for there to be happiness without rule; whether rulers *themselves* can be happy; or whether the ruled, *once* they are happy, can rule themselves without the need for rulers; or whether happiness is merely *secondary* and rule *primary*—or the other way around: to such questions we find no answers in the Talmud, nor any of the commentaries, nor in any of the Christian, Islamic or secular authorities that I have diligently consulted. For in some places it is written that *"Affliction is a blessing"*; elsewhere however it states that *"The unruly man is miserable."* While some implore God to *"save the innocent from harm,"* others lavish praise on heroic figures who have openly defied temporal law in a just cause.

"Since the Talmud has abandoned us on such questions, I have labored to exert my own feeble wit" (exclamations of denial from the audience) "to resolve them in my own way. But even at this late hour I cannot honestly say whether it is better to be ruled or to be happy, or whether one is possible without the other, or which of the two is more important. After long inquiry and reflection, I have come to the conclusion that it is best that such matters be left to the citizens of Chelm for themselves to decide. *I therefore propose that Chelm should be ruled when it wants to be ruled, and not ruled when it doesn't want to be ruled."*

The conclusion of Rabbi Yonkel's dissertation was followed by long applause. His proposal was placed on the floor and immediately passed without further discussion, or even the formality of taking a vote. Chelm was now going to be ruled when it wanted to be ruled, and not ruled when it didn't want to be ruled. It was in this fashion that democracy came to the legendary town of fools.

## A Free Society isn't a Free Lunch

Townsfolk milled about the main square of Chelm, their minds in confusion, their world in chaos. When would they ever be allowed to get on with their lives?

"This obsession with government has brought us nothing but *tsuris*!" the baker sighed. "Why can't we go on living the way we've always lived? I *bake* bread?; you *buy* bread! If I steal, I go to jail. If I've got no way to earn a living, I become a *schnorrer* or, if that's below my dignity, a Council elder. Before they started all this *groisse tumel*, this *narrishkeit*, about government, we never quarreled. Now we fight over which end of a pickle gets eaten first! Like we hear today, you never heard such accusations!

"It wasn't so long ago either, that life was pleasant: *Yeshivabuchers* rocked back and forth all day in *schul*; *schnorrers* lay in the gutter and dreamed of being aristocrats; *schlemiels* spilt hot coffee on *schlimazls*; green pickled herrings hanged on the walls whistling; *chazzans* lulled themselves asleep listening to old Yosele Rosenblatt records; *moels* soaked heaps of foreskins in formaldehyde; *yentas* banged ears; *maggids* scared us out of our wits with hellfire and brimstone; *goniffs* stole from *groisse machers*, who cheated you and me.

"The point is, everybody was happy. I tell you, this insanity has shortened all of our lives twenty years!"

"What are you saying, Schmuel?" Isaac, the synagogue *shammas* (sexton), replied: "Have you ever heard tell of any place in the world without government? It's simply unheard of. Look, it's obvious: *You* want to build a house? *I* want to build a house. So what happens? We go to the government! If my friends are higher up than your friends, *I* get the house and you don't. Society can't function without government; it's as simple as that. There's no other way to get things done."

"Sure, sure," retorted Meyer the innkeeper. "But what kind *mishegass* is this funny idea of being ruled when you want to be ruled, and not ruled when you don't want to be ruled? Suppose, just to take an example, I *want* to be ruled?"

"*Nu?* So you're ruled!"

"And if I don't want to be ruled?"

"*Nu?* So you're not ruled!"

"But, and I bet you never thought of this: *suppose I want to rule!*"

"*Nu?* So, go ahead and rule, who's stopping you?"

Which sums up, more or less, what happened to Chelm. Within a short time the villagers found themselves in the category most congenial to them. By far the largest group consisted of those people who wouldn't have understood the new arrangement if Elijah had suddenly reappeared on earth and gone wandering through Chelm trying to explain it to them. Going about their daily round as if nothing had changed, they made the best adjustment to this perplexing state of affairs. Indeed the majority of them could not later recall that Chelm had ever gone through a crisis of authority.

The second group consisted of those who needed somebody to rule them. They scrambled to pay their taxes on time, submitted their letters for censorship, labored at menial jobs like worker ants in exchange for empty promises of modest but guaranteed pensions at the end of the road. In their spare time they attended great rallies at which they shouted praises to their rulers.

Those who didn't want to be ruled canvassed petitions and organized demonstrations against the rulers. They distributed tracts and pamphlets denouncing them. During synagogue services they gathered in the central downtown plaza for ostentatious demonstrations and public burnings of Bibles, Torahs and Talmuds. They were to be found hanging out in Chelm's kosher deli, talking politics and agitating for revolution.

Those who wanted to rule soon installed themselves in the seats of power. They levied exorbitant taxes, gave summary justice, established ministries stocked with their friends, cronies and sycophants. They were perpetually embroiled in elaborate conspiracies against one another.

All disputes between the rulers, anarchists and subjects were arbitrated by the Council of wise elders. As the Council discovered, most of its efforts were diverted to censuring those who didn't want to be ruled, for bullying those who wanted to be ruled into standing up for their rights against the rulers.

# The Fortunes of War

*So? Noch amol: What else is new?* The Russians invaded Poland. As the saying goes, if you want to avoid old age, hang yourself when you're a kid. While the Polish landed aristocracy fled, their pitiable, hastily assembled army left Chelm to its fate. If these Jews wished to defend themselves they were welcome to do so: it was no business of theirs.

At night all cows are black.

From their side as well, the Council of Elders sat by and did nothing. War was not a branch of philosophy; invasion was a pragmatic, not a theoretical, reality. Such things were best left in the hands of the government they'd established with such deliberate care.

There now being four categories of Chelmites, it was only to be expected that responses to the crisis would follow on four different lines. The bulk of the population, those who found even the subject of government uninteresting and made little distinction between Polish, Russian or Talmudic rule, lived as they always had, from day to day. Potatoes they ate, five days a week, sugar beets on Fridays and potato soup on Saturdays. How did they survive? by "crawling up the walls!"

Those who hated rule organized themselves into battalions. Armed with pitchforks and clubs, they spread out along the banks of the Uherka River to defend Chelm to their last drop of blood.

Those who needed to be ruled patiently awaited the transfer of power.

Those who wanted to rule used the opportunity to patch up their differences. In private meetings they determined how to best exploit the Russian presence to advance their own ambitions. This conspiracy resulted in a directive to those who needed to obey rulers to sabotage the efforts of those who were out fighting the Russians. In this they succeeded very well, so much so that the para-military gangs of thugs that the Russian Army had assigned to the task gained control of the village with no loss of life to themselves.

As their only motive for conquering Chelm was plunder, they slaughtered the population indiscriminately, ignoring all distinctions between soldiers, rulers, subjects, rabbis, merchants or scholars. Nor did they spare the Council, murdering Rabbi Sobel himself right in the assembly rooms of the Council, huddled on the floor in the midst of the prayer of *Schema Yisroel!*

## Tyranny, on Delivery

Staying just long enough to exact a ruinous tribute, the invaders moved on. Apart from the sporadic *pogrom*, the Russians had no further use for the *shtedl* of fools. In accordance with its time-honored historic destiny, it was left to its own devices.

The vexing issue of the appropriate form of government for Chelm surfaced again at the wake following the funeral of Rabbi Sobel:

"We must have government!" pleaded Rabbi Rubin. There were no murmurs of dissent. The notion of a people living together without government was something of which no mental image could be formed.

"Maybe *we* should govern?" Rabbi Lefkowitz timidly suggested.

"That's a notion!" snapped Rabbi Yonkel with undissimulated sarcasm: "And, Rabbi Lefkowitz, you tell me, to whom can the people turn to resolve the really big issues? Suppose for a moment that we *do* agree to accept the burdens of government? After spending the whole day worrying about Schmuel's goat, Leah's horse, Pincus's son's *bar mitzvah*, the potholes in the roads and the salary of the town undertaker, where do we find the time to debate matters of tradition, law, justice and religion? Even a stupid ox cannot be forced to move in two directions at once: we cannot be concerned with practical concerns!"

"I have a suggestion," said Rabbi Abramowitch, who had replaced Rabbi Sobel on the Council: "Since it is impossible, indeed a logical contradiction, that a people should rule itself—for who can persuade himself to do what he will do only under compulsion?—I propose that Chelm be ruled by someone who is not a Chelmite."

Speculation ran high as to likely candidates for this honor. Who would agree to such a thing? Whom could they find, other than a resident of Chelm, to accept the frustrations of worrying about Chelm's business?

Rabbi Yonkel was the first to grasp the implications of the new idea:

"My esteemed colleagues," he said, "learned, sagacious, holy, humble and wise *chochems*! Not knowing how to solve the problems of their own country, the Russians have wasted many lives to take over ours. Since ruling Poland is so important for them, I suggest that we ask them to govern Chelm also."

The resolution passed by a narrow margin, and only after prolonged and strenuous debate. Rabbis Rubin, Lefkowitz and Abramowitch volunteered to form the delegation to Lublin to hand the village administration over to the Russian Army.

# On Widows, Goats and Other Matters

It may appear strange to some of us who are accustomed to think rationally (though one may search long and hard for a rational definition of rational thought) but it appears that the Russians, despite having invested so much energy in the conquest of Poland, were somewhat less than pleased with the prospect of governing Chelm.

## THE GOVERNMENTS OF CHELM

"You Jews handle your own affairs," grumbled the regional military commander.

"But sir, speaking to you with the greatest respect," explained Rabbi Rubin, "That's just what the problem is; we've failed in every attempt to do so! And think of what will happen if Chelm remains without a mayor? Anarchy is certainly the next step. And after that? Well—revolution for one thing! What else?

"And, even if the revolution fails—a sure certainty, Chelm being Chelm—you still have to make an example of us! Without rulers there can be no rule. Without rule there can be no order. Without order there can be no command. Without command there is no possession. Without possession there is no ownership! And without ownership—without ownership . . . well, what was the point of your invasion in the first place?"

"Get your smelly backsides and your Yid dialectics back to Chelm!" roared the garrison commander, "and don't let me ever see your faces again!"

But as they backed out the door with a profusion of gestures of obeisance and obnubulation, he shouted after them, "Expect your new mayor the first thing tomorrow morning!"

True to his word, their new Russian mayor arrived shortly before noon the next day. It quickly became evident that he was neither Jew nor Pole. Within a few weeks, he and his underlings had raped the wives of all the leading men of the village. The poor were rounded up and organized into chain gangs. Working around the clock they built him a grandiose mansion in an outlying neighborhood. The jails were emptied of thieves and cutthroats to stock his goon squads. Most of the members of the political opposition were put to death. The Council of the Elders was dissolved, the synagogue boarded up. All teaching of Jewish law was forbidden.

For the townsfolk of Chelm, in such sufferings there were no surprises and were readily assimilated as the order of the day. Public opinion held it better to make a bad bargain than no bargain at all.

Yet the tyrant of Chelm, Ivan Ivanovitch Petrov, after a reign of less than two months, fled one night under cover of darkness and never returned. Once again, Chelm found itself mired in anarchy.

The Council reconvened the day after his mysterious abdication. The rabbis could not fathom what had motivated him to quit a situation where he had but to raise his voice for people to come running to fulfill his every command. However, there is little doubt that his departure had been precipitated by the accumulation of a number of minor incidents, of which the following may be taken as typical:

One of the few services that Petrov had provided for the townsfolk was in the maintenance of a tribunal, three days a week between the hours of eleven and one. People were encouraged to come to him at these times with their grievances and disputes. For those willing and able to pay, Petrov's vanity was gratified when he sat, a modern-day Solomon dispensing justice in all matters great and small.

On a certain Monday morning, two months or so into his tenure, Petrov opened his doors to a delegation consisting of Rabbis Abramovitch and Lefkowitz, the town's kosher slaughterer, and the widow Greenberg.

"Pani Petrov," said Rabbi Abramovitch, in tones mixing respect with obsequiousness in equal amounts, "The matter I bring to you today concerns the very future of Chelm itself."

"Hey! Yid! So what? *Svolitch! Spit it out!* I haven't got all day!" His legs crossed and riding boots resting on the desk top, Petrov picked his teeth with the point of a sheath knife. "If it's important, Reb Hamflesh, I listen to you." he held up a glass of vodka and shook it in his face, "But, if it's not?—Woe unto all of you!"

"Sire: it is a indeed matter of great urgency. Far be it for one such as I to waste the time of a high dignitary such as yourself, Pani Petrov! For rightly has it been said that, *A wise man keeps silent as long as he can,'* and *'It is good for a wise man to be silent. How much more so for a fool?'* and I am but a fool, who passes his days studying the Tal . . . "

"Go to hell with you and your Talmud!" Petrov screamed, "and I want no more of your introductions, Reb Abrahamster and Reb Laugh-Shits!" Petrov pointed ostentatiously to his watch: "You have exactly five minutes to state your case."

"Yes . . . Forgive us," they replied together. Rabbi Abramovitch went on, "Far be it for us to consume your rare moments of leisure with nonsense. For, if I remember correctly, it is said of Solomon that . . . " Rabbi Lefkowitz silenced him with a stern gesture, then picked up the story:

"*I* will come right to the point: This women here, a poor widow whose husband, Meyer Greenberg, *Boruch Hashem!*, died six years ago leaving her nothing, that is to say, some cows and chickens, one ass and a few dozen goats, the latter being the object of our visit.

"Honored mayor, worrying about goats may seem nothing more than a petty nuisance for you, but to a poor widow like Mrs. Greenberg they are everything in the world. Once a year she fattens up two or three of them and arranges to have them slaughtered. The meat she sells to the grocers. All this by way of explaining why we have our slaughterer, the *shochet*, with us today.

"It may seem like nothing to you, Pani Petrov, but Mrs. Greenberg has no way of carting her goats into town without assistance. She is therefore obliged to pay somebody to take them to the kosher butcher. Then she must pay an additional sum to a rabbi, usually one of us, to examine the meat and give his approval in the form of an official stamp testifying that it has been slaughtered and dressed in accordance with our kosher laws. We of the nation of Israel have always taken pride in our humane customs with regard to the killing of livestock. As you will find it written in the book of the prophet Elijah: *'There will come a day when the wolf will lie down with the lamb, and . . . '*"

"Rabbi Lefkowitz!" interrupted Rabbi Abramovitch, "I cannot understand why you have deemed it suitable to take up the mayor's time with such tedious displays of erudition! If you will now permit me, *I* will relate the rest of the story in a more thoroughly businesslike fashion!"

"And if you do not tell me immediately," screamed Petrov, "what all this has to do with me, my high tribunal, or your filthy town, I will have all of you locked up!" He slammed his knife on his desk and jumped out of his seat.

"I will stick to the point," Rabbi Abramovitch continued, "Well: it just so happened that the man to whom the goats were entrusted was a worthless *paskudnyak*!" (the Russian word caused Petrov to burst out into loud guffaws) "and, what was worse (no criticism, by the Torah! of your Lordship!) he was a Gentile and knew nothing of our customs. Or perhaps he did know them, but since he intended to steal the meat, it made little difference to him. Once out of her sight he drove the goats to another town and had them slaughtered by a Polish butcher in an utterly atrocious fashion. He did not return, after this, to the widow Greenberg, but took the freshly slaughtered meat home for himself."

"Fortunately, Mrs. Greenberg learned of the theft in time, and was able to have the man arrested the same day. This brings us up to date, and to our reasons for appearing before you today."

"The widow Greenberg came to us with the slaughtered meat, bringing along this butcher (an honorable tradesman of Chelm, sir, if there ever was one!) They wanted to find out from us if there exists some official procedure for *unslaughtering* the meat, so that it can be *reslaughtered* with our benediction. If this turns out to be possible, she may then either sell it or keep it for her own use. You must understand, honored mayor, Mrs. Greenberg is a *very very* poor woman, left all alone in the world. She would like to convince the *shochet* that, since her intentions were kosher, the meat really is also kosher. But our *shochet*, your Lordship, is an honest man; and not once in all his

## THE GOVERNMENTS OF CHELM

days had he heard of meat being reslaughtered, and refuses to do unless we prove to him that it's allowed by the Torah."

Petrov was hopping about the room on one foot by now, stammering with pent-up rage, his sweating face red as borscht. Removing a boot, he threw it against the wall:

*"And what is the name of blazing hell has anything of this got to do with me?!!"* he roared.

"Well, your honor, it is, in the strictest sense, a religious matter. But, as the *shochet* will not abide by the religious authority, it becomes a matter for the civil administration. We've come here, to you, Pani Petrov, to beseech you in the humblest manner to draw up some kind of legal certificate that will testify that the goat has somehow been unslaughtered, thereby opening the door for the *shochet* to have it reslaughtered in any way he deems fit. That much we should be able to do to save Mrs. Greenberg from starvation!

"Your refusal to do this will leave us with no choice but to concur with the orthodoxy of the *shochet* and condemn the meat as *treff*."

"*Get out of my sight this very instant, all of you!!*" Petrov screamed. The four visitors raced to the open door.

"But your reverence," pleaded Rabbi Lefkowitz as they backed out into the street, "It's because of problems like these that we wanted you here in the first place. And, if you don't imagine that the fate of Chelm itself is involved, you're much mistaken! Suppose the *shochet* refuses to work for us any more, and leaves for another village! Suppose we forget the observe of our kosher laws! Suppose our good *shochet* has to start competing with *goyische* butchers? What will happen if the citizens of Chelm believe that we've neglected our duty to protect the widow and the orphan? What then, Pani Mayor? What then, I ask you?"

"*What then?? I'll tell you, what then!! Get the hell out of my sight!! If I ever see another filthy Yid face here again, I'll hang a dozen hostages! I'll shoot you all!! I'll set fire to this pig-sty!! I'll ... I'll ... I ... !*" The tyrant of Chelm having exhausted his store of imprecations, collapsed into a chair speechless and gasping for breath.

A week later, Ivan Ivanovitch Petrov's horse was nudged out of Chelm at three in the morning, to carry him back to Lublin and the train to St. Petersburg.

# And Why Not?

The wrangling over the causes of Petrov's precipitous departure went on for some time. Eventually the Council, recognizing that it never would understand what had impelled him to leave, turned to the next item on the agenda: the perennially vexing issue of government.

"Reb Yonkel!" Rabbi Yehudah was an elderly, much-beloved sage, conspicuous by a scruffy beard which looked as if tufts of cotton had been placed at different places around his face. Lame for more than a decade, he gesticulated with his cane, but without malice, in the direction of his audience: "What sense is there in continuing these fruitless experiments in government? Before we began with this government here, government there business, if my memory serves me aright, everybody was happy. Then there was only laughing and singing. now there is only *rachmones*—endless woe and lamentation!

"Our succession of failures have taught us nothing, yet we appear almost eager to engage ourselves in an enterprise that is only bound to bring renewed grief. My advice to this venerable assemblage of sages, whom I demean by my very presence," (a prolonged fit of coughing) "is that Chelm dispense with government altogether."

"We've grown accustomed to hearing nonsense from you, Reb Yehudah!" snapped Rabbi Yonkel, in good form as ever, "yet never before has such a thoroughly ridiculous proposition been heard during a meeting of the Council! To live without government is simply unthinkable. A people without government is like a law book that isn't the Torah. It has some sort of scribbling on its pages, and once in awhile it may even say something—but so what? In the same way, Chelm without government is nothing. It is not even Chelm!"

The effect of this final phrase in Reb Yonkel's discourse was to give Rabbi Lefkowitz a sudden inspiration:

"That's a splendid idea, Reb. Yonkel! A *mitzvah* from heaven! My brethren, defenders of the Law, laudable in all things—let's change the name of Chelm to something else!"

Everyone stared at him as if he'd lost his mind:

"Why?"

"*Nu?* if Chelm without government is not even Chelm, it can maybe be called something else?"

"Like what . . . for instance?" snarled Rabbi Yonkel, in a tone that conveyed all that possibly can be conveyed of withering sarcasm.

"Like . . . like . . . like *Elchem*!!"

A motion was therefore placed on the floor which, in effect, allowed that Chelm could call itself Elchem whenever it chose to be ungoverned.

This strange motion carried with a single vote. Indeed it was Rabbi Yonkel himself who cast it at the last moment.

"We've tried everything else," he sighed.

## What's in a Name?

It was at the synagogue services on the following Friday evening that the villagers heard for the first time that they would henceforth be living in a single place, but with two names: *Chelm* and *Elchem*. Chelm was governed, Elchem ungoverned. Since every resident, if he lived in either place, lived in both, all were both governed and ungoverned.

Justifications for this procedure were drawn from comparisons with the condition, both free and unfree, of the soul in the body; with the bride and bridegroom in Solomon's Song of Songs; with the Diaspora, combining as it did the sufferings of Exile with the promise of Return; and so forth and so on.

The more philosophical inclined among the wise elders devised a tightly reasoned rationale to prop up this peculiar fabrication. Long experience had shown that all systems of government were eventually self-defeating. Whenever a new form of government replaced an earlier one, it always turned out to embody features which, though the opposite of whatever had been wrong with its predecessor, were just as bad, if not worse.

Any flaw in the governance of Chelm could now be sidestepped simply by moving all aggrieved parties to Elchem. As the present system of government contained a loophole for every contingency it might, it was to be hoped, evolve in such a way that only the best features were retained.

For Chelm's mayor the wise elders reappointed Chiam. It was understood that, although Chiam wielded authority in Chelm, he was just an ordinary citizen in Elchem.

Chelm/Elchem collapsed in two days. In the middle of the night, sometime around 2 A.M., all the Council's rabbis were rudely summoned from their beds to a meeting in the Assembly with a delegation from the public demonstration gathered in the town square. Their spokesman was none other than Chiam himself:

"Learned rabbis," he said, "this *mishegass* has got to stop."

Rabbi Lefkowitz's head was bowed in contrition: "We are prepared to hear the worst. We accept your admonition."

"Honored sages: I don't know where to begin to relate to you all the miseries I've suffered since I was reappointed mayor of Chelm—or is it Elchem? To tell you the truth I don't honestly know! Anyhow, I'm mayor of one and not the other.

"Well: suppose (this actually happened, by the way) Ziskind the tailor and Yitzhak the shoemaker accuse each other of robbery. First one, then the other, they come to me demanding that the other one be locked up. What can I say? Both the bartender and the drunkard smell of whiskey! What they actually did to each other, you can't learn by any means. When I question Ziskind about Yitzhak's accusation, he says:

"'I don't have to answer to you, because I'm a citizen of Elchem.' (That's right. *Now* I remember: Chelm is governed, Elchem is not governed.) But then I return to Yitzhak, who cries, 'I *demand* my rights as a citizen of Chelm!' And when I go back to Ziskind he says the same thing. What is really happening is that Yitzhak, while in Chelm, accuses Ziskind of a crime, which Ziskind admits he *might have done* in Elchem, over which I have no jurisdiction.

"Everyone knows, when you talk to a fool, it's a conversation between two fools. When Ziskind accuses Yitzhak, then *he* is in Chelm, and *Yitzhak* is in Elchem! I tell you, wise teachers, whom I have not once ceased to revere since the days of my youth, it's too much for me. I resign."

"And that's not the whole story either!" interrupted another villager, "because Chiam himself, though he may speak against others, has raised the price of milk in Elchem, and demands his money in Chelm!"

The rabbis were readily forthcoming in their apologies to the community. After hearing all points of view, they excused themselves to retire to the inner chambers for prolonged deliberation. Although they recognized that something had gone terribly wrong with their ingenious construction, it turned out to not be an easy matter to lay one's finger on it. Rabbi Yehudah was the first to discover the fallacy in their reasoning:

"Venerated and estimable colleagues," he said, "among whom it is my great privilege to sit, you whose powers of illumination are so vast that even the Sanhedrin of ancient Jerusalem would have been embarrassed to come into your presence: when we decided to change the name of Chelm to Elchem, we did not really expect that Elchem would be ungoverned. Our real intention, which we failed to grasp at the time, was only that Elchem's government should be *different* from that of Chelm!"

The rabbis congratulated Rabbi Yehudah for his astounding powers of penetration. The Council returned to the populace the next day to announce that everyone subject to the laws of Chelm would also be subject to those of Elchem. Elchem's government was somewhat different from Chelm's, although they had not yet gotten around to determining in what ways they would differ. Rabbi Lefkowitz had been proud to enunciate the catch-phrase of the new innovation: "One village, two systems!"

For mayor of Elchem, they reappointed Yitzhak.

## Identity Crisis

Several weeks passed. Then before the Council stood Horowitz the landlord.

"Holy rabbis!" he began, "May you inspire awe among the angels! May the heavenly host bow down before your feet! May . . . " Rabbi Abramowitch stopped him, "Mr. Horowitz," he chided, "if you want to flatter the beings of the supernatural realms, it's quite all right with me. But if you please, leave us out of it."

"Mentors and teachers, truly I meant no offense." His voice was trembling and his eyes overflowed with tears. "If I overreach myself, it is only because it is my sad duty to bring you dreadful news: *Chelm and Elchem have declared war on one another!*"

"That's ridiculous!" Rabbi Lefkowitz barked, glowering at him as if he'd been personally offended, "How can Chelm and Elchem fight a war when the citizens of the one are also citizens of the other?"

"*Narrishkeit* it is indeed, and even worse than that as it must appear to such wise dignitaries as yourselves, if you choose to think so. Unfortunately it's also true. I prayed all night long that I would not have to appear before you today.

"It started with the old bickering of Chiam and Yitzhak over milk and shoe leather. Begging your pardon, both of them have grown more cunning through experience. Now they dare to do whatever they merely fancied before. Whenever Chiam issues a law, Yitzhak brings out a law nullifying his law. And Chiam does likewise.

"Yet somehow they were able to get together long enough to raise taxes. And together they lowered the minimum wage. Honored sirs, to have to pay higher taxes to both Yitzhak and Chiam, yet work for nothing at the same time, it's impossible! Need I remind you that it affects me too, because how are my tenants supposed to pay rent if they don't earn anything?

"So some people go to Yitzhak, the rest to Chiam, begging for mercy. Chiam gives the matter some serious thought. Then he decrees that the citizens of Chelm don't have to pay taxes to the town of Elchem. And Yitzhak does likewise. Naturally, when the tax collectors come around, people tell them they'd already paid taxes to their own town, which is always the opposite from the one the tax collector claims to represent. To both Chiam and Yitzhak this is insubordination, and they order out the police (the same in both towns) to arrest anyone who didn't pay taxes to them.

"Finally, outraged at the arrest of their citizens by the police from another village, Chiam and Yitzhak send out more police to arrest the ones who were making the arrests! It was only a matter of time before they accused each other of invasion and commanded their subjects to take up arms! Since all the inhabitants of Chelm also live in Elchem, they were, in effect, demanding that the people declare war against themselves!

"And gentlemen, excuse me for saying this, but, following this logic to its conclusion, even Chiam and Yitzhak should be fighting themselves, since they may be mayors of Chelm and Elchem, but they're also citizens of Elchem and Chelm!"

"*Schema Israel!*" Rabbi Yonkel cried and rent his garments, "*Adonai Elohenu, Adonai Echod!*"

## Reinventing Socialism

The Council dissolved the government and hostilities ceased forthwith. No pitched battles had been fought and no-one was injured.

"This Chelem-Melem, Elchem-Melchem *mishegass* has got to stop!" Rabbi Silverstein insisted. "Already we're the laughing-stock of all Jewry!"

"We've tried absolutely everything! The situation is hopeless!" wailed Rabbi Abramovitch.

Rabbi Yonkel, a tall man of erect posture, rose to his full stature. Between stroking his long, silver-streaked patriarchal beard, he grasped the lectern with trembling hands. Fixing his audience with the sharp eyes of an eagle (their piercing gaze no whit diminished by years of studying far into the night) he commanded silence. Then he began a speech in that style of flat-footed ponderousness familiar to those who'd listened to him over the years, and which had made him famous even beyond the borders of Chelm:

"My dearest friends! Ye mighty founts of erudition, sages all! Scions of genealogies of no less eminent sages, stretching back to the dawn of time! Your Reb Yonkel feels nothing but shame from having to lay these evidences of his feeble capacity of thought before the accumulated sagacity and intellect, like a fabled treasure of so many precious gems, herein assembled before me!"

This time no-one bothered to contradict him. They were not in good humor. After glancing uneasily about the room he went on:

"The issues that confront us this day are very grave. Our endeavors have come to a complete halt, and we are obliged to return to first principles. Speaking frankly, it has always been obvious to me that most of our troubles stem from the fact that we have never resolutely dealt with the fundamental dilemma of government: *happiness versus rule*.

"Even a certain notorious anti-Semite, an Englishman I believe, knew a thing or two when he wrote: 'Uneasy lies the head that wears the crown!' Does not Solomon himself state that rule is a burden? When subjects are happy, rulers are miserable. And usually, when rulers are happy, their subjects live like slaves.

"And if we're going to have rulers—and rulers above rulers—and even rulers above those rulers! Very soon it becomes impossible!"

"Rabbi Yonkel"—it was the voice of Rabbi Yehudah as his most ingratiating—"May I be permitted the audacity to ask again: Does Chelm really need a government? People didn't know that they wanted to be governed until we told them they did. Not a single one of our ideas has succeeded. Even tyranny doesn't work in Chelm! Life was so horrible under the Russian Ivan, that if the ten plagues that Moses inflicted on Pharaoh had descended upon us, it couldn't have been worse.

"And are we going to continue to pile Yitzhaks upon Chiams, and Horowitzes on top of Yitzhaks? Let's forget these silly notions of government and go back to living the way we've always done!"

As Rabbi Yehudah spoke the Council sat immobilized. For no little time they all stared at him in cold and stony silence. Then as if on cue, they all started talking loudly against him together.

"No government?" cried Rabbi David, a young man in whom senility had not yet made significant inroads. He'd joined the Council but recently; already, however, he'd developed the habit of compulsively readjusting his glasses with his right forefinger while speaking: "Reb Yehudah, do you realize what you're saying? Not since the days of Sabbatai Zevi, the false Messiah, has such infamy been spoken!"

"As the Talmud says," sing-songed Rabbi Silverstein, "Man is like the angels in three ways, and like the animals in three other ways. If you want us to start living like the animals, Rabbi Yehudah, you're certainly welcome to do so on your own. But I, and I believe the rest of this distinguished congregation, haven't forgotten that the better half of us is angel! We intend to do all that we can to bring back government!"

"In the final analysis," snapped Rabbi Yonkel, "Reb Yehudah is talking nothing but insolence and ignorance! I, too can quote Talmud: *A wise man knows what he says. A fool says what he knows.*' Let me suggest to you, Reb Yehudah, that you return to *Yeshiva* for a few months before making your voice heard among us again. Ignoring this unfortunate digression, it happens that I've come up with a way out of our perplexities." The assembly quieted down.

"As the twin functions of government are happiness and rule, which are rarely identical, although they may overlap, being as distinct as smoke and fire, or leaves and twigs, both of which arise from the same source yet have little in common; and as any exclusive pre-occupation with one is bound to bring disaster upon us by neglecting the other; and as it appears that all functions of government need to be brought under the same roof; and that, furthermore we will have to govern ourselves since nobody else seems to want to do it for us . . . I therefore propose that Chelm's government be divided between three autonomous, albeit inter-related, branches.

"Firstly: we must have a ministry of rule. Then we want a ministry for happiness. An independent branch of government will then be necessary to administer these ministries. I have thought long and hard about this, and reached the conclusion that it is only in this fashion that we can guarantee that the people of Chelm will be secure, happy, and unconfused!"

"Not since the days of Solomon has such wisdom been spoken!" cried Rabbi Lefkowitz with elation, his enthusiasm reciprocated by all the other members of the Council. Even Rabbi Yehudah, formerly so critical, clapped his hands and improvised a little dance. Rabbi Yonkel's proposal, cast into the form of a motion, was carried by consensus.

"And let it also be resolved," cried Rabbi Abramovitch, "that the name of Chelm be forever changed to Elchem!!"

His motion was seconded and passed without a murmur of dissent.

It was in this way that Socialism came to Chelm—or Elchem—or whatever it chooses to call itself.

# In Pursuit of Happiness

And so the municipal buildings of Elchem were soon crammed with bureaus, each with half a dozen or more offices under its command. There were offices in the basements, offices in the attics. There were offices even in the bathrooms and coat closets!

And if there are bureaus, there have to be bureaucrats—no? Before long, there wasn't a citizen of Elchem who wasn't some kind of bureaucrat. There were directors and sub-directors, administrators and subalterns, division supervisors and district coordinators, civil servants and case workers, executives and secretaries, activators, implementors, facilitators, commisioners, arbitrators, ombudsmen, negotiators, hangers-on, layabouts, flunkies, stooges, lackeys, running dogs, cranks, and—have I forgotten anyone?—all the trappings of a modern democratic polity in a state of advanced civilization.

Hierarchies, chains of command, balances of power and intricate mechanisms of countervailing forces were everywhere in evidence. While law and order were enforced by police, lawyers and judges, social workers of every description dedicated their lives to seeing that everyone was happy. Finally, administrators at many levels, grades and ranks monitored the smooth workings of government.

In these sorry times, any person who stole as much as a crust of bread was more miserable than one who, in former days, had stolen the Menorah from the synagogue.

The magnitude of the theft is of no relevance; the entire police force of Elchem works around the clock to track him to his lair. Even in the middle of the night, when all good citizens are safely inside their homes, when even the mice in the synagogue are fast asleep, the suspected *goniff* is liable to be dragged from his bed in his pajamas and made to walk on bare feet to the police station.

One can be certain that the police convoy, after traveling half way across town, is brought to a halt. A social case worker sent from the ministry of happiness is there to confront them with orders that their captive, innocent until proven guilty, be accompanied back to his bed and allowed to stay there until dawn. Then and only then can a proper summons be delivered. Even at this moment, the case worker says, the ministry of administration is debating whether to charge the police with trespassing.

While, with that close attention to particulars and addiction to casuistry for which Chelmites are noted, the police and the case-worker debate the merits of their respective positions, the poor *nebbish* of a *goniff* will be left standing out on the street corner in the wintry night, turning into a block of ice. Were some kind-hearted *kibitzer* to suggest that, since the prisoner has already walked halfway to the jail, it would be better for him to continue on to the police station rather than contract pneumonia, the town officials might stop quarreling just long enough to tell him to mind his own business. Otherwise, the police suggest, he may be in danger of being locked up himself. And if that happens, even the case worker won't put in a good word for him!

The argument goes on for quite some time, but eventually a mediator arrives from the ministry of administration. He soon reaches the same conclusion as the friendly outsider: that the prisoner be walked the shortest distance that will secure him from the cold. Now, however, a new problem presents itself: being halfway between his home and the jail, between happiness and rule, the choice of which of the two directions to send him is impossible to make—this being Chelm (Elchem for now).

Therefore the prisoner may be forced to stand on the street corner for the rest of the night until the sun comes out, an arrest warrant is delivered to him, and he can be taken to the station.

In the short term, being in jail is better than standing out on a bitterly cold street corner. But, honored and attentive readers: don't imagine that the troubles are over for this pitiable *schlimazel*. For we defy anything to arouse compassion in the hearts of decent people more readily than his trial the next day! Can you believe it? a law-and-order bureaucrat for prosecutor, a happiness-bureaucrat for public defender, and an administration-bureaucrat for his judge!

According to the law, the *goniff* can be sent to jail: he did steal, indeed he admits to stealing the little thumbnail of a heel of pumpernickel lying on the floor of Chelm's bakery. The judge is not obliged to punish him, mind you; it is the prosecutor who is determined to pressure the judge into applying the maximum sentence.

The defender has no motivation for establishing his client's innocence, a moot point since after a night on the street, the *nebbish* is ready to confess to anything. His reason for being there is to defend his client's right to happiness. The final verdict doesn't interest the judge any more than it does him. His only reason for presiding is to make sure that the intricacies of the trial don't become too complicated.

*Nu?* So the *schlub*, the hapless wretch does serve out his sentence, *kinohoira!*, although his indefatigable social worker is able to provide him with so many privileges, comforts and amenities that, *schlemiel* that he is, he briefly imagines that being a *goniff* is pretty clever after all.

The presence, or the imagined presence, of such arrogance did not please the forces of law and order, and it wasn't long before a law was passed stating that stealing a crust of bread was punishable by hanging! But—and I don't expect you to believe this but it's true—the social workers saw to it that when *goniffs* went to their final reckoning, the noose was braided in such a way that it didn't scratch their necks!

And the complications within the legal and penal systems ended up causing problems within the rest of the bureaucracy as well. While the social workers did what they could to keep the police—citizens of Elchem in their own right—happy with their work, the prosecutors aggressively sponsored laws making a social worker's job all but impossible.

So that even as the rulers were bringing back ancient punishments like flogging, tattooing, ear-cropping, mutilation and branding, the likes of which had not been seen for hundreds of years, the social workers went around building clinics, hospitals, day care centers, homes for retired *shammases*, ski resorts for *Yeshivabuchers,* pensions for *schnorrers,* and free psychiatry for *yentas.*

It got to be so bad in Elchem, that nobody could decide if he were happy or miserable.

Than this, greater misery does not exist on earth!

# Concluding Remarks

Surely the saga of Chelm's many valiant attempts to govern itself is without end! The name "Elchem" never found favor and everyone went back to calling it by its former name—which, as its origins lie in the sources of all true myth—will never be anything but CHELM, the Yiddish village of fools.

The Council of Wise Elders never will arrive at a workable form of government; indeed, those that last the longest are worse than those which immediately fall flat on their faces. And, although a wise rabbi or two may, from time to time, draw from their failure a lesson in politics, they never stay around long enough to put their ideas into practice. As the composition of the Council changes frequently, the same blunders are destined to be repeated time and time again.

So Chelm advances in years but never in wisdom.

Yet one is not inclined to say that Chelm fares any worse from its inability to do anything right, or get anything done, or even to organize a system for doing so. Its citizens may all be simpletons, but no-one ever lives there who is really bad at heart.

Indeed: A legend relates that a *Lamed-Vov,* one of the thirty-six clandestine angels whose earthly presence alone spares this world from destruction, took a fancy to visit Chelm. A residence of a few months was enough to convince him that the good folk of Chelm were, without a doubt, the most foolish of all the beings he'd encountered in his endless travels. Before his departure (for as the Baal-Shem informs us, the Elect never stay in any one place for long) he paid a visit to the Council president, at that time one Rabbi Baruch.

"Reb Baruch," he asked, "Why is it that Chelm, in living memory or recorded history, has never produced anything but fools?" Rabbi Baruch answered him thusly:

"Your question is normal, coming as it does from someone who has lived in our village for a short time only. We of Chelm have come to look upon our foolishness, as you call it, as a sign that we have found favor in God's eyes. Reflect upon those many persons who, exceedingly shrewd in the ways of the world, cease never to betray His commandments day after day? They do not hesitate to imagine themselves superior to Him, while we dwellers of Chelm, through our very incompetence and ignorance perhaps, are incapable of such presumption. Unable to devise laws to govern ourselves, we somehow manage to adhere to those laws which were not made by Man."

This made the *Lamed-Vov* thoughtful. Then he said: "Excuse me, Reb Baruch: but isn't it true that, in a certain sense, no-one ever really breaks the laws God handed down to Moses. Soon enough he comes to such grief that he must begin again, and yet again, until he learns how to keep them? How does that make this little village of yours better than others?"

"I will tell you," replied the rabbi: "In all respects save foolishness, we surely are no better than anyone else. Yet Chelm possesses one characteristic through which it will always retain the esteem of Heaven. Tell me, sir, whoever you are," (for Rabbi Baruch, nor anyone besides a few chosen saints, would ever see in the *Lamed-Vov* anyone but the most ordinary of mortals) "can you name me another settlement which, through the sorry account of its mishaps and woes, fills mankind with such laughter and joy? Somehow what the world calls wisdom draws such a long face that we may be forgiven, I think, if we prize our foolishness above most of what passes for intelligence elsewhere.

"And consider this: could any people for whom God does not nurture a special fondness, have survived centuries of lamentable disasters from all its undertakings?"

And when the *Lamed-Vov* heard this, he thought: "Truly I have lived in a village of saints."

And when, in his frequent returns to Heaven, he sits at the table of the Most High, the *Lamed-Vov* pleads for leniency for every citizen of Chelm who, leaving the transitory governments of this world for the perfect one above, comes into His presence.

*MacDowell Colony, 1962*

*Roy Lisker at the San Francisco Dada Festival, 1985*